BECAUSE
WHISPERS MATTER

JESSIE SWIERSKI

Copyright © 2016
Single Pen Press, LLC
Jessie Swierski, author

Cover photo: Kayla Swierski
Cover layout: http://melchelledesigns.com

Single Pen Press, LLC
6620 S 48th Ln, Laveen, AZ 85339

jmswierski@gmail.com

ACKNOWLEDGEMENTS

Mike, my husband. Thanks for your patience as I lost myself inside of Caitlyn and Victor's world so many evenings.

Alysa and Kayla, my wonderful daughters. Thanks for believing in me. Your encouragement means more than words can express.

Kayla, thank you for the gorgeous photo that became my cover. You have a great eye.

Mom and dad. You've always told me to write. So, I listened and wrote.

Pam Huf, sister, friend and fellow writer. You have been cheering in my corner from the very start. Thank you!

Lori Law Daou. You were the first person to meet Caitlyn. Thanks for your honest and encouraging feedback after meeting her and learning about her journey.

Dawn Gunn. I smile every time I think about the way you fell in love with Victor.

Avondale Ink Slingers! I would be hard pressed to find a better group of encouraging writers.

To all the wonderful women who read this story and shared reactions, feedback, and encouragement. From the bottom of my heart, I thank you.

National Domestic Violence Hotline **Call** **1.800.799.SAFE** (7233)

National Human Trafficking Hotline **1 (888) 373-7888**

1

The blinking light signaled a new friend notification. Caitlyn opened it and gasped. There he sat, with the nerve to flash bright eyes and a huge smile, indicating everything in his world is wonderful.

"You have some nerve contacting me, Justin! What part of stay away from me don't you get? This is so not a great way to start my day. Argh!"

Caitlyn lifted her hair off her neck and fanned the beads of perspiration that caused hair to cling to her damp neck, then opened the privacy settings for her account, blocked him, and shut down her computer. She picked up her cell phone, pulled up her mom's number, hesitated and shook her head, then turned it off and set the phone down on the desk.

Heading into the bathroom, she stared at her reflection and started a pep-talk.

"I *will* get it together. Today is the first day of my dream job and thoughts of Justin will not screw it up. I'm strong and this will be a great day. The past has no hold on me. I'm looking ahead and I claim everything positive waiting for me." She took a deep breath, squared her shoulders and exhaled slowly through pursed lips.

Caitlyn splashed cool water on her neck, refreshed her make-up, grabbed her purse and cell phone, and then headed out the door. After starting her car, she forced her fingers to unclench the death grip they had on the steering wheel, closed her eyes and rolled her head from side to side. After shrugging her shoulders, she turned up the volume on her stereo, checked her mirrors and pulled out.

* * *

Navigating the streets of Phoenix during early morning rush hour traffic turned into a teeth-grinding job of managing frustration. "More blasted construction," muttered Caitlyn as she turned to avoid the detour that tried taking her in a direction she didn't want to go.

She managed to arrive twenty minutes early at the building where the magazine, Dante's, operated. The tall building in central Phoenix had lots of windows and beautiful granite floors.

Caitlyn took a moment to compose her face and calm her thoughts before striding into the building, determined to present a confident demeanor. She hoped her nervousness didn't show in her eyes or smile as she introduced herself to the brightly dressed young receptionist.

"Hi. My name is Caitlyn Matthews and I need to meet with Mrs. Crebb, please."

"Yes, I was told you would be starting today. Welcome to the magazine. My name is Lilly and if you need anything, be sure to let me know." Lilly told Caitlyn how to find the department she needed and turned to greet the next person.

Caitlyn took the elevator up to the fifth floor, walked through the double doors and found herself standing in a large, square room filled with half-walled cubicles in the center. Several offices lined the outer walls of the room. Janice Crebb, a senior writer and her assigned mentor, beckoned her inside.

"Hi Caitlyn. It's good to see you again. I'm glad you accepted this position. I enjoyed meeting you during your interview and Jack, the magazine's owner, liked the essay you wrote on your application."

Caitlyn let out a small breath and felt her smile relax. "I'm really excited to have this opportunity, and I intend to make the most of it by working hard. I'll be trying to learn as much as I can, so be prepared for lots of questions."

"Bring 'em on, I'm ready." Janice brushed her hand over the center of her stomach and Caitlyn saw she was pregnant. Janice didn't mention her pregnancy, and Caitlyn stopped herself from bringing it up. They walked over to a nearby desk, and Janice handed Caitlyn the new employee handbook to review and left her alone to get started on the required reading.

After she sat down, Caitlyn smiled and took a deep breath as she rubbed her hands across the cool smoothness of the gray desk. A familiar voice interrupted her musings.

"Caitlyn? As I live and breathe. It's good to see you. I heard someone new was starting today. Tell me it's you. I haven't seen you since our last group project at NAU. Ugh, I hate group projects. You remember how crazy that last assignment was? I couldn't wait to be done with that class. How've you been?"

Laughing, Caitlyn watched Penny's hands move up and down, keeping time with the rapid rate of her words.

"Oh my gosh, Penny, it's so good to see you. You work here, too? This is totally awesome." Caitlyn smiled and stood up to greet Penny.

Penny appeared as vivacious as Caitlyn remembered, her dark shoulder length, wavy hair bounced with every hand flutter.

"I've been working here for a month as a junior writer. We have to get together soon. Being able to work together again is going to be great. Man, I have an appointment, but I'll stop by later."

Penny gave Caitlyn a tight hug then walked over to her desk, picked up her purse and left. Caitlyn sat down again and began opened the new employee handbook.

Wow, what a small world. It's nice to know someone already.

Caitlyn smiled as she thought about Penny. They had taken a few classes together and hung out some at NAU. Penny had made it a little easier to get through those last, painful months of school. Caitlyn put the brakes on her thoughts and stopped herself from thinking about Justin.

She repeated the words that proved to be her source of strength for the last two years.

Today is my day. It's going to be great. I'm a strong, loving person and nothing will destroy my joy. I'm in control of how I feel and I will not be defeated. Breathe.

Caitlyn resumed reading and before she knew it, June had blazed away and July sizzled its way into August while Janice made sure Caitlyn researched and wrote a wide variety of stories while she mentored.

* * *

"Caitlyn, get in here." Jack Wingate's voice sounded irritated and Caitlyn's stomach clenched. She wondered what had caused him to be in such a foul mood this early in the morning.

She grabbed her notebook and hurried to his office. Neither Caitlyn nor Penny had much to do with him. They spent their time with their assigned mentors and only senior staff spent time in his office. There wasn't much yelling that took place, but when things weren't up to his standards, no one had any doubt that something needed to change, and change right now.

Jack didn't look up when she entered. "Close the door and sit down. I need to speak with you."

"Sure, Mr. Wingate," Caitlyn replied. Her voice shook slightly. After closing the door, she sat down in one of the plush, upholstered wing back chairs that adorned the office.

Jack tapped an open calendar on his desk. It was the one Janice Crebb used to write her daily appointments. "Caitlyn, as you know, we were all set to get an interview with Victor Knoble."

Caitlyn nodded her head. She knew about Victor's work with slavery rescue organizations. She thought about some of his photos. The faces of rescued children were captivating. Their eyes made it difficult to look away.

Jack continued. "Unfortunately, Janice went into labor last night, Phil left yesterday for his assignment in Portland and Becca and Sean are swamped with their departments. Since you helped Janice prepare the background information about Victor, I want you to finalize the details and conduct the interview."

Caitlyn sucked in a deep breath, her mind racing. She bit the inside of her lower lip on the right side of her mouth to keep a smile from breaking out on her face.

I get to interview Victor Knoble. I can't believe it. Okay, focus, breathe.

Jack continued, "Janice said you typed up the questions and can handle this without her. Just stick with those notes. I want this assignment completed as soon as possible the way Janice would have done it. Just do the interview the way she taught you, with the professionalism that reflects this magazine. Got it?"

Without waiting for her to respond, Jack went back to reading the papers he had scattered about on his desk, totally forgetting, or ignoring the fact that she was still in the room.

Caitlyn tried to wrap her thoughts around this turn of events, then gasped as she noticed the stern gaze Jack gave her when he glanced up and cocked an eyebrow.

"Be sure you close the door on your way out," Jack said and promptly went back to the papers on his desk. Dismissed.

Caitlyn got to her feet, went back to her desk and sat down. She tried to contain a sudden sense of panic, mixed with an overwhelming tingle of excitement. Her dream of doing an important interview, on her own, was finally going to happen. Not just any interview, but the chance to interview Victor Knoble, of all people.

The most sought after photographer around these days, he was young, but showed great skill and imagination. Victor's work inspired words like remarkable, poetic, and provocative. He had a keen eye and knack for capturing extraordinary images. He was also good looking, single, and tabloids ran stories about the women he loved. Caitlyn frowned.

I hope he takes me seriously.

Caitlyn sorted through the notes about the interview, found his contact number and tried to keep her smile under control as she dialed the number.

"Victor Knoble's office. This is Sheila. How may I help you?" Sheila had a soft, smooth, voice.

Caitlyn took a deep breath.

"Hi. I'm calling from Dante's on behalf of Janice Crebb. Mrs. Crebb had an agreement to interview Mr. Knoble. I will be filling in for her and would like to set up an interview with Mr. Knoble at his earliest availability. If you would be so kind as to give me a date..."

"I'm sorry. Mr. Knoble does not give private interviews," interrupted Sheila.

"Oh, but I was told Mr. Knoble had agreed to be interviewed by Mrs. Crebb." Caitlyn grimaced when she heard the higher pitch of her voice.

"I'm looking at Mr. Knoble's calendar and there is no mention of a meeting with Mrs. Crebb," Sheila continued calmly.

"Well, I'm sure if you could just let me speak with Mr. Knoble, I'm sure he will remember ..."

"I will be sure to let Mr. Knoble know you called." Click.

Caitlyn called every day for the rest of the week with the same results. Sheila continued to be an immovable wall.

* * *

Jack's patience began to wear thin as the humid days of August continued to march along. He reminded Caitlyn that Victor's publicist, Tom, had agreed to this interview.

"I've known Tom a long time. We go way back and he said we have an exclusive. Make sure Sheila knows and get this interview done. We're behind schedule on this thing."

Caitlyn nodded and left his office. She bit her lip as she went back to her desk. She sat down, leaned her chin on her hand, then reached into her middle drawer and pulled out a piece of dark chocolate. Chewing the creamy chocolate, Caitlyn doodled on a note pad, eyes squinted as she circled, scratched, out and boxed words.

* * *

Coming into work the following Monday, the last one in August, Caitlyn pulled Penny aside and told her about the unsuccessful attempts to get the interview with Victor.

"I haven't been able to get past Victor's assistant, Sheila, to set up an interview. I'm so aggravated."

Penny nodded her head as she listened to Caitlyn. "I've heard about Victor's assistant. She's tough. She isn't about to say, 'okay', over the phone. I think you should go in person and let her put a face to the voice on the phone. Then you'll be able to show your Dante's ID and have her talk to Jack on the phone if she wants. He'll be able to verify the fact that you really are trying to get a date for a prearranged interview Victor's publicist already approved. What do you think? I could go with you. We might get to see 'The Man' himself. That would be awesome."

"Well, I guess I could stop by tomorrow morning before coming in. Maybe I should bring some doughnuts or something." Frowning and biting her lip, Caitlyn narrowed her eyes as she thought about professional ways to approach Sheila.

"If you come by the office first, you can pick me up and we can both go." Penny smiled and rocked back and forth, heel to toe.

Caitlyn chuckled and shook her head as she walked back to her desk. The need to secure the interview weighed heavily on her all day as she worked.

There has to be a way to get this done.

Later, Caitlyn looked up and saw it was after six o'clock. She made a decision to stop by Victor's office right away. There was a chance Sheila would still be around. Caitlyn looked down at her outfit with a frown and let out a small sigh as she looked at the plain black skirt and pale lavender, scoop necked top. Her low comfortable heels were the ones she wore on most days.

"Oh well. I'll either convince Sheila and get the interview or she'll toss me out on my ear. At least she won't be able to hang up on me," Caitlyn muttered as she grabbed her purse.

Caitlyn took a deep breath and left the building. She rehearsed possible openings to use with Sheila as she drove.

After she arrived, Caitlyn took a moment to smooth her skirt before she reached out to try the doorknob of Victor's office.

Fantastic, the door is still unlocked.

She squared her shoulders and walked confidently toward the nondescript looking desk near a window open to a breathtaking view of the city. Caitlyn opened her mouth and prepared to state her case in a firm, no non-sense, manner.

Sheila looked up from the papers on her desk and stopped Caitlyn with an icy, irritated look that froze her on the spot.

Before Caitlyn collected her thoughts, the door to Victor's office opened and he strode out with one of the most beautiful women Caitlyn had ever seen. Her long, brunette hair was perfectly coiffed and her make-up, flawless. Everything about the woman screamed 'model', outfit, mannerisms, and disdainful look. Victor gave Caitlyn a long, slow, up and down look as he handed Sheila a paper, then they turned and walked out the door.

* * *

As soon as her eyes met Victor's, Caitlyn caught and held her breath. She tried to calm her breathing and hoped her eyes did not betray the erratic beating of her heart. The door closed quietly behind Victor and the woman, and Caitlyn exhaled.

"Excuse me..." began Caitlyn, only to stop when Sheila put up a finger to silence her as she read the paper Victor had given her.

"Now then," asked Sheila after looking up. "What can I do for you?"

"My name is Caitlyn and I'm here from Dante's. I came by hoping I could speak with you in person, to set up an interview with Victor Knoble. Mrs. Crebb was going to interview him but she is currently unavailable and I've been assigned to handle the interview. Mr. Wingate arranged it with Mr. Knoble's publicist, Tom Sherman. If you could please give me a date for the interview, I would appreciate it."

Sheila looked at the flustered young woman in front of her without speaking, pursed her lips, then looked over Victor's scheduled shoots and rattled off an 11 o'clock appointment on September 12th.

Caitlyn bit her lip to keep a grin from breaking free as she thanked Sheila and left the office.

Yes, I did it. I got the interview date.

Outside the closed door, Caitlyn leaned back against the door and closed her eyes for a moment. She sighed and smiled as she strode out the door and walked back to her car.

* * *

Caitlyn came into work a week before the interview and found a message from Sheila waiting for her. Victor wanted to meet with her to clarify some of the questions. He was expecting her to stop by his office at 11 o'clock.

As she was reading the message, Penny came over. "Hey, Caitlyn. Let's have lunch early today because I-am-starving. Jarrell and I had a good time at Palisades last night. That place is so fun. You know you should go out with us. I keep telling you Jarrell can hook you up with one of his friends and then we can all have a good time. I need to eat before I head over to the zoo this afternoon."

Penny didn't wait for Caitlyn to say anything. She just kept rattling on about how awesome Jarrell was and how fun the night had been. Caitlyn waited for her to take a breath and jumped in, letting Penny know she wasn't sure about lunch since she had to meet with Victor.

"I don't know how long it'll take, so don't wait for me. I'll call you if it looks like I can break away. Okay?"

"What? You get to talk to Victor Knoble? Man. Lucky you. I would love to be in your shoes right now. Want me to come with you? We can tag team him and he won't even know what hit him." Penny was jubilant with excitement over the possibility of sharing this interview.

Penny grabbed her purse, all set to head out the door with Caitlyn.

"Penny, you know I love you, but I'm doing this on my own. You go take care of your story on the new exhibit at the zoo and have fun. Mr. Knoble and I will be just fine." With a smile and a wink, Caitlyn left Penny standing there with a pouty look on her face. Victor didn't give many interviews, so this was not a chance Caitlyn was going to miss or share.

2

Glaring at Connie, Tom's assistant, Victor tried to control his irritation. It wasn't her fault Tom refused to let him out of yet another interview with some butt-kissing journalist, eager to make a name for herself.

"Tell Tom this is the last one of these damn interviews I do. I can't stand them and I don't want to do anymore. They are a waste of my time. And what happened to my Africa assignment? When do I leave? Why-can't-I-see-Tom?" Victor tried to control his frustration as he paced back and forth in front of Connie's desk waiting impatiently for satisfactory answers.

Arching her eyebrows, Connie smiled and replied, "I can only answer one question at a time. Which one would you like me to answer first?"

Victor took a deep breath. "Connie, try and get me out of this, please?"

Connie shook her head and laughed. "Sorry, my friend. Jack is an old acquaintance of Tom. You're doing the interview, so be good or you might not like your next job."

Like Sheila, Connie was an impenetrable fortress where Tom was concerned. Victor knew he was beaten and left. He felt frustrated at having to do this interview. Tom granted the interview for his friend, Jack, but he became the token pawn, shuffled around at their whim. As a managing publicist, Tom was great, but this interview irritated Victor. As he left Tom's office, he wondered who was working for whom.

Back in his studio, Victor leaned back in his chair and tried to get his irritation under control. His door opened and Sheila stuck her head in to announce that Ms. Matthews had arrived. Victor scowled and nodded for her to show the person in.

Victor watched the young woman walk into the room and motioned for her to sit down. He felt himself smile as he took in her unassuming appearance. He remembered seeing her before. This time she had her hair pulled up in a bun, but there were pieces that had managed to escape their confinement. She also had a tiny smear of chocolate on the left side of her face, just below her bottom lip.

"Mr. Knoble, thank you for meeting with me. I understand you wanted to clarify some of the questions Mrs. Crebb prepared for the interview."

Victor watched the speck of chocolate as it moved with every word Caitlyn spoke.

Attending to the question asked, Victor responded. "Yes. I noticed there aren't any questions dealing with the pictures of children who have been trafficked. Can you tell me why?"

"Yes. Mrs. Crebb didn't want to sensationalize the horrors the children suffered. If you want, I can come up with additional questions and bring them by prior to the interview next week."

"That would be fine. I think it's important to talk about trafficking. The pictures I've taken celebrate the victories of lives that finally have a future. I think people care when they can look into the eyes of those children. They matter."

Caitlyn heard seriousness and passion in Victor's voice as he spoke about those child victims.

"I'll have those questions available for your review by tomorrow. Thank you, Mr. Knoble."

Caitlyn stood up and presented her hand. Victor shook it and watched as she turned to leave his office.

After she left, Victor walked over and leaned on Sheila's desk.

"Hey Sheila. I feel like having a chocolate doughnut. Want one?" Victor laughed as he waited for Sheila's reply.

"Since when do you eat chocolate doughnuts in the middle of the day?"

"I guess since now because I really want one. You in?"

"Pass." Sheila glanced up at Victor over the top of her glasses and lifted her left eyebrow. Her lips turned up in a tiny smirk.

"Okay. Don't say I didn't offer. You know you want one."

"Yeah well, maybe next time. Before you go, any changes to your schedule?"

"No. The interview is still on. So, what do you think about Ms. Matthews?"

"Well, she's got spunk, I'll give her that." Shelia nodded her head and a gave a little chuckle.

"It should be interesting. She seems nice. I think she was nervous, though." Victor's gaze seemed distant.

"I would be too if I were her."

"You, nervous? I don't think so, not a dragon slayer like you. Okay, I'll catch up with you tomorrow. I have a meeting this afternoon. Later."

Victor left the office to grab some lunch and a doughnut before scouting his next shoot location.

* * *

Caitlyn headed back to her office and went to the bathroom before starting work to look up the organizations Victor routinely worked with when taking photos of rescued children.

"You have got to be freakin' kidding me!" Caitlyn groaned when she saw the chocolate smear under her lip.

"This is great. Just great. I finally get a chance to meet Victor Knoble and I end up going into his office with chocolate all over my face. Wonderful." She washed the chocolate off and pointed at her reflection in the mirror. "You just had to eat part of that doughnut, didn't you?" Caitlyn continued to fuss at herself as she finished up in the bathroom.

She went back to her desk and sat down, determined to find enough information to generate great questions. Caitlyn spent the rest of the afternoon researching organizations and some of the children highlighted by Victor's work.

She stopped by Victor's office early the next morning on her way to work.

I bet Sheila is already at work. I hope I don't see Victor.

She looked around, crossed her fingers and rubbed her face, still embarrassed about the chocolate smear.

Caitlyn walked into the foyer of Victor's office and Sheila looked up from behind her desk. Her left eyebrow rose slightly when she saw Caitlyn.

"Yes? How can I help you?"

"Good morning. I told Mr. Knoble I would provide him with questions to consider addressing in the interview."

"I will take those for Mr. Knoble. If he has any additional questions, I will contact you later today."

A thud came from Victor's office just as Caitlyn was about to hand Sheila the questions.

"Sheila!"

The door to Victor's office flew open and Victor came hurtling towards Sheila. Caitlyn's mouth fell open and her eyes widened as she looked at him.

He stopped when he saw Caitlyn.

"Hi. You're here awfully early. Do you mean to tell me you have those questions already?"

"Um, I mean, yes. I have them right here." Caitlyn handed Victor the copy.

"Great. Sheila can hang onto those for me. How about grabbing a cup of coffee with me. I was just about to leave."

"No. I mean, sure." Caitlyn stammered.

"Great. We can go to the coffee shop downstairs. They do a great breakfast special."

Caitlyn looked over at Sheila and saw that her left eyebrow was even higher than before. She shrugged her shoulders and nodded. Caitlyn looked at Victor, "Okay, sure."

They headed toward the door, but Victor stopped, snapped his fingers, and turned back to speak to Sheila.

"Sheila, Tom called me a few minutes ago and said I'll be heading to Ghana in a couple of weeks. Can you call Connie and find out the details?"

"Yes, I will take care of everything." Sheila jotted down a reminder note. "You're awesome. I'll see you later."

Victor headed to the door and placed his hand on Caitlyn's waist as they continued toward the elevator.

"Thanks for bringing over those questions. I wasn't expecting you to come by so quickly. Do you always start your day this early?" Victor looked at her and noticed that the top of her head reached the top of his shoulder. He cocked his head to the left and met her gaze as he waited for her reply.

"No. I wanted to make sure you had plenty of time to look at the questions. This way, I have more time if I need to tweak them further. They were on my mind."

"I'm sure they're great. Is it casual Tuesday at your office?"

"No, why?" Caitlyn looked up at Victor with a slight frown on her face. Then she realized he was referring to her shorts and tee-shirt.

"Oh, you're talking about my outfit. I figured since I was getting an early start, I might as well hit the gym near the magazine before work."

"Where do you work out?"

"Fitness First Gym on Central."

"I haven't tried that one. Do you like it?"

"Heck no, but I like the results, so I make myself go."

Victor chuckled at the grimace on Caitlyn's face. "Is it the gym you dislike or the exercising?"

"It's definitely the exercising. The gym itself is fine, no complaints."

"So, what's your torture of choice?" They reached the coffee shop and Victor held the door for Caitlyn.

"I mostly do Zumba classes. That way, I get to dance around and get a cardio workout at the same time. What about you? What's your poison?"

"I do some weights, hiking, and play basketball. My schedule requires me to be flexible because I travel a lot. Sometimes I have to be creative."

Victor ordered breakfast and Caitlyn ordered some toast, tea, and fruit. They continued to talk after they sat down.

"So, Ms. Matthews, can I address you by your first name?"

"Sure. It's Caitlyn."

"Great, and please call me Victor. I hate Vic though. Do you like working for Dante's?"

"I love it. It's the one place I had my heart set on after I graduated and now that I'm there, it's even better than I imagined. What about you? I've seen some of your work and it's amazing."

"Thanks. I'm lucky because I get to do something I love and it's nice knowing that some of my work helps people who need a boost. It feels good to photograph the rescued kids and I love giving them a voice. I get to meet a lot of people and tell their stories through my work."

"I think it's great that you showcase the faces of the children. Sometimes, when reading about child trafficking, it's easy to read the words and feel nothing. It's harder to remain untouched when you actually look into the eyes of those children. Some are beautiful, but some have haunted, sad eyes. I can't imagine the horrors they must have endured."

"Your reaction is the one I'm looking for. When people are touched, lives are changed. Sorry. I don't mean to get all serious on you." Victor smiled and took a bite of his toast.

"I don't mind," replied Caitlyn. "I can tell you really care."

As they enjoyed chatting, Caitlyn looked at her watch and exclaimed when she saw the time. 7:30 a.m.

"Victor, this was great. I look forward to the interview. If you need any tweaks to the questions, please let me know. I have to hurry and get to work." Caitlyn stood up and grabbed her keys.

He started to stand, but Caitlyn put her hand out to stop him.

"Please don't get up. I hate to run, but I have to go. Finish your breakfast and excuse me." She turned and started toward the door.

"Wait, this was nice. I had fun sharing breakfast with you. How about going hiking with me sometime?" Victor called out. He smiled when Caitlyn turned back to face him.

"I like the idea of hiking, but the actual work of hiking? Not so much." Caitlyn smiled, the right side of her lips tilting up crookedly.

"I tell you what. I'll let you set the pace and if you hate the hike, breakfast is on me."

"I guarantee you won't like my pace. I tend to stop, a lot." Caitlyn shook her head as she replied.

"No problem. Like I said, if you hate it, you still end up with a nice breakfast. It's a win-win situation." Victor watched Caitlyn's eyes.

As she stood there, Caitlyn looked down and fiddled with her keys. She tucked some stray hair behind her ear and tilted her head toward her left shoulder, then looked up when Victor spoke again.

"I tell you what, just to make it fun, we can decide the when and where next week when we meet for the interview. That way you don't need to feel like you have to give me an answer right away. Okay?"

Watching Caitlyn's face, Victor saw her face relax as she nodded her head.

"Okay, that sounds great. We'll talk about it next week. Thanks again for breakfast."

Caitlyn smiled and turned to leave. As she reached the door, she turned back and saw him still standing beside the table watching her. She gave a half wave and walked out the door.

His last glimpse showed the curls and waves of Caitlyn's thick ponytail bobbing from side to side as she walked out the door. Victor sat down and finished his breakfast. As he smeared jelly on his last slice of toast, he smiled.

3

Caitlyn woke up the morning of the interview, anxious to look her very best. The interview with Victor was important for her, the magazine, and the children who received the benefits of his efforts.

She changed her outfit three times, finally settling on one that provided the confident and able image she sought. The ankle-length golden brown dress with a few large flowers scattered throughout had cap sleeves, a scoop neckline, and a knee-length slit on the right side. A wide belt around her waist completed the look.

In the office, she tried to concentrate on her other stories but found it difficult. Before leaving for the interview, Caitlyn went to the bathroom, looked in the mirror, and gave herself a much needed pep talk.

I can do this. I've studied his work, I know the questions and I know what to do. Okay, don't be nervous. Deep breath. Here I go.

Caitlyn stopped by Penny's desk on her way out the door. "See you later, Penny. I'm off to interview Victor. Wish me luck."

"Wow, you look awesome. Victor isn't going to know what hit him when you walk in his office, that's how good you look. I wish I was going with you," Penny lamented.

"If I ever get another interview with him, I'll try and take you along. See you later." Caitlyn headed out the door to drive over to Victor's office.

Penny gave a little wave as she picked up her ringing phone and started writing.

* * *

Victor finished perusing his latest photos as he waited for Caitlyn to arrive. Sheila rang into his office to let him know she had arrived. He told Sheila to have her come in and put away the proofs while he waited in the chair behind his desk.

As Caitlyn walked into the room, Victor felt his breath catch in his throat.

Pulse pounding, his eyes never leaving her, Victor remained seated while Caitlyn approached the desk and took a seat. Gone was the girl with the plain outfit, chocolate smudge, and crooked ponytail.

* * *

Caitlyn's chest felt constricted. The blinds in the office created a bright light behind Victor's head and made it difficult to see his face clearly. After she sat down, she got a good look at him.

Just freakin' great. He's as gorgeous as the last time I saw him. How am I supposed to get through this without looking like some lovesick schoolgirl?

Her train of thought broke off as Victor spoke.

"Can I offer you any refreshments? A drink perhaps?" came his low, smooth voice.

"No, thank you" she replied while trying to remember what to do next.

Oh yes. Interview, notebook, voice recorder, questions, write.

Caitlyn fumbled around in her bag and brought out her notebook, pencils and the small digital voice recorder. Laying them on the desk, she braved a glance in Victor's direction along with a small smile. He was still watching her, unsmiling.

Caitlyn cleared her throat.

"Shall we get started? I know how valuable your time is and I want you to know just how much I appreciate this opportunity."

"Is that what I am? An opportunity?" he asked softly. Victor's eyelids closed a little.

"I don't understand." Caitlyn frowned and shook her head.

"To tell you the truth, I don't have time for this interview. I do, however, have time for lunch, so if you want to interview me, you'll have to do it while we eat."

"But this interview has been set for weeks. You said last week we were good to go." Stuttering, Caitlyn did a quick calculation of cash and checking account and grimaced as she thought about the small amount of money she had from her internship.

"I'm sorry, but I didn't come prepared to take you to lunch Mr. Knoble."

"Since I changed the circumstances of the interview, lunch is on me. Come on. I know this really great place to eat."

Walking around the desk and grasping her arm above the elbow, Victor led her out the door and down to his car before she had a chance to protest further.

Caitlyn felt her stomach clench. Her breath became shallow and she pulled her arm free of Victor's grasp but continued to walk beside him to the garage.

"Wait a minute. We left in a hurry and I didn't bring my notebook or the recorder."

"Don't worry. I'll make sure you have what you need."

Caitlyn was surprised to note he drove a modest gray sedan. Opening the passenger door, Victor waved his hand and motioned her inside.

What the heck am I doing?

Caitlyn tried to calm her breathing as she settled onto the passenger seat. When she looked at Victor, all efforts at controlling her thoughts went right out the window. His hair, lush with dark brown curls, screamed an invitation to run her fingers through them. Victor's strong neck joined his broad shoulders and deep, expansive chest. He looked handsome in a blue shirt and gray slacks that accentuated his long legs. Victor turned to glance at her, and once again, she felt lost.

"Let's go, shall we?" Victor started the car and they headed out of the parking garage. Caitlyn smiled and nodded her head.

"Okay."

Victor looked at her lips as she smiled.

Suddenly feeling as if she were on a rollercoaster, Caitlyn turned to look out the window and wondered where they were going.

* * *

The city streets soon turned into lush green expanses of farms as Victor continued to drive west on Interstate 10.

"Do you mind if I put on some music?" Victor paused and glanced at Caitlyn before pushing the button.

"No, go ahead. I don't mind." She enjoyed the soothing sounds of the Miles Davis, Sketches of Spain CD.

"Exactly where are we going for lunch?" She managed to ask after clearing her throat again.

I'm glad my voice didn't squeak.

"Trust me. You'll love the food. It's my favorite place to eat when I just want to be myself," Victor replied instead of answering the question.

"Hmm. You're being very mysterious. I think you should give me a clue." Victor chuckled. "We'll be there soon, I promise. Relax and enjoy the ride."

Caitlyn laid her head back against the seat and tried to still the trembling in her stomach, wondering what made Victor Knoble tick.

She thought he would prefer one of the trendy eateries in Scottsdale, but here they were, driving out to the middle of nowhere.

The restaurant, more of a remodeled home than a typical place of business, looked quaint and inviting. The sandy beige color of the building blended in with the surrounding landscape.

The yard in front contained saguaro, prickly pear, and cholla cacti. There were also several hibiscus bushes with flowers of varying colors. The front porch contained an inviting lounge swing and a few high back wicker chairs for waiting guests.

There were a few expensive cars in the parking lot, a couple of trucks, a jeep and a car that looked like it had seen better days.

Victor opened her door and gently held her arm as they proceeded into the brightly decorated restaurant. There were serapes and landscape paintings on the walls that depicted the beauty of Arizona. Hanging behind the cash register was a scenic photograph signed by Victor, alongside a smaller photo of a shorter man and Victor standing side-by-side.

"Victor. It is so good to see you again, my friend. I didn't know you were back in town," greeted the same man from the photo. He grasped Victor's hand and gave him a half hug with a little slap on the back.

"Come, come. We will seat you and your lovely friend right away." He led them to a corner table near the back of the restaurant beside a window that offered a view of the garden on the east side of the building.

Caitlyn wondered if this table had seen a lot of action from Mr. Victor Knoble. She didn't plan on forgetting about his reputation.

"Mr. Knoble, I like your taste in eating establishments. This is very nice. I would have thought that you'd prefer the more popular hot spots in Scottsdale instead of a small place in Buckeye."

"There's a whole lot about me you don't know, yet." replied Victor as he watched her. Victor waited a moment, then continued, "I happen to like this place very much. I met Felix, the man who seated us, on a flight when I moved here from Virginia. He sat next to me and we hit off. He invited me to his restaurant, so I came, had dinner and we continued talking until I got in touch with Tom. We've been friends ever since. Besides, the food here is great. It's the real stuff without all the fluff and fancy names attached to meals in other restaurants. What kind of places do you like?"

"I like eating at places that are off the beaten path. The journalists from Dantes almost always choose someplace in Scottsdale when they go out to eat or socialize. They say if you want to be 'seen', those are the places to frequent." As she spoke, Caitlyn lifted her napkin off the table and looked down as she placed it on her lap.

"Is that important to you? 'Being seen?' There's a price to be paid for goals like that. Sometimes, it's a high one, but if it's what you want, I can help you succeed." Victor watched Caitlyn's face carefully to see her reaction.

She stared at him, eyes wide.

What am I hearing? Is he flirting with me? Me! An intern trying to muddle through her very first interview without the watchful eye of Janice.

Feeling her cheeks begin to flush with anger, Caitlyn wondered if Victor could really be so arrogant as to think she would fall at his feet just because he was famous and good looking.

"The only thing I want you to give me is the interview I came here to get. I'm sure I can manage to get anything else I want on my own," Caitlyn replied with as much dignity as she could muster.

Dipping her head slightly, Caitlyn added, "Thank you anyway for whatever it is you were offering."

Victor suppressed a smile.

"Why don't we order and see where things lead, shall we?" He had been in the company of beautiful women before, but for the first time, he felt his very breath taken away.

* * *

Caitlyn snatched up her menu and tried to concentrate on the words before her. She noticed her hands shaking so she sat the menu down and excused herself from the table.

She leaned her head against the wall in the bathroom. The other women in the office would have melted into a puddle at Victor's feet if they thought he was flirting with them. She knew she would too if she didn't get away from him soon.

"I don't want to be just another puddle," she told herself. "Just ask the questions and try to remember his answers. Paper. Yes, I'll ask Felix for some paper, that's what I'll do. Okay, now breathe. Victor's just a man like any other man, okay, maybe not like any other man, but still, a man. This will be a point in my favor if I can pull this off. I *can* pull it off. No matter what, I can't let him see I melt every time he looks at me!"

Turning on the cold water, Caitlyn rinsed her hands and wiped some of the cold water on the front and back of her neck. She dried her hands, smoothed her hair, squared her shoulders and left the bathroom, determined to keep the interview on track.

Having given herself a much-needed pep talk, she walked back to the table and sat down. As soon as Victor looked at her, the talk went right out of her head. There he was, mesmerizing her again with a gaze that seemed to penetrate her inner most thoughts.

How can I do this when my insides feel like liquid fire?

"I asked the waiter to give us a little time before ordering. I hope you don't mind," Victor said after she sat back down.

"No, I don't mind," Caitlyn answered as she began to look around for Felix. "Do you think Felix might have some paper I can use? I want to be sure I quote you correctly."

"I'm sure that can be arranged. I'll take care of everything as soon as we finish our lunch.

Since you'll be asking all the questions later, do you mind if I ask a few now?"

Surprised, Caitlyn wondered what kind of questions he had in mind, but fair was fair, so she nodded her head.

"If you could plan the ideal weekend, with someone you care for romantically, what would it include?"

Mind whirling, she looked at Victor and wondered how she could answer without sounding foolish and young.

"I'm not really comfortable talking about something so personal. Besides, I don't think you'd be impressed with my idea of the perfect weekend. It wouldn't include anything exotic or fancy at all." Caitlyn averted her eyes from Victor's face and bit her lip as she tried to calm down.

"Come on. You agreed and I think fair is fair. I always have to talk about things I'm not comfortable with. It comes with the territory. Just for fun, tell me anyway. I want to know about you." Victor lowered his head and tilted it to the left as he tried to make eye contact with Caitlyn's down cast eyes.

"I can't tell you something that personal. It isn't professional and I really want to do a good job. I was so excited about this interview and now..." She cleared her throat a little as her voice trailed off.

"You're not excited anymore? Why not? I can't wait to hear what you have to say."

Victor leaned back a little in his seat.

"Are you serious? Do you even have to ask?" Caitlyn hated the higher pitch in her voice.

"I'm totally serious. Tell me about your weekend. It's only fair. After all, if you want to pick my brain I should have a chance to pick yours. Play along with me." Victor smiled a little as he tried to make his voice sound playful.

"No way. I still remember the way you looked at me the first time I came to your office."

"Tell me what you remember." Victor sat there watching Caitlyn, his gaze never wavering.

"I came, determined not to leave until I had gotten this interview set up for Janice. You came out of your office with a beautiful, polished, model-type on your arm. You barely even acknowledged me. You glanced at me like I was some bug you wanted to flick away. I know your type." Caitlyn tilted her chin up as she looked at Victor, her lips pressed together in a line.

"You only know what the tabloids want you to know. And just for the record, I could never think of you as a bug," laughed Victor.

"Well, maybe not a bug then. Of course, someone like me wouldn't even be worth the brain cells you'd have to activate in order to take notice of me in the first place," sniped Caitlyn.

"What do you mean, 'someone like me'?" Victor leaned forward again and interlaced his fingers together.

"I'm not the beautiful, polished, model-type. Just look at me. I'm pretty ordinary. You would never be seen with someone like me," laughed Caitlyn. She shook her head and rolled her eyes while her mouth formed a smirk.

"Um, hello. Here I am, out in public, with you. So much for your grand theory about me not wanting to be seen with you." Victor stared at Caitlyn with an intensity that felt like it went straight to her soul. Picking up Caitlyn's hand, he linked his fingers with hers. With his free hand, he began stroking the skin on the back of her hand.

Not knowing what to say, Caitlyn looked down, took a deep breath, and tried to still her scattered thoughts. Her heart was beating fast and her breathing was shallow and hurried. As his fingers moved, her skin felt like a trailing blaze of fire remained.

"I don't care who sees me with you. Let the whole world know. I don't care. Come on. Tell me about that weekend," whispered Victor.

Without realizing it Caitlyn had started on her second prickly pear margarita while nibbling the chips and salsa. She felt a little daring and decided to play along with this gorgeous man who was hypnotizing her with his eyes and touch. It felt good to have that smoky look pointed at her. Where was the harm in having a little fun? Shaking her head, she realized she shouldn't have consumed her first margarita so quickly. She felt more relaxed than she had been in a long time. Taking a sip, Caitlyn's eyes took on a dreamy look as she began to speak in a whisper.

"Okay, whatever. Well, I guess it would have to start on a Friday morning. He'd call me right before my alarm goes off to tell me good morning, followed by something really sexy, like how much he can't wait to hold me and kiss me during our weekend together. Then, when I arrive at work, he'd call to tell me he can't stop thinking about me. At lunch, I'd go shopping for a cute little something to wear during the weekend."

"What does this cute little something look like?" asked Victor quietly.

"I change my mind a lot on what I would buy."

"Do you have a cute little something waiting to be used?"

"No, of course not. This is my dream weekend, remember? Stop interrupting." Caitlyn frowned at his interruption.

"I'm sorry. Please, go on." Victor sat back and crossed his arms.

"Where was I? Oh, yes. Friday night, we'd talk on the phone while sipping wine. We'd talk about anything and everything, just to hear each other's voices. Then Saturday morning, we'd leave for our weekend. It'd be in a secluded little bed and breakfast nestled in a wooded area. We check in and then we take a long walk, holding hands. He'd touch me in little ways, all day and stroke my hand, my arm, my cheek. I'd touch him also. First his neck, then his chest, and knee. We'd keep it light on purpose, to build anticipation. We'd have a picnic and feed each other strawberries, bread, and cheese. We'd have a candlelight dinner and spend the next hour slow dancing in the lounge of some small little hideaway where jazz played softly in the background. Finally, we'd go back to our room and share long, slow kisses. We'd end the evening by making heart-stopping love with each other."

When Caitlyn finished, she realized she was leaning on the table with one arm, her food all gone and Victor staring at her with a fierce, unwavering look of fire. She shook her head, amazed she had shared a private fantasy with Victor, of all people. What must he be thinking?

* * *

Victor forced himself to uncross his arms and unclench his fists. His heart was pounding furiously and he couldn't breathe. His skin was hot and he felt sweat running down the back of his neck. Any chance of answering questions was gone. He sucked in some air and pushed himself away from the table.

"We'll have to do the interview another time. Right now, I need to get back to my office. Let's go."

Victor held out both hands. Caitlyn placed her hands into his and he pulled her to her feet. He walked up to the cash register, paid the bill, ushered Caitlyn out the door and was once again putting her in his car and driving off.

* * *

Caitlyn tried to shake off the effects of those two delicious margaritas and cursed herself for being all kinds of a fool and blowing this chance.

What is Jack going to say when he finds out I blew this interview? She wondered if she was going to be able to save her job as an intern, let alone get a job as a journalist. *What now? How can I fix this?*

"Victor. I'm sorry for sharing my private thoughts. I don't know what got into me. I really need to do this interview. Jack was counting on me to do a good job since Janice is out. If I go back with . . ."

"You'll still get the interview. I'll square things with Jack. Tell him I came down with a sudden touch of fever. I just can't do it today," Victor interrupted with a grimace.

Caitlyn slumped down in her seat. All she could do was hope the return ride would pass swiftly.

So much for being a professional. I blew that, and why? Because of a pair of smoky brown eyes, a voice of soft velvet, and the face and body of this one man, Victor Knoble.

* * *

Victor parked his car in the garage and turned to look at Caitlyn. Her chin was practically on her chest and she looked small and dejected as she sat hunched in the seat.

Placing a finger under her chin, he encouraged Caitlyn to raise her head and meet his gaze. He could see from her eyes that she was not pleased with the way things had turned out.

"Caitlyn, I'm sorry I changed everything. I promise Jack won't go ballistic. You'll get this interview. There's no one else I want to do this interview, only you." Shaking her head, Caitlyn started to speak.

"I can't believe I spoke about something so personal with you. That isn't like me. I don't want you to think ..." Victor placed his finger on her lips.

"I don't think anything. I've never done this before and I don't want you to think I'm playing some kind of game, because I'm not. I'll have Tom, my managing publicist, call Jack and tell him you were great. I'll handle things, I promise. Are you okay to drive?"

Victor sounded sincere, but Caitlyn hated feeling like the situation was out of her control, especially because of her loose tongue.

Getting out of the car, Caitlyn nodded and started the long, slow walk back to her own car. The drive back would give her the time she needed to rehearse different conversational possibilities.

Victor watched her leave and took a deep breath to ease the clenched muscles of his stomach, then turned and headed back to his office. Pulling out his phone, he pulled up Tom's number. He had to contact him fast, before Caitlyn made it back to her office.

Sprinting, Victor bounded into his office, greeted Sheila and asked her to give him some quiet time this afternoon. Ever composed, she simply nodded.

* * *

Caitlyn knew she wasn't ready to face Penny, with all her questions that probed for details. They had been casual friends for over a year, starting as students at NAU, and she was the one person who would see right through any story to explain the lack of interview. Even though Penny was a talker, she wouldn't hesitate to say she had blown it big time.

Dragging her feet, Caitlyn made her way into the office. She put her purse in a drawer, sighed, then grabbed her purse again and made her way into the bathroom to freshen her make- up before going to see Mr. Wingate.

I might as well face the music.

Caitlyn breathed a sigh of relief when she saw he wasn't in his office after she came out of the bathroom and put her purse away for the second time. Luckily, Penny was still out so she didn't have to worry about making something up before being pestered for the truth. Drumming her fingers on her desk, she realized she wasn't going to get anything accomplished. Signing out for the day, Caitlyn headed over to Janice's house. If anyone could help her figure out a way to turn this mess into something manageable, she could.

* * *

"Janice, what a beautiful baby. I can't believe you had this wonderful little person inside you all this time. I hope you don't mind me stopping by."

"Not at all! And thanks. She is great, isn't she? I feel like the luckiest woman in the world right now. But tell me, how did things go with the interview? I feel bad I couldn't be there to help you. Babies just have their own time-tables."

At the mention of the interview, Caitlyn's eyes grew large and her breathing became constricted.

She avoided Janice's gaze. Janice had so much integrity and had tried to show Caitlyn that hard work, high ethics, and guts were the tools she needed to make it as a top-notch journalist.

How can I tell Janice I ended up talking about a sexual fantasy with Victor?

"It must have gone really well. Victor sent over these beautiful flowers this afternoon and the card said he was glad the interview hadn't been canceled. He said you were the right person for this assignment. I'm glad it worked out. Once this piece runs, you'll be recognized in your own right." Janice continued talking but the words sounded like buzzing in Caitlyn's head as she tried to comprehend what had taken place.

Victor had covered up her professional slip. Why? Chewing her bottom lip was a nervous habit Caitlyn had developed as a young girl. She did it now as she continued to ponder this unexpected reprieve and wondered what price she might have to pay. After all, gifts like this were not free and she had no doubt Mr. Victor Knoble would be expecting some kind of thank you.

What game are you playing Victor? She frowned while pondering possible reasons for his actions.

As she thought about Victor's possible endgame, memories began to surface of Justin's expectations and his ability to control their relationship. Her involvement with him had started out great, but his demands had turned out to be life altering. Caitlyn balled her hands into fists.

I will not let life repeat itself.

4

Back at her apartment, Caitlyn took a shower and began putting her apartment in order. As she sorted laundry and cleaned up the dirty dishes from breakfast, she thought about the day. She frowned as she tried to figure out why she had slipped up at lunch. There was Janice, the new baby, work, and the fact that she had not been on a date in a very long time. Thinking about Victor made her flush.

She thought about the smoky, veiled look of his eyes as she shared her fantasy. *Justin used to look at me that way. Maybe that's why I slipped up and started talking the way I did at lunch. It isn't sex I miss. I miss knowing I'm desired and wanted.*

* * *

Justin. She wondered where he was now, and what he was doing, besides stalking her. Caitlyn leaned back on the couch, listened to the quiet operation of the washing machine and dishwasher, and sipped a glass of Sangria. She took a deep breath as she realized, and admitted, that since Justin, she had deliberately cut herself off from any, and all, possible relationships that would lead to romance. Memories began to flood in.

Can I think about Justin without feeling like breaking glass inside? Do I want to take that chance? I have to do this or I might find myself slipping up again and again in the company of someone as magnetic as Victor. How long has it been? Twenty-two months.

* * *

Caitlyn met Justin when she worked in one of the school dining rooms in March of her junior year at Northern Arizona University. He was tall and blonde with brilliant hazel eyes, and a smile that went on forever. He had dimples in both cheeks and his personality reminded Caitlyn of a playful puppy.

Justin approached Caitlyn one day with a single daisy that he held out as if it were a precious diamond.

"Please go out with me fair Caitlyn. You are the most beautiful woman in the world, and I will be your knight in shining armor if it's the last thing I ever do." He placed his hands over his heart, left over right, and arched his eyebrows as he waited for her answer.

Caitlyn saw the twinkle in his eye and knew he was joking, but there was no way she could resist his charm. She took the daisy and gave it an exaggerated sniff while looking at Justin. Then she laughed and agreed to go out with him. That was the first of many dates. Dating him was so much fun.

His sense of humor was nonstop. April and May flew by, and all too soon it was time to pack up and move home for the summer.

* * *

"I can't believe you have to go back. We just started going out. Why did I wait so long to ask you out? You know I love you, right?" Justin continued to hug and kiss Caitlyn between loading boxes into his car.

"I have to get enough kisses to last me through the summer."

He drove her down to Phoenix and managed to stretch a two and a half hour drive into five hours. Justin stopped every time he saw an interesting sign, a strange boulder, or an unusual tree. He stopped at Sunset point and insisted on having a small picnic. The fresh fruit salad was a wonderful surprise.

"You can thank me with another kiss."

Caitlyn was all too happy to oblige and enjoyed the soft, silky feel of Justin's lips. When she pulled back, Justin sighed and gazed at her with hooded, sleepy-looking eyes.

During their summer apart, Justin called almost every day, close to the half hour after he expected her to be home from work as an intern for Channel 10. They talked on the phone for hours, and Justin always told her how much he was thinking about her and missed her. His position as a tutor in the math department ended in July, and he headed back to San Francisco for the remainder of the summer. Justin's constant attention, while long-distance, made her feel special and cherished.

The start of August brought a nice surprise. Justin came down for the weekend to celebrate her birthday. He arranged the surprise with her mom and arrived mid-morning. Caitlyn came home from work and walked in to find him standing by the door with balloons, flowers, and a small, black, rectangular box. Her mom, brother, and stepfather were standing behind him, all beaming, waiting to see how Caitlyn liked her 'surprise'.

"Happy birthday, Caitlyn. I hope you like your presents," Justin whispered as he leaned over to plant a soft kiss. Gasping, laughing and crying, she threw her arms around his neck and hugged him close.

"Oh my gosh! You're the best surprise ever. I can't believe this." She squeezed Justin again and relished feeling his strong, solid body pressed against hers. She turned and looked at her mom and saw a huge smile on her face. Her brother, usually absent at family events, also watched her reaction to Justin's surprise visit.

"Honey, why don't you and Justin come in and sit down. Dinner is almost ready. I made your favorite." Rosie, animated and talking a mile a minute, ushered everyone into the kitchen.

The smell of vegetable lasagna teased everyone's nose and made stomachs rumble in anticipation. A vase sat ready for the flowers, and her brother tied the balloons to a chair near the door. A chocolate-hazelnut birthday cake with chocolate-coconut frosting sat ready for dessert.

"How long can you stay?" *He must love me.*

Justin beamed. "I can only stay two days. I had to get time off work so I could celebrate the birthday of my best girl."

Leaning over, Justin kissed her. She started to pull back because she didn't know how she felt about kissing him in front of her family.

Justin laughed, caught the back of her head and forced her to continue kissing him. "It's all right. They know I love you."

Looking at her mom, Caitlyn saw a smile on her face as she gazed at their embrace.

Justin had completely charmed her.

She felt confused by her mom's reaction.

I know she wants me to be happy, but she just met Justin. Can she really be okay with this display of affection?

Caitlyn wondered how her mom could just set aside all the lectures of the past.

What happened to her advice about going slow after meeting someone I might want to get to know in a romantic way?

"Hurry and open your present. I hope you like it," Justin continued. He shuffled from foot to foot as he waited for his present to be opened.

Caitlyn felt the heavy thud of her heart. She slowly opened the box. Inside was a beautiful copper bracelet, inlaid with small, smooth, polished rocks. She laughed. Of course they were rocks. It was a gift from Justin after all and she knew how much he loved all kinds of rocks. They were brilliant in color. The stones consisted of varying shades of purple, red orange, soft pink and golden brown. A rock bracelet was just the kind of present Justin would get and she was completely in love with it. She didn't know what she would wear it with, except maybe jeans. Looking up into Justin's shiny, expectant eyes, she smiled and whispered, "I love it."

"Yes! I knew it. I knew she would love it. Didn't I tell you? Do I know my girl, or what?" Justin winked at Rosie and leaned over to kiss Caitlyn again.

"Ah, young love. It's the best," Rosie said, then laughed as she turned and began placing dinner on the table.

Justin made the most of his visit. Rosie doted on him. She anticipated his needs and filled them before he asked. He, in turn, charmed her at every encounter.

"You look so beautiful today. That color is really becoming on you. I can see where Caitlyn gets her charisma." The compliments to Rosie continued the entire time he was visiting.

During Justin's visit, they had a lot of fun. They went Go Kart racing, horseback riding, and boating at Tempe Town Lake. Bowling was even more fun. Justin proved to be very bad at it. In fact, he totally sucked, but every time he threw a gutter ball, he ended up making everyone laugh as he groaned and wailed about his blasted luck, his sticky shoes, and the slick lanes. The excuses went on and on, but no one cared because he ended up making everyone nearby join in the fun. Justin didn't even care when Caitlyn beat the socks off of him. It just gave him another excuse to grab and kiss her as he offered his congratulations.

On his last night, they spent the evening watching scary movies with Rosie and Darius, Caitlyn's stepfather. Justin kept sighing and making soft groaning sounds as Caitlyn spent most of the evening with her head buried against his chest or neck. She peeked every now and then at the horrible images on the screen. Justin kept his arms wrapped around her and took the opportunity to caress her arms and back and kiss her cheeks, the top of her head, and her lips.

Rosie glanced at them while pretending to watch the movie. She still had a little smile on her face.

Caitlyn couldn't believe how comfortable Rosie appeared with all the physical contact. Justin seemed intent on touching her in front of everyone, almost as if he were establishing his right to touch her whenever and wherever he wanted.

When he walked her to her room later, he leaned her against the wall near the door and pressed his body firmly against her.

"I don't want to leave tomorrow. I don't want to be without you. Can I stay in your room tonight?" he asked as he continued to plant kisses up and down her neck.

"Justin, I can't. Not here in my parent's house."

"Please." Kissing her lips, Justin began gently rubbing his fingers up and down her arms. "Please," he whispered. He slid his fingers up to her throat and she felt his fingers trace the curves of her neck and collar bone down to the tops of her breasts. He slid his leg between hers and ground his pelvis against her. Her body felt warm and open. "Justin, no. Please don't push me. I just can't. Not here, not now."

Justin pulled back and stared into her eyes for a long, silent moment. Then, he turned and walked off without saying a word.

Caitlyn took a deep breath and slowly entered her room. Sleep? Impossible. She had a lot of questions and no answers.

What is Justin thinking? Did I blow it? Will he still like me? He came all this way to see me. Maybe I should have said yes.

Caitlyn tossed and turned all night. Three a.m. rolled around and the questions continued to badger without offering any answers. The blasted alarm went off way too soon. Dragging herself out of bed, she paused, listening for movement to indicate Justin had gotten up. She had no idea what to expect and nibbled on her lower lip, nervous about seeing him.

Will he talk to me? Is he still angry? What should I do?

Caitlyn closed her eyes and took a few deep, cleansing breaths as she tried to find a sense of peace. A cloud of uncertainty continued to linger at the edge of her consciousness.

Justin planned to take a shuttle to the airport. Caitlyn found him eating breakfast when she came to the kitchen. Rosie and Justin were quietly talking but stopped when she came in the room. Rosie said good morning, and then excused herself. Justin continued eating his breakfast without looking at her. He stared down at his plate and stabbed at each morsel of food before shoving it into his mouth and chewing slowly, eyes squinted, lips tight.

"Justin. I'm so sorry about last night. Please don't be mad at me. You made me happy with your visit and I don't want you to leave while you're still mad."

Silence, no eye-contact.

Caitlyn walked over and laid her hand on his shoulder, then leaned down to kiss him on the cheek. Justin froze as soon as she touched him. He laid his fork down and sighed, then scooted his chair back and pulled her down onto his lap. Holding her face between his hands, he kissed her, and then placed his forehead against hers. "I'm sorry I acted like a baby. I just love you so much."

Justin tucked her head under his chin and continued.

"I have to leave and I don't want to, but I'll call you every day, okay?"

"Okay." Caitlyn smiled and snuggled closer, rubbing her nose back and forth across the front of Justin's neck. *My Justin still loves me.*

True to his word, Justin did call every day. He said his day wasn't complete until he heard her voice. He took time to charm her mom on the phone at least once a week.

* * *

Those daily checks should have been her first warning. If she came home from work late or had an unplanned outing with her family or, heaven forbid- went out to have fun with people from work, Justin was quick to give her the third degree.

"Where were you? Who were you with? What were you doing? Why did you get home late?"

Sometimes it took half an hour just to get him to calm down. Justin always said he got upset because he worried about her safety and he only knew she was safe if she was there for their phone calls as planned. Then he would talk about how his days were dragging by because he couldn't be with her. He remained dissatisfied with their separation until they made plans to meet on August 25th, when Caitlyn planned to arrive at NAU and check into her new dorm room.

* * *

Back at campus, Justin met her arrival with bagels, cream cheese and tickets to the football game scheduled for the next week. Caitlyn felt special walking around campus holding hands with such a beautiful boy. Girls always looked their way and Caitlyn experienced a burst of pride knowing Justin only had eyes for her. He spent most of his free time with her as they began to date in earnest. Their dates included walks in the rain, picnics in the mountains, carnival rides, and double feature movies with lots of popcorn. Slow, sweet kisses, feather light touches, and a feeling of being special were a part of every encounter.

Justin had a habit of placing his nose just under her chin. From there he could run his nose up and down her neck while tickling her with his breath. Sighing, Caitlyn could still feel the slow travel of his nose from her ear to her chin and back again. Shivers traveled up and down her spine and she sighed from the warmth of her memories. It all felt so good.

* * *

What a crock. Caitlyn took a deep breath as she continued to think about the lessons she had learned from Justin. She knew now that those phone calls were Justin's way of controlling her. All of it was his way of wrapping silky bands of iron-clad control around every part of her life. Being new to a serious relationship, Caitlyn thought all relationships were like this. Didn't all men want daily check-ins? Didn't all men want to know where you were, what you were doing and who you were with?

Caitlyn shook her head, tears coursing down her cheeks. Her fingers gripped the stem of the wine glass so tight she was afraid of snapping it in half. She took a deep breath and carefully set the glass down on the table but had to steady it with both shaky hands. Breathing rapidly, she rubbed her churning stomach.

I can't go any further into those memories, not yet.

Taking a deep breath, Caitlyn tried to still the thoughts rolling around in her head and the thumping of her racing heart. Going to the bathroom, she decided to take another shower. This time, she hoped the warm water would soothe both her body and soul.

5

Sheila stopped Victor when he returned to the office after his lunch with Caitlyn. "You've been booked on a late flight. There's an emergency meeting with representatives from five countries interested in battling human trafficking. Here's your e-ticket, hotel information, itinerary, Ghanaian currency, and contact information. Is there anything else you need?"

"Sheila, you've worked your usual magic. I see I'll be traveling and working with Alan Fromm. That's great. He's been following the horrors of human trafficking for six years. I'm glad he'll be writing about the meetings. Okay, I have to pick up some more mosquito repellant and a couple of shirts. I better check my schedule in case anything needs to be rearranged."

Victor looked at the notes as he walked into his office. He frowned as he realized he wouldn't have an opportunity to see Caitlyn before he left, then smiled at the thought of her.

"How to make sure she keeps thinking about me. Hmm. Flowers? No, that's too ordinary. Candy? No, not personal enough."

Victor ground his teeth as he thought of, and then discarded, idea after idea. He didn't have her phone number so he couldn't even call her and tell her he was leaving. Then, it came to him. Looking at the clock, Victor realized he would have to work fast. He still had to finish packing and get to the airport by 11 pm.

* * *

The alarm blared. Caitlyn groaned and sighed, then forced herself to get up.

"Oh great. I would have to go to work looking like a hag today," grumbled Caitlyn when she saw her reflection in the mirror. Her eyes looked tired with dark circles underneath her eyes, attesting to her troubled, restless night. She downed three cups of tea, threw herself together and trudged out the door.

Caitlyn checked to see if Mr. Wingate had arrived. He was usually in his office well before the rest of the staff and he was always the last one to leave. He expected his staff to be the very best, but he didn't re-quire them to be married to their careers, as he was. Jack Wingate was the first one to admit that being obsessed with starting, running, and building this publication into what it was had cost him his marriage. He found it impossible to split his passion for work from his life at home. His marriage became a distraction he refused to nurture.

Today, Caitlyn noticed he must have decided he to stop for one of those things most people take for granted, breakfast. Breathing a small sigh of reprieve, she wondered how she was going to tell Mr. Wingate about the failed attempt to interview Victor Knoble. Caitlyn said a hurried hello to the receptionist who was conversing with a delivery-man and headed quickly toward her desk. She set her purse inside her drawer and started looking through her To Do list.

"Excuse me. Can you tell me where I might find Caitlyn Matthews?"

Caitlyn looked up to find a young man staring at her from across her desk, just outside of her cubicle.

"Yes, I'm Caitlyn. How can I help you?"

"This is for you, ma'am." Handing her a small basket, he quickly turned to leave.

"Wait. I haven't ordered anything. I'm sure you must have the wrong department, office, or something." The young man turned back and verified the location.

"Are you Caitlyn Matthews?"

"Yes," Caitlyn answered. It was obvious the basket was for her. *Hmm. Why? Who was it from?*

"Then this is for you. I'll see you again tomorrow."

Caitlyn had no idea what his cryptic remark about "... seeing you to-morrow," was all about or why some mysterious basket had been deliv-ered to her. The sweet cinnamon smell wafting up from the basket was heavenly. Lifting the cloth, she discovered small, freshly baked Mexican pastries. Noticing a small envelope tucked inside, Caitlyn quickly popped a pastry into her mouth as she opened it and took out the note. She almost choked as she read the message it contained inside.

"Caitlyn, as you enjoy these sweets, know that I'm thinking about you. I'm sorry the interview and hike will have to wait."

Victor

Caitlyn took a sip of tea to clear her throat and frowned as the scalding liquid burned her tongue and the roof of her mouth. With unsteady hands, she set down her cup as she realized the room sud-denly felt overly warm.

"Hey Caitlyn. What have you got there? How come you didn't say you were stopping for treats? Man, am I starving," exclaimed Penny. She came over and started snacking on the pastries without waiting for a re-ply and started telling Caitlyn all about her latest and greatest guy. With Penny, there was always a latest and greatest guy. Caitlyn quickly put the note in her desk as she tried to focus on what Penny was saying.

"So, you know I was going out with Jarrell. He's so nice, but I met this guy, Len, while I was on the treadmill and we started talking. We went out last night and I think I like him. I just don't know what I'm going to do about Jarrell..."

Penny continued to ramble on, not concerned about the fact that she was doing all the talking.

Caitlyn's mind was racing.

Why did Victor send over the pastries? What did the delivery guy mean when he said he would see me tomorrow? What does all of this mean?

Caitlyn felt like a deer blinded by the headlights of an oncoming car. She had to get away from Penny and the constant mind-numbing chatter. She had to think. Excusing herself from Penny, Caitlyn started walking toward the bathroom.

"Caitlyn. Get in here!"

Oh no, thought Caitlyn. *This is all I need.*

Turning, she headed into Mr. Wingate's office with slow, hesitant steps. Biting her lip, she felt like a child dreading the reprimand of a student heading to the Principal's office.

"Caitlyn. I got Victor's message. Sorry your first assignment didn't work out. We'll have to run his preliminary statements now and do the in-depth interview later. Tom said it was unfortunate Victor couldn't finish the interview and they both feel bad. Thanks for doing your best. Your assignments for the next two weeks are on your desk. We'll be getting you hooked up with a new mentor within a few days since Janice won't be back for another two months." Jack ended his speech and quickly went back to his papers, dismissing her as quickly as he had beckoned her.

Caitlyn left the office and walked, in a daze, to the bathroom.

What the heck just happened? Mr. Wingate didn't ask me to say anything at all about the interview. What has he been told and by whom?

Suddenly, everything was spinning out of her control and she didn't like that feeling one little bit.

Splashing cold water on her face, Caitlyn looked in the mirror. Good. There was anger in her eyes, along with determination. She didn't know what kind of game Mr. Victor Knoble was playing, but she was not going to be some little pawn he could move around and manipulate at will.

Been there and done that. "*What are you up to, Victor?*"

Taking a deep breath, Caitlyn marched out of the bathroom with a determined tread, reached her desk, picked up the phone and dialed Victor's number before she lost her nerve.

"Yes, I'll hold."

Well, so much for quickly speaking my mind. At least now I'll be able to have a moment before I let him know what's what.

"May I speak to Mr. Knoble please? My name is Caitlyn Matthews."

"I'm sorry. Mr. Knoble is unavailable for the next two or three weeks. Is there some urgent matter which would necessitate contacting him?" Sheila's voice sounded as smooth and unflappable as ever.

"No. No, that's all right. Thank you." Caitlyn said quietly, as she hung up the phone.

Feeling as if the wind had been taken out of her sails, she popped another pastry into her mouth.

"Oh well. Nothing to do now but get on with my day," Caitlyn said as she picked up her assignments. At the top of the list, she found she was to research the free reading programs at the Phoenix Public Libraries and to write a brief highlight on the ones she found most interesting.

While the task seemed mundane, Caitlyn realized she had to start somewhere, and the memo from Jack did say she would get the byline once Victor's interview appeared in print. Picking up the phone, Caitlyn called the library closest to the office. She would be able to stop by within the hour and get to at least two other libraries before the day was over.

* * *

The first stop was Middleton Children's Library, named for the late Henry James Middleton.

He was a local resident who had spent his entire adult life searching for great children's stories. When he found stories he liked, he would buy as many copies as he could afford at the time and share them with the children who lived in his neighborhood, at parks, or any other place where he found someone who shared his enjoyment of the written word. He and his wife had been unable to have any children of their own. Upon his death, she donated the rest of his books to the public library near the Capital. His gift was more than enough to start a small library for children and had prompted many generous donations to add to the legacy of literature he began.

"We also offer a wonderful puppet theater for our younger patrons," continued Mrs. Sanchez. Caitlyn realized she had missed some of the information. Her low voice had a droning, nasal quality Caitlyn found hard to listen to for very long. She found herself thinking of Victor instead of concentrating on the task at hand. It was going to be a long day. Just thinking about his dark, mesmerizing eyes and smooth, silky voice caused her heart to beat faster and her mouth to go dry. Caitlyn took a deep breath, tried to still her pulse and concentrate. The interviews at all the libraries seemed to take forever, and Caitlyn ended up downing two large coffees before the afternoon wrapped up.

* * *

The following morning, Caitlyn found herself blushing as she read Victor's note of the day.

"I close my eyes and I see your beautiful face. Think about me."
Victor

"Caitlyn, what's with the sweets? Is that a note? Did you order this stuff? What gives?" The questions from Penny seemed non-stop and Caitlyn had no intention of showing her the note. She wasn't ready to let anyone know Victor Knoble was expressing an interest in her.

Besides, she didn't even know where he was since he was 'unavailable' for another thirteen days.

Every morning became a routine. The young deliveryman appeared at her desk with yet another gift, along with a love note. The staff was going crazy with curiosity about the mystery man who was so in love with her that he sent something new each day. Caitlyn wondered how he could be doing all of this when Sheila said he was out of the country. The big question remained, why?

Two weeks flew by and October graced everyone with some needed relief from the heat.

Caitlyn looked for the young deliveryman on Friday. In fact, everyone anticipated this daily game. The staff had been enjoying the treats and suspense of wondering what was next, not to mention the chance to tease Caitlyn about her very generous mystery man. When the deliveryman didn't show, Caitlyn sighed.

I guess it's finally over. It was fun while it lasted.

Penny tried extra hard to take Caitlyn's mind off her disappointment and invited her out for the evening.

"Caitlyn, I met this really great guy while I was picking up dinner last night. He just moved here from California. He said he went to NAU. Anyway, we started talking and really hit it off. I invited him out to Palisades but if you don't come, it'll just be the three of us and that'll be weird. Besides, you need to get your mind off your mystery man, whoever he is, which you could tell me, you know. I am your best friend after all."

Giving in, Caitlyn forced a laugh as she concentrated on the details for the night.

"All right Penny, I'll go. Geez. And I'm not going to tell you anything about my mystery friend because I don't have it figured out yet. You know I love you, though," Caitlyn replied with a smile as she told herself Victor didn't matter.

So what if she hadn't been able to get him out of her mind? It didn't help that work was extra slow and the day seemed to drag.

6

As she left the building later that evening, Caitlyn regretted her agreement to meet Penny, her latest guy and the great man she just met. Then, there was that nagging disappointment she had tried to ignore all day. She half expected to hear from Victor since she heard he had returned.

Why send treats and love notes for two weeks, and then stop suddenly? What am I supposed to think?

Deep in thought, Caitlyn made her way out of the building. As she walked toward her car, she noticed someone leaning against it. Victor. He watched her with an intense look that never wavered.

A smile burst out on her face and Caitlyn felt her breathing become shallow and her step slowed. He was just as handsome as she remembered, and he still took her breath away. Her bones felt like they were melting, and she felt a tingling warmth radiating from the pit of her stomach.

"I missed you while I was gone. Could you tell? You look so good to me right now all I want to do is grab you and never let you go. I didn't know how much longer I could wait for you to come out. I didn't know if you were ready to be seen with me." Victor spoke softly with a small smile.

"I was wondering if I would hear from you. The deliveryman didn't come, and I thought maybe you weren't ..." Caitlyn stopped herself as she realized she was babbling.

"I wanted to give you my latest gift in person," Victor replied. "Can we go somewhere quiet? I need to be alone with you."

Groaning, Caitlyn remembered she was supposed to meet Penny in two hours. Now, more than ever, she regretted her agreement to go out, but Penny had been a good friend.

"I'm sorry. Since I didn't hear from you, I made plans to meet Penny later. I can't back out now, it's too late. Can we talk tomorrow? I know tomorrow is Saturday, but I really want to give you all of my attention. I have so many questions. Questions about why you sent all those gifts and those notes. What did they mean? Please..." Caitlyn ended quickly as she saw a change in Victor's eyes.

He started to frown as soon as she mentioned going out with Penny, and Caitlyn found herself drawing back in the face of his obvious anger. As she saw his expression darken, she stepped back, further away from him and clutched her purse to her chest. She glanced down at his hands and saw them balled into fists. His eyes were narrowed and his lips were pinched tightly together.

Feeling as if she couldn't get enough air into her lungs, she took a couple of steps back and prepared to run. Her muscles became tense, tightly wound coils of strength, ready to spring.

* * *

Victor started to let her know just how angry he was over her plans, until he saw how large her eyes had grown and how pale her face had become. She seemed to shrink in size as he continued to stare at her. He realized she was truly terrified at seeing his anger and he took a deep breath to control himself before she ran away screaming. The last thing he wanted was her running away from him, instead of to him.

Taking another deep breath and rubbing his hands through his hair, Victor tried to reassure Caitlyn. "Sure. We can talk tomorrow. Just tell me you'll be thinking of me while you're out having fun." He flashed a reassuring smile and reached out to smooth her hair back but dropped his hand when she flinched away from his touch.

"By the way, where are you going? Is this a double date or just friends getting together?"

Caitlyn forced herself to relax as she watched the effort Victor was making to control his emotions. His restraint showed he could be sensitive and was man enough not to threaten her with his anger, size, or physical strength.

"We're going to that new jazz club, Palisades. Penny wants to show off her newest love so I said I would go along. Thank you, Victor." Caitlyn stretched up to give him a gentle kiss on the cheek.

Victor quickly turned his head and captured her lips softly while gathering her into his arms for a soft, gentle embrace. Breathing in the scent of her hair, Victor slowly released her.

"Sorry. I just had to let you know how much I missed you. Will you please, please give me your cell number? If I'm going to see you tomorrow, I need to be able to call you." Victor ended his request with another tender kiss.

Head swimming, Caitlyn sighed as she took out her phone and handed it to him. He made sure they had each other's numbers while she tried to get her breathing under control. Victor took her keys, unlocked her car door and assisted her inside, then leaned over and whispered, "Until tomorrow, Caitlyn."

Caitlyn watched him walk away and wondered how she was going to listen to Penny and her new friend when images of those wonderful kisses were fresh in her mind.

* * *

Back at her apartment, Caitlyn settled herself into a hot, steamy bath scented with lilac oil. She tried to be excited about the evening ahead as she thought about her outfit choices. It couldn't be the cute little red dress. The cap sleeves and sweetheart neckline tapered down into a narrow, gathered waist, then flared into an a-line bottom. That one screamed, 'look at me'.

Caitlyn still couldn't believe she had let Penny talk her into buying it. Nope, it would remain in the closet until just the right occasion. The blue pants outfit seemed to say, 'I'm superwoman'.

Caitlyn tried on and discarded various options. *What to wear, what to wear?*

She finally selected burnished gold pants, along with a golden brown tunic that clung to her waist while offering a modest hug to her neckline. This was the first date she had allowed herself to be talked into since last year. Poor Roger. He was a nice guy, but he didn't stand a chance against her perception of what a relationship was like. He had clearly been interested in trying to have a relationship, but Caitlyn wasn't ready to trust her emotions after Justin. She shut down any interest Roger may have had and declared no more dating, until tonight.

But tonight doesn't really count, does it?

After all, going out with Penny wasn't the same thing as going out with someone on a date with the potential of a relationship. This night was just for fun. Nothing more, nothing less. The pep-talk helped her calm down as she continued to get ready.

Caitlyn took extra care with her hair and makeup, making sure every hair was in place. She took the time to apply fragrance to the insides of her elbows, the backs of her ears, and the backs of her knees. Looking at her reflection in the mirror, Caitlyn smiled.

I look good.

* * *

Victor spent the next two hours trying to keep busy. Even though she said she was meeting her friend Penny, he figured Penny would bring along a male friend for Caitlyn to make it a foursome. Grinding his teeth, Victor put down the photos that he kept moving from pile to pile. Showering quickly, Victor changed and headed to Palisades.

* * *

Palisades looked crowded. Tables for conversation were on the far wall, along with couches and lounge chairs arranged to invite people to sit down and get to know each other. Near the center of the room sat an island bar and the bartenders knew how to put on a show. The dance floor was near the front of the room and off to the side of the dance floor sat a small stage for bands and the disc jockey. Caitlyn saw Penny as soon as she entered the club. Penny was dancing close to her latest guy but stopped and came running over as soon as she spotted Caitlyn. Panting and out of breath, Penny grabbed her hand and pulled her over to one of the couches to introduce her to the man she had recently met and invited along.

Caitlyn found herself laughing at her friend's enthusiasm. "Caitlyn, I'd like you to meet . . ."

* * *

Caitlyn heard Penny's voice, but it seemed as if she were far away and speaking in a tunnel. Her palms started sweating and her feet felt heavy and leaden. Her mouth felt so dry she couldn't even swallow.

No, it can't be. Of all the men in the world, why does it have to be Justin?

Caitlyn tried to back away but Justin reached out and grabbed her hand. His hold looked like the soft caress of a lover, but Caitlyn flinched with remembered pain.

"Caitlyn," came the soft raspy voice she remembered so well. "I was so glad to hear you and Penny are friends and that you were willing to come tonight. I've missed you, babe."

The words, so familiar. Caitlyn gasped for air. She couldn't breathe. Her heart raced and she felt small and helpless, trapped like an animal in the grip of a predator. The mind box she had used so often in the past as her place of safety couldn't be found.

Caitlyn heard a voice inside her head whimpering but no words came out of her mouth.

Never in her wildest dreams had she imagined herself in the same room with him again.

The voices of the others faded away, as did the sounds in the room. The lights seemed to dim and Caitlyn felt as if she were peering through a narrow hole, with Justin as the only sight she could see. Her fingers felt icy cold and stiff, yet she could feel sweat pouring down her back. Then, there was Justin's voice, coming in a low whisper, as if he stood a great distance away.

She would never forget his raspy voice, not as long as she lived.

"Come on babe. Let's dance. I want to feel you in my arms again," Justin said as he began to lead her toward the dance floor.

"Justin, no," whimpered Caitlyn. Pulling back, she tried to resist.

Justin turned to look at Caitlyn. Instead of giving a reply, he just smiled and continued to lead her to the dance floor.

Caitlyn felt too weak to pull away and felt herself drawn relentlessly forward. A sense of helpless panic began to overwhelm her.

* * *

Sitting on a bar stool on the other side of the room, Victor scanned the room and felt his heart quicken when he spotted her. Victor ground his teeth as he watched the hand that caressed her back. Sipping his lime-flavored club-soda, he continued to watch Caitlyn from across the room.

"Maybe I should just leave instead of sitting here feeling like an idiot," murmured Victor.

* * *

Caitlyn felt Justin's hand sliding up and down her back. The touch felt like the heavy hand of oppression. Looking up into his eyes, she felt an urge to run screaming from the room, yet paralyzed at the same time. Caitlyn didn't know how much longer she could remain standing.

Her legs became shaky and her stomach began to churn with an ever-increasing urgency. Salty, bitter bile rose up from her stomach and filled her mouth with hot liquid that was difficult to swallow. Breathing through her nose, she tried to calm down.

"Caitlyn, love. What's the problem? You knew I would come back someday. I told you it would never be over for us. Let's get out of here so we can be alone ..."

Justin's voice continued but Caitlyn no longer heard the words. All she heard reverberating in her head were the words, "be alone."

Be alone? With you? No, never again!

Caitlyn tried pulling away from Justin and felt him tighten his grip on her hand and waist. "Let me go. I have to go, *now*," said Caitlyn as calmly as she could.

"We'll go together."

"I am not going anywhere with you. I want you to let go of me so I can leave," said Caitlyn in her strongest, most polished, professional voice.

"Caitlyn. You're starting to piss me off. You always do that. Now, let's try it again. Caitlyn my love, let's go somewhere so we can be alone," Justin repeated softly.

"Not this time. You can't just come in here and make me do what you want. Now, let me go! I swear Justin. I will scream and yell and make the biggest scene ever."

The old panic intensified as she saw the flushed cheeks, narrowed eyes, and clenched jaw, the signals to announce the start of pain. She began to pull away even harder, but the more she pulled, the harder Justin's grip became. Caitlyn began looking around wildly, desperate to see someone she could call out to for help. There were people dancing, laughing and talking all around, but no one seemed to notice the battle of wills between her and Justin. She didn't know if anyone would help her or if they would even be able to hear a scream because of the loud music and noise.

* * *

Victor's eyes narrowed when he saw Caitlyn try to pull away without success. Her complexion had lost all color and she seemed very stiff. He noted the change in Justin's face as well and saw flushed skin and clenched teeth. Victor forced his hands to relax and slowed down his breathing as he walked onto the dance floor.

* * *

Caitlyn felt giddy with relief when she saw Victor's face. That feeling gave way to fear for his safety. As she tried to take a step toward him, Justin tightened his grips on her wrists to hold her in place.

"Excuse me. It looks like Caitlyn is tired of dancing for the moment. I'm sure you won't mind if she sits down," said Victor.

"Who the hell are you? Mind your own damn business," snapped Justin.

"My name is Victor and I'm a friend of Caitlyn's. Now, I think she'll be going."

"I don't think so. You'd better leave now because Caitlyn and I have some unfinished business," snarled Justin.

Justin's hands squeezed her wrists even harder as he turned aggressively to face Victor, yanking her off balance when he moved.

Victor glanced, unspeaking and unsmiling, at Caitlyn. He took a deep breath and turned to meet Justin's angry gaze. Victor stared him straight in the eye, then looked down and noted Justin had released one of Caitlyn's wrists. The other one was still held firmly in his grasp.

"Caitlyn. Are you ready to leave?" asked Victor gently.

"Yes. I'm ready to leave," said Caitlyn softly. She kept her eyes on Victor's face, her eyes pleading.

Grabbing Caitlyn's free hand, Victor attempted to pull her behind him as he began to back away from Justin.

Dropping Caitlyn's wrist, Justin squared his shoulders and pushed out his chest. He looked angry and confused as he watched the confident, controlled, physically fit man lead his Caitlyn away.

Clenching his jaw, he turned and stalked off the dance floor. Heading back to the table where Penny and her date sat, Justin snarled out a nasty, "Thanks for nothing Penny," and strode away.

Penny looked over to the dance floor and saw Caitlyn leaving with Victor Knoble of all men. Jumping up, Penny ran out the front door to make sure Caitlyn was all right.

* * *

"Caitlyn, tell me where your car is parked," Victor requested quietly.

"I came by cab," she managed to tell him before running to the nearest trash can where she became ill.

Victor waited a short distance away while she composed herself.

Penny started to rush to her, but Victor stopped her and said he would take her home. He asked where Caitlyn lived and assured Penny that Caitlyn would be all right and he would take care of her. He walked over and took Caitlyn gently by the arm, then led her toward his car and placed her gently inside.

The ride flew by and Caitlyn found herself standing in front of her door before she knew it. Her legs felt shaky and her insides were still quivering and her body felt weak. Tears kept leaking from her eyes. She turned to thank Victor for his help, but he slipped her keys out of her hand and unlocked the door.

Ushering her inside, he locked the door and led her to the couch. He stretched her legs out after she sat down, removed her shoes, covered her with a blanket, and sat down on the floor near her head, still without speaking. When she tried to speak, he placed a finger on her lips, then caressed her hair.

"It's okay. You're safe and I'm not going anywhere. You don't have to say anything. I just want you to relax."

With tears slipping quietly down her cheeks, Caitlyn nodded, took a deep breath, and tried to sleep, but every time she closed her eyes, Justin's angry face filled her mind. Reaching out, she found Victor's hand and entwined her fingers with his. She held onto his hand and tried to wipe Justin's image from her mind by concentrating on Victor's strength. Sighing, she felt her body slowly begin to relax.

Victor leaned his head back on the sofa and continued to sit in silence, holding her hand and stroking her hair. He didn't force her to talk.

As she slept, Victor sat there watching her, the scene from the dance floor replaying in his mind.

When he was sure she was asleep, he grabbed a couch pillow and a blanket off the back of a chair and went to sleep on the floor by the couch, listening to the quiet, rhythmic, sound of Caitlyn's breathing.

7

Caitlyn awoke to the soft hum of the ceiling fan but remained still and kept her eyes closed. She stretched slowly and winced at the soreness in her muscles. As memories began to flood her mind she jerked upright and glanced around to locate Victor. She saw him stretched out on the floor beside the couch. He was on his back, long legs straight with his ankles crossed. She felt like crying all over again as she thought about how tender and caring he had been. She felt safe with him and frowned, surprised at the realization. She glanced at his face and met his gaze.

Victor watched her, not saying a word, as she looked at him. His hands were under his head, accentuating his flat, taut stomach and the broad expanse of his chest.

Caitlyn's breathing slowed down and became shallow as Victor continued to gaze into her eyes. Then he smiled and whispered her name. The room seemed brighter and warmer as she returned his smile and ducked her head.

"Thank you for staying with me. You must have had an awful night's sleep down there," said Caitlyn while swinging her legs off the couch.

"It wasn't so bad. I wouldn't like to sleep down here every night, but you just say the word and I'll make camp any time you want."

"I don't think that will be necessary," said Caitlyn as she lifted her chin and turned her gaze away. She got off the couch and took a couple of steps toward the door, then stopped to look back at him.

Victor heard the change in her voice and took a slow breath.

"I don't know about you, Caitlyn, but I'm starving. It feels like I haven't eaten in ages. Are you hungry?"

"Yes. I am a bit hungry. Would you like breakfast before you leave?" answered Caitlyn as calmly as she could.

Victor didn't answer right away. Instead, he got up, folded and stacked the blanket and pillows neatly on the couch.

"Well. I had something different in mind. I need to test my newest equipment and was hoping we could drive out to Lake Pleasant and eat breakfast there. I know a great bakery where we can pick up some fresh bread, coffee, cheese, and fruit. How about it? I have spare clothes in the car that I keep on hand in case I go to the gym or need to work after exercising. I can change and off we go."

Victor stayed in front of the couch and held his breath as he waited for her reply.

Caitlyn remained silent and watched as Victor ran his fingers through his hair. She flicked each fingernail across the pads of her thumbs as she considered Victor's words and wondered what to think.

What if he can see my attraction for him? Will that give him power over me? Will he use those feelings to hurt me?

Caitlyn started shaking her head as she backed away, arms crossed over her stomach.

Victor walked over and cupped her left cheek with his right hand as he leaned forward to gently capture her lips with his. Pulling back, he looked into her eyes and smiled.

"Please. We can have a great day, no stress. We're just two friends hanging out, enjoying each other's company. What do you say? Are you game for some fun?"

"Okay," sighed Caitlyn as she met his gaze.

Releasing her hand, Victor stepped back, told her he would get his clothes, grabbed Caitlyn's keys off the table by the door and left in a flash.

Caitlyn watched him leave, then went to change. She showered and changed quickly, then went to let Victor know he was free to use the shower and the spare toothbrush she had received at her last dental cleaning. Time flew and he soon came back out, dressed and ready to go.

They stopped at Geno's Bakery, the most popular bakery on the west side of Phoenix, so they had a small wait. Victor bought enough food.

He also went to the store next door and picked up sunblock, a cooler, and drinks. "Feel free to pick any station you'd like," invited Victor as he turned onto the Carefree Highway toward Lake Pleasant.

Reaching over, Caitlyn flipped through several stations and settled on a jazz station. She sighed, relaxed from the warmth of the sun streaming in through the tinted window. As she listened to the soothing sounds of the music, she leaned back in the seat and drifted off to sleep.

Victor looked over at Caitlyn several times during the drive out to the lake and smiled.

He began tapping his fingers on the steering wheel to the beat of the music.

The lake, a beautiful rippling blue, remained a popular place for people with boats and jet skis. It also provided nice areas for families to spread a blanket out and watch kids play in the water.

Victor drove west of the boating docks to an area with a small sandy beach. Not many people went to that area because they had to travel over rough terrain to get there. It was public enough to make Caitlyn feel safe but secluded enough so they would not be disturbed.

Caitlyn spread out the blanket while Victor grabbed their bounty of food and supplies from the car.

"Caitlyn. I brought this in case you forgot to bring some. This sun feels great, but burns are dangerous. I put some on when I dressed," said Victor as he held the bottle out for Caitlyn to take.

"Thanks. I did forget to bring some along." She began applying the lotion to her arms and heard the tale tell clicking of a camera. She looked up and saw the camera aimed at her, so she made a face and stuck out her tongue.

Victor laughed as he continued to snap pictures of her. He turned the camera upside down, sideways, moved in close and stood far away in order to capture various angles and background images.

"Hey. I thought you wanted to get pictures of this beautiful lake," laughed Caitlyn. She felt a little self-conscious being the sole object of Victor's focus.

"No. I said I wanted to test out my new equipment and you happen to make a wonderful subject. I hope you don't mind," answered Victor.

Breakfast became a game. Victor would pop a bite into his mouth while trying to capture pictures of Caitlyn eating. She kept laughing and threw some grapes at him. She laughed so hard that she made a snorting noise in her nose and made them both laugh even harder. Caitlyn found herself rolling around on the blanket holding her stomach. Jumping up, she grabbed a pillow and started posing in funny positions, using the pillows and the chairs as props. She picked up handfuls of sand and threw them in the air. She threw shells into the water, tried to skip rocks and waded in the water while she tried to splash Victor. All the while, he kept snapping pictures.

Victor felt his body becoming tense as he watched her through the camera lens. His throat felt dry and his breathing was becoming increasingly shallow with every passing moment. His hand became shaky and the camera started to feel heavy. As Caitlyn posed once more on the blanket, Victor knelt beside her.

He set the camera down as he captured her eyes with his. Leaning over her, he kissed her.

He brushed his lips back and forth, then pulled back, looked into Caitlyn's half-closed eyes and waited.

Her hands slid up into his hair and she gave a little sigh as she captured his lips.

Groaning, Victor stretched out beside her and placed a leg across her body. He deepened the kiss and caressed her stomach. Slanting his mouth across hers, Victor slid his tongue along the ridges of her lip.

Caitlyn tipped her head back and waited for his tongue to enter her mouth, but Victor continued to tease her by refusing to go in. Caitlyn teased back by nibbling on his lip. She slid her fingers through his hair and gently scratched his scalp.

Caitlyn wanted to be closer to the solid warmth and strength of Victor's body. Her mind was whirling and for the moment, she forgot they were at a public lake. All she knew was that it had been a long time since she felt these wonderful sensations. Caitlyn felt warmth radiating all over her body as her mind continued to whirl with wave after wave of delicious sensation.

Turning her toward him, Victor wrapped his arms tightly around her as he pulled his mouth from hers. He breathed in the scent of her hair, eyes closed, body still and tense. Victor smiled as he rubbed her back and felt her quivering legs. He frowned as he recalled the image of Caitlyn being held, against her will, in the club. He started to ask her about it, then bit his lip.

As Caitlyn's breathing began to return to normal, Victor pulled away and looked into her eyes. He kissed the tip of her nose, her cheeks, her forehead, and her chin. Victor looked down, then he gave her lips a soft kiss.

"I think I like you just a little bit," he said with a small smile.

Caitlyn exhaled and smiled, then snuggled against him. "I think I like you, too." Victor rolled onto his back and tugged Caitlyn over so that she was laying against his side. He kept his left arm under her neck and played with her hair while resting his head on top of his right hand.

Caitlyn began to doze and Victor eased from her side without disturbing her. He placed a pillow under her head, picked up his camera and began to head a short distance away.

There were several boats out on the water. Victor began to photograph the boats and spent some time concentrating on getting shots of people in the boats and water. He snapped some pictures of children playing on the opposite shore and photographed them as well. The air was dry, the sun was warm and the woman he wanted was asleep nearby.

The lap of water greeted Caitlyn as she woke up and stretched her arms and legs, then looked around. Victor was some distance away and she rolled onto her side and watched him as he concentrated on his work. She loved the way his hair curled at the nape of his neck. She was glad he didn't wear it long, the way many photographers did. She found him much sexier with shorter hair.

Caitlyn bit her lip as she thought about her lack of control earlier.

What in the world came over me? Why does he get to me? What is it about Victor that makes me want to seize the moment? Would I have this reaction with another man? What's next? What does he want?

Thinking about his tenderness of the night before, Caitlyn wondered how Victor had known where she lived. He had driven her home even though she didn't tell him where to go. She made a mental note to ask him about it later.

Why was he at Palisades?

Caitlyn looked down at her wrists and saw faint impressions, discoloration from Justin's tight grasp. Those would bruise later. Not that she hadn't had bruises like that before. She had experienced bruises like this too many times before and had vowed that never would she let any man bruise her again.

Justin looked as handsome as he had the first time she saw him, when he had charmed her with that stupid flower, but it didn't matter because she knew the man inside the skin. Caitlyn felt a moment of panic as she wondered if Penny had told Justin where she lived. That was one conversation she determined to have with Penny right away.

Victor walked back over to the blanket, sat down, and began to eat some of the food. He looked over at Caitlyn and saw her lost in thought. From the pensive look on her face, he figured the thoughts weren't good. He placed his finger under her chin and tipped her face up so he could capture her gaze.

"Hey you. Today is a no stress day, remember? What are you thinking about?"

"Oh. It's nothing really," replied Caitlyn.

Holding her gaze, Victor reached out a hand and caressed her face.

"Caitlyn, I promise you can trust me. I'm not some creeper hoping to have a hot and heavy hook-up with you and then leave you hanging. I feel like with us, there could be more .... I don't know what yet, but just more. I know I want more. More time with you, more time for us, more time for everything."

"I'm just not sure about myself right now. Last night, it was such a shock seeing Justin and then you've been so great. I just don't know what to think." Caitlyn bit the inside of her lower lip on the right side as she held Victor's gaze.

"Will you tell me about him? You don't have to tell me anything you feel uncomfortable about, but I would like to know if you still have feelings for him."

"No. I don't have feelings for him and I know I don't want him anywhere near me. When Penny invited me to meet her at Palisades, she said she wanted me to meet this new guy. I didn't know Justin was the person Penny met and I hope she didn't tell him where I live. I don't know what I'll do if he finds out. I didn't know..." Her voice sounded shaky and strained.

Victor moved closer, cupped the back of her head, and silenced her with a gentle kiss.

Pulling back, he met her gaze.

"Did he hurt you Caitlyn?" Holding his breath, he waited for her to answer.

Blast it all, not tears again!

"I can't talk about it, Victor. I'm sorry. Not yet."

Catching a tear on the tip of his finger before it fell, Victor smiled as he looked into her eyes.

"It's all right. Just know that when you're ready, if you ever want to tell me, I'll be ready to listen. I'm here and I don't want to go anywhere. As long as you let me, I'm going to stay close. I really like you. Give me a chance, please. I'll try never to hurt you." Leaning over, Victor captured her lips in another gentle kiss.

Sighing, Caitlyn gave herself over to the warm feelings that came with Victor's gentle kisses and felt her body relax.

They shared cheese and crackers, along with the grapes and left over apple slices. Victor had flavored water to drink and it was wonderful with the food, a nice change from soda.

They spent the rest of the day lounging around the lakeside. Neither Victor nor Caitlyn, were interested in being in the water, so they tossed aside the idea of renting a boat for the day. Later in the afternoon, they gathered their things, returned the Jeep and headed back to Caitlyn's apartment before the evening traffic became too heavy.

"How about some dinner? We could stop and grab some Chinese food, rent a couple of old movies and relax. What do you think?" asked Victor quietly.

"It sounds great to me, but I remember reading that you usually like to spend your weekends dancing the night away. Won't you find an evening filled with rented movies kind of dull and boring?" asked Caitlyn. She found herself holding her breath as she waited for his reply.

"I won't find it boring if I'm wrapped around you. And don't believe everything you read, because most of it is hype and conjecture. If tabloids and headlines were all true, I would have a string of beautiful women with me all the time. That's not what I want or what my life is really like. I'm a simple man and all I want is to spend some more time with you."

Caitlyn sucked in her breath at his heady reply and felt herself melting into a hot puddle of liquid. Instant heat radiated through her body again as she looked into his eyes and remembered the sensations evoked during their last embrace. Caitlyn took a breath, not sure she was ready for that level of involvement yet.

Victor read the changing expressions on Caitlyn's face. Her dreamy, breathless and flushed expression slowly faded to one of doubt and uncertainty. Reaching over, he picked up a hand and kissed her fingers.

"We won't go any further than you're ready to go. I promise. No stress, remember?"

Caitlyn smiled and her eyes lit up once more. Nodding her head, she relaxed and looked forward to a wonderful evening.

Stopping at Ming Lee's on Glendale, Victor and Caitlyn each placed an order. Victor ordered spicy, seared sea scallops, brown rice and a side of vegetables. Caitlyn ordered Kung Pao shrimp, brown rice, egg foo young and seasoned vegetables.

"A little hungry are ya, Caitlyn?" teased Victor.

"I love egg foo young for breakfast and this saves me trip. So there," quipped Caitlyn.

"I get it. Two meals taken care of in one trip. Very smart."

Grabbing the food, they continued on their way back to Caitlyn's apartment. She checked her messages and found that Penny had called several times.

"Hey Caitlyn. Are you there? Are you okay? What happened last night? I didn't know you already knew Justin. Are you going to tell me about it? Call me and let me know you're okay. . . Okay? Bye."

"Caitlyn. It's me again. Where are you? I know you left with Victor. Was he the one sending you all those treats? . . . What's the deal? . . . What's going on? Are you okay? Call me before I go crazy. Okay, bye."

Caitlyn smiled when she heard the messages. Penny was a good friend. She wasn't looking forward to telling Penny everything, but it was nice to know that Penny cared enough to call not once, but twice. While Victor went about setting out the food, Caitlyn went into her bedroom to call Penny. Perfect, the answering machine.

"Hi Penny. I'm so sorry I didn't call you back sooner. I'm okay and yes, Victor sent the treats. I'll tell you all about it when I see you Monday. Let's have lunch. Don't tell Justin where I live or give him my number, okay? Bye."

Victor and Caitlyn ate dinner quickly and cleaned up the dishes. They selected a couple of movies and Caitlyn arranged the couch for comfort while Victor showered and changed into a pair of sweatpants and a tee-shirt he kept stored in his trunk.

When he walked out, Caitlyn felt her heart begin to thud and her mouth went dry as she realized all over again, just how handsome he was, no matter what he was wearing. The sweatpants showed the lean length of his legs and the tee-shirt showed the deep expanse of his chest and muscular shoulders.

Victor told Caitlyn he would fix some drinks and relax while she showered and changed.

Speechless, she nodded her head and headed to the bathroom.

Walking back into the living room following a nice warm shower, Caitlyn saw Victor stretched out on his side, on the couch. As she entered the room, he looked up and met her gaze, then smiled and patted the space on the couch in front of him. Victor felt his body growing tense as Caitlyn advanced across the room. Each step she took caused his heart to beat faster and his breathing became shallow.

Caitlyn felt a warm surge of heat flood her body as she walked toward the couch. Sitting down in front of Victor, she leaned back against him, lifted her feet, and stretched out in front of him. She could barely breathe as she felt the muscular hardness of his chest against her back.

Victor shifted slightly so that her hips settled firmly against his pelvis and there was no mistaking his state of arousal. He closed his eyes and suppressed a groan as he took a deep breath and forced his body to relax.

"Concentrating on this movie is going to take every bit of effort I can muster." Victor kissed her neck then adjusted the pillows they were laying on.

Caitlyn felt the tension easing from Victor's body even though his arms continued to tremble ever so slightly. As she listened to him take slow, deep breaths, she felt her own body start to relax. A sense of serenity stole over her as she realized that, true to his word, Victor didn't press her to move too quickly. Smiling to herself, she contemplated her growing feelings for this wonderful man and settled herself fully and firmly, against Victor's length.

Gritting his teeth at her movements, Victor forced himself to speak softly. "Careful, my love. You have to help me by staying still."

Caitlyn felt no concern at hearing his words, but felt her whole body vibrate as his words rumbled against her back.

"I promise to do my best sir, but I do have to say that this is the best snuggling I've ever had and I plan on enjoying it," quipped Caitlyn with a small chuckle.

"Okay brat. You've been warned," replied Victor. Grabbing a pillow, Victor smacked Caitlyn on the top of her head.

Scrambling off the couch with a shriek from Victor's surprise attack, Caitlyn quickly grabbed one of the pillows off the floor and started hitting back at Victor. He lunged and grabbed her around the knees. As they toppled over on the floor, they both doubled over with laughter.

Caitlyn could not remember the last time she had felt so relaxed and at ease. Looking up into Victor's eyes, she saw his eyes slowly darken as he gazed at her mouth.

"I could listen to you laugh forever," he said softly.

Slowly, the little space between them disappeared as Victor leaned down and gently captured her lips with his. He gently settled his body on top of hers as their kiss continued to deepen.

She felt very comfortable with Victor and longed to languish in this warm, sultry feeling forever. But, a small part of her began to feel afraid.

Will Victor feel like he has the right to keep going even if I say no?

Justin had, and Caitlyn began to worry. Feeling tears begin to form, she tried to remind herself this was Victor, not Justin.

Breathe Caitlyn, she told herself. Trying to calm down, she forced herself to remember how tender Victor had been.

Pushing gently on Victor's chest, Caitlyn sought to put some distance between them before things went too far, too fast. She wasn't ready, not yet.

"It's okay Caitlyn. You have control, and we'll stop whenever you want. Just try and trust me not to hurt you," whispered Victor as he looked into Caitlyn's eyes.

Nodding, Caitlyn let Victor pull her close again for another soft kiss.

He continued to give kisses as he slowly stroked her stomach and gently caressed her body. Each movement of his hands brought shudders of pleasure and sighs from her parted lips.

Caitlyn felt herself slipping further and further into a sea of whirling pleasure. His touch felt so light and thrilling at the same time. She felt torn. Part of her wanted these delicious feelings to go on forever, but then, there was another side of her that whispered again.

Be careful. Remember the last time you trusted.

"Caitlyn, look at me," Victor urged. "I think I need you forever, not just for this moment. I will never hurt you or force you to bend to my will." Capturing her lips again gently, Victor continued in a soft whisper, "Please trust me."

Pulling back, he looked into Caitlyn's eyes and smiled. His face looked strained and tense and Caitlyn could feel his body shaking. Sitting up, he pulled her onto his lap and leaned back against the couch.

Victor started forcing himself to breathe deeply, then tucked Caitlyn's face into the cradle of his neck.

Caitlyn nuzzled and kissed Victor's neck as he continued to slowly and gently stroke her body. She could not believe he had stopped right when part of her had finally decided to consider giving in to the pleasure he was making her feel. As the tension slowly eased from her body, Caitlyn could feel Victor start to relax.

Sighing, Victor rested his forehead against hers a moment, then eased Caitlyn off his lap and got to his feet when he felt his legs would once again support him. Pulling Caitlyn to stand against him, Victor held her quietly. Slowly, still without speaking, Victor helped Caitlyn to adjust her clothing, and she in turn, helped Victor to fix his clothing.

"I have to go now. I want to stay so badly, but if I stay, I may blow it because I really want you. You set me on fire Caitlyn. The more time I spend with you, the more time I want. After I leave, don't close up on me, okay? If you start to have doubts, just call me and talk to me."

Walking slowly toward the door, they paused a couple of times to share slow, soft kisses before Victor finally turned to leave.

Catching his hand, Caitlyn pulled him around to face her. She forced herself to meet his gaze and took a deep breath before speaking.

Victor saw a frown form on her brow.

"I don't know if I want you to go. I feel so confused right now. But, I do know that I don't want to think about not feeling this way with you again, and I don't know if you'll come back if you leave now." The words came out in a rush and Caitlyn gulped a breath after she finished.

Laughing softly, Victor replied, "Don't worry. I'll never be gone for long," and kissed her again. "Remember what I said earlier? With you, I want more."

"Can you tell me why we stopped? I think I would have let you... us, happen."

Is this what the possibility of rejection looks and feels like?

Victor paused a moment before answering her. Cupping her face in his hands, he whispered, "With you, there can never be any regrets. Not with me. When we come together, you'll know beyond any shadow of doubt that you feel about me the same way I feel about you.

There won't be any hesitation. Like I said before, this isn't just a chance, momentary encounter or a quick hook-up. I want more than that. I want you to want me for more than a little while. Think about me while I'm gone." He kissed Caitlyn on her forehead, cheeks, chin, nose, and finally, on her lips. Then he turned and walked out to his car.

Leaning her head against the doorjamb, Caitlyn watched as Victor climbed into his car.

As he drove away, she couldn't help feeling that a part of her heart was also missing.

Am I falling too fast? I can't believe the feelings I have for him are so strong already. Am I crazy to feel this way so soon?

She could still smell his lingering scent, could still feel the tingling warmth of being held in his arms. Smiling, she slowly closed the door and wondered how she was ever going to sleep.

* * *

Victor ran a finger across his lips as he pictured their kiss. Instead of heading back to his lonely place, he decided to head to the gym to lift some weights and go swimming.

* * *

Back in her apartment, Caitlyn reflected on the differences between Victor and Justin. She hated comparing them, but she didn't have any other relationships to use as comparison.

Victor stopped just as he said he would.

Thinking about his control brought back memories of her times with Justin; how he first approached her, swept her off her feet, and then caused pain.

Justin fooled me. I can't let that happen again, not ever. I can't believe it took me so long to see the real Justin.

Caitlyn settled into bed and picked up her computer and opened her notifications. As she stared at Justin's face, she frowned as memories began to flood her mind.

8

Dates with Justin were usually good times, full of fun and laughter. He was not above acting a little goofy just to make her laugh, but not enough to cause embarrassment about being seen with him in public.

Dating between classes became tricky to accomplish. Justin would have a class or Caitlyn had class and they both worked hard to find time to be together. Justin often showed up at Caitlyn's classes with muffins, coffee, and silly notes. He even showed up one time with a sign that read, "I'm dreaming of my beautiful, brown-eyed girl." Forget concentrating after that one. She left in the middle of class.

Heading to her room, Justin kept one arm wrapped tight around her waist. Caitlyn's head and senses swam with warm tingles while he nuzzled her neck, rubbed her stomach, and breathed heavily between soft kisses that made her skin sizzle. The walk seemed to take longer than usual because of her shaky legs.

Melinda, Caitlyn's roommate, was in class for the afternoon, so they took advantage of their time alone. Justin kept caressing her and telling her how much he loved her. Rational thought was becoming impossible, so before things went too far, Caitlyn started to pull away.

"I can't, Justin. Please, slow down." It took some time, but Justin finally pulled back and allowed space between them. He looked at Caitlyn for a moment, then left without a word.

Worried, Caitlyn sent him multiple texts throughout the evening, but he never replied and didn't talk to her for two days. When he finally replied to one of her texts, he said she had broken his heart and he needed some time, but everything was 'okay' now. She didn't know what that meant.

A week later, the second week in September, he surprised her with a trip down to Phoenix just to play miniature golf at Castles N' Coasters, a local amusement park. They left right after Caitlyn's last class and the drive flew by as they laughed, talked, and sang the whole way down to the valley. Justin didn't have a great voice, but he made it fun to sing together. Once they arrived at the park, he insisted on paying for all of their activities.

Justin was terrible at mini-golf and kept hitting the ball too hard. Twice the ball hit the target and bounced back toward him with lightning speed. He ducked out of the way with amazing acrobatics to avoid injury from the whack of the ball. He fell to his knees and cried out, "Why oh why?" with a wail and a moan, then he tried to sweet-talk the ball into the hole. Caitlyn doubled over with laughter.

He made friends with players in front and behind as everyone laughed at his silly antics. It was hard to be angry with someone having obvious fun and inviting everyone else to join in at the same time. Justin cracked jokes the whole time and never seemed irritated, even when he managed to hit a ball over the tall perimeter fence. He watched Caitlyn every time she putted and offered his assistance, then demanded a kiss when Caitlyn managed to sink a ball.

They enjoyed nachos and soda after they played the final hole, before heading back up to NAU. Caitlyn's family lived six miles from the park, but she decided not to stop by on a spur of the moment visit.

"Do you want to stop by and see your mom? We have time to stop by before heading back up the hill."

"No. She'll ask way too many questions and she'll probably think you're my Mr. Right or something like that. She's a romantic."

"It's okay by me if she thinks we have a future together. I kind of like the sound of that."

"Not this time."

"I've already talked to her on the phone a couple of times and I know she likes me."

"Ha, and that's exactly why I'm not taking you anywhere near her yet." Caitlyn threw her head back and laughed.

Justin's next surprise was a trip to the Lowell Observatory in Flagstaff. The huge telescope gave a great view of the solar system. Justin brought blankets and a thermos of hot chocolate flavored with cinnamon and chili. He even brought two paper cups instead of Styrofoam.

After gazing at planets through the telescopes at the observatory, they drove north of the campus for about an hour. Caitlyn didn't know where they were, but Justin found a nice secluded area for them to lay down and snuggle together in the sleeping bags he zipped together. The pitch-black sky gave the shooting stars a marvelous canvas to display their beauty.

Caitlyn snuggled close to Justin and they spent the next hour sharing kisses, until the cold made it impossible to stay out any longer. Even cuddling failed to keep Caitlyn's teeth from chattering.

"Come on. I guess it's time to go. It's only going to get colder."

Grabbing her hand, Justin hauled Caitlyn up and wrapped the sleeping bag around her shoulders while he gathered their picnic items.

Are you the one, Justin? Okay. You did get mad that one time, but who doesn't have a bad day once in a while? This feels right.

* * *

Spending the evening with Justin became the routine. When he wasn't with his friends or in class, Justin made it a point to spend time in Caitlyn's dorm room. Luckily, Melinda, her roommate, was involved with her own relationship, so she was gone most evenings and weekends.

When she was there, Justin tended to ignore her and insisted on cuddling and kissing Caitlyn as if they were alone. Melinda became annoyed.

"Some people should go get a room and be considerate of others."

Those evenings ended with Justin and Melinda arguing and Caitlyn spent her time apologizing to Melinda and trying to calm Justin down. Telling him it was Melinda's room, too, meant nothing to him.

"Choose. Do I stay or does she stay?" Justin growled through clenched teeth.

"You know I can't do that. This is Melinda's room, too. Can't we just cool it for awhile?"

"Why should we? I think I like you more than you like me," said Justin petulantly.

Folding his arms, he waited impatiently for Caitlyn to make up her mind. "You know that's not true. I like you a lot..."

"Then tell Melinda to piss off. I want to touch you and if I can't, then I'm leaving!" Caitlyn saw the anger continue to build on Justin's face. He squinted his eyes, pinched his lips tight, and clenched his jaw. His whole body appeared tense and coiled.

"Justin..." Caitlyn held out one hand toward Justin and rubbed her stomach with her other hand.

"See ya," Melinda said with a sneer.

Justin glared at Melinda and waited for Caitlyn to make a choice.

That was the first time he grabbed her. Holding her wrist, Justin tried to pull Caitlyn out the door, demanding she go with him.

Melinda wasn't having any of that. She picked up the phone and yelled that she was going to call security if Justin didn't let go right then and there.

When Caitlyn didn't make the choice he wanted, he grabbed his coat and stalked out the door.

The arguments and demands began to occur more frequently and every time Justin stormed off, his phone calls started. He didn't care about keeping Caitlyn up all night on the phone; after all, he was up, too. If she didn't talk as long as he wanted her to, he pouted and sulked for days.

When Caitlyn stayed on the phone with him, he talked about how sorry he was and promised the arguing and grabbing her wrists would never happen again. He said he loved her so much and wanted to spend as much time with her as he could. He ended those phone calls by saying he loved her and felt like he couldn't breathe when they were apart. Caitlyn ended up forgiving him and then he would surprise her with something cute and unusual.

One time, he gave her a shiny black, polished rock. It was just a rock, but for some reason, it was important to Justin. He was so proud of it and treated it as if it was a precious jewel. She couldn't help but laugh and accept his peace offering.

Melinda, rolled her eyes when she saw the gifts. "He gives you lame junk so you'll think he's cute even though he treats you like crap!"

Melinda took every opportunity to tell Caitlyn Justin was a jerk and control freak. She pushed Caitlyn into defending him and then Melinda wouldn't speak to her for a couple of days, walking around muttering about 'stupid girls.'

* * *

Underneath all her bravado, Melinda really was a sweet person and Caitlyn enjoyed knowing her. She was a walking poster board for self-confidence and people never noticed how tiny Melinda was because her personality was huge and made her seem bigger than life.

Caitlyn thought they might be friends after college, but that was before Justin. Melinda had no patience for women who refused to defend themselves or let men push them around, physically or emotionally. She felt Justin was that kind of man and as long as Caitlyn chose him, her patience had its limits.

Tanya, another girl, lived next door and proved to be an invaluable source of solace during those turbulent months. There were many nights when Tanya came over after hearing Melinda and Justin screaming at each other, neither one willing to give an inch or see things from the other's perspective. She never approached Justin while he was angry, but she was able to help diffuse his anger with a quiet word here, or some reasoning there and he would finally agree to leave for the time being.

Caitlyn started taking refuge in Tanya's room after that because it was one of the only places where she felt any sense of peace. Tanya let Caitlyn share feelings without talking about her own views. She accepted Caitlyn for the mixed up, insecure person she was without demanding an instant metamorphous into something stronger, confident, or mature.

* * *

Over the next six weeks, Justin became more persistent with his embraces. It wasn't enough to spend the evening exchanging long, slow, kisses with cuddling and caressing. He was pushing more and more for a complete physical relationship.

Caitlyn resisted.

I want to be sure Justin is going to be in my future before giving away a part of myself I will never get back. Sure, I will still be my own person, but there is only one first time.

The Monday after Thanksgiving break, they spent an evening watching a movie in Caitlyn's dorm room. Melinda was gone and Tanya was studying with friends. She curled up next to Justin, sharing kisses and enjoying their time together. As the movie ended, Justin became more amorous. Trying to calm him down, Caitlyn left the bed and went to put in a comedy, hoping to lighten the mood.

"Caitlyn, you know I love you. If you love me, then there's no reason why we shouldn't be together. Do you love me or not?"

"Justin, I just want to be sure. I told you about how my mom has been married twice. I don't want that for myself. My brother has been married and divorced and my sister is living with a man who won't marry her even though they've been together for six years. I want to know where this is going first..."

Her voice trailed off when she saw Justin's face tense up with anger. His eyes narrowed and she saw his nostrils flare. His teeth clenched, his lips were pinched together and his cheeks showed red splotches. Justin got off the bed and grabbed Caitlyn's wrist. Then he pushed her against the wall and slammed his mouth down on hers. Grinding himself against her, he muttered between kisses.

"Haven't I been good to you? Haven't I taken you out and bought you presents? How come you don't love me the way I love you? I need you so much." Justin continued to squeeze Caitlyn's wrists between mutters. He pushed a leg between hers and his hand joined in the pain.

She froze as she realized Justin was assaulting her.

What the crap? God help me. No, no no, this can - not be happening. Did I do something wrong? What can I do?

Justin pulled back and took several long, slow breaths. He released his grip on Caitlyn's wrists and stepped back as he started to apologize. His voice was rough and hoarse.

"I'm so sorry Caitlyn. I don't know what happened. You just make me so crazy. Say you forgive me, please."

He reached out to stroke her hair and then continued in a whisper.

"You shouldn't piss me off. I know you didn't mean to, but you did. You know I love you. Right?"

Caitlyn nodded without saying anything as tears streamed down her cheeks. She looked at Justin, silent and rubbed her wrists. After a few moments, she answered.

"I need some time alone. Please leave, now."

Justin nodded his head and leaned over to kiss her again, but Caitlyn flinched away, turning her head to the side. Justin hesitated, then kissed her on the cheek and walked out the door.

Caitlyn stood frozen against the wall for what seemed like an eternity, her mind frozen and blank. She held her breath, afraid she would shatter into a thousand tiny pieces if she moved. Finally, shaking, she stumbled toward the shower. Cold inside and numb, she sought the soothing warmth of a shower. Her gaze, blurred by a constant flow of tears, seemed fixed on some distant point of light.

In the shower, Caitlyn doubled over, crying and shaking as she thought about Justin. She was glad he had stopped when he did because she couldn't bear to think about what he might have done if he had kept going. Dragging herself to bed, she crawled under the covers and drew the blanket up to her chin. Shivering, with tears slipping quietly down her cheeks, she finally drifted off to sleep as she tried to block the evening from her mind. One question continued to whisper in her mind.

What just happened?

* * *

"What in the world happened to you?" Caitlyn opened bleary eyes to see Melinda leaning over, peering at her arms. She sat up and started to place her arms under the covers but Melinda grabbed the cover and held it back, looking at the marks. Her short-sleeved tee-shirt revealed them along the length of her arms and circling her wrists.

Melinda's face showed anger and concern. Meeting Caitlyn's gaze, she asked again, "What happened? Did he hit you? Tell me."

Shaking her head, Caitlyn tried to answer Melinda, but tears started streaming down her face again.

Melinda wrapped her arms round Caitlyn and held her until she was able to talk about Justin's assault.

"You need to file a report against that prick. He has no right to treat you this way," fumed Melinda.

"He said he was sorry. I don't know what I want to do. Please, just be my friend right now. Okay?"

"Fine, fine. Okay, I have an idea. Why don't we drive down and see your mom? It'll do you good to have some momma love. I'll drive," offered Melinda.

"No. I can't let her see me like this. She'll be so disappointed in me. I feel like this is all my fault. Maybe I let him think we would be together even though I didn't mean to send that message." Caitlyn looked down, plucked at the blanket, and chewed the inside of her lower lip on the right side.

"Listen up. This is not your fault. Justin has left bruises on you before and he always says it's you who pisses him off. He can't control his temper and every time you let him come back, he thinks the way he treats you is okay. You need to lay it on the line that you aren't going to tolerate abuse, period. Do you like getting bruises?" asked Melinda. Hands on her hips, Melinda's voice raised in volume and speed as she spoke to Caitlyn.

Caitlyn drew her knees up, wrapped her arms around them, and placed her forehead on her knees. She sighed and closed her eyes.

"No. Of course not. I try not to make him mad. I don't know what happens. It's like he just snaps. I don't know what to do."

"You need to tell him to take a hike and cry as you walk away for good. What about seeing a counselor? You can see one here on campus." Melinda walked over and sat down in her desk chair as she waited for Caitlyn's reply.

"I can't do that. People would see me going in there and then, when I have classes with them, they'll know. No, counseling would be way too humiliating."

"Just think about it. If you can't talk to your mom, you should have someone to talk to. But remember, this wasn't your fault."

"Thanks Melinda." Caitlyn closed her eyes and pulled the covers back up over her head.

Is this my fault? How did this happen?

* * *

Justin called three times, but Melinda convinced Caitlyn to go to the movies with her so she wouldn't have to deal with him just yet. Dinner followed and the girls arrived back at the dorm around 11:00pm.

Justin was waiting by the door and Caitlyn saw that he was seething. His pinched lips, narrowed eyes, and flushed cheeks left no doubt about his feelings. Caitlyn's pulse began to pound and her mouth went dry. Without speaking, she began to rub her wrists. Her stomach began to rumble and gurgle.

Melinda went up to Justin and whispered.

"If you don't leave, now, I'm going to call campus security and re-port you. I'll show them Caitlyn's wrists. Do you really want to ex-plain that?" she asked with a sneer.

Justin muttered a curse and left after telling Caitlyn he would see her later. He smacked the door frame as he walked out.

* * *

Caitlyn managed to avoid Justin for three days with the help of Melinda and Tanya. They decided they needed Caitlyn's company for everything, from shopping, to eating, to doing laundry. Melinda was great. She went out of her way to make Caitlyn laugh and put her at ease. They gave each other a facial and painted each other's nails. Tanya needed new make-up, so they all went shopping and spent hours looking at the new fall colors.

* * *

Caitlyn found her thoughts dark and disturbed. She pictured Justin's face and her mind kept replaying the way he looked. Skin flushed, nostrils flared, eyes squinted into little slits: all signs that he was infuriated. Instead of love shining from his eyes, the only look coming from them was a look of fire. It felt like his eyes could blaze right through all her defenses.

Caitlyn found herself avoiding eye contact with people in the store. She felt like everyone was looking at her. Going through the checkout line, she found it hard to meet the eyes of the clerk. It was easier to keep her eyes averted and fiddle with the money in her purse, the zipper.

She knew she would burst out crying if anyone else was kind. Then again, she might cry if anyone gave her an angry look.

Can people tell I've been assaulted? Will they think I asked for it? Was it my fault?

That last question wouldn't go away. No matter how hard she tried to look objectively at the events leading up to the assault, she couldn't help thinking she had done something wrong. It couldn't all be Justin's fault, could it?

* * *

Justin continued leaving phone messages but Caitlyn didn't return his calls. It was hard to listen to the pleading in his voice. He sounded sad and sincere.

Melinda watched Caitlyn's face every time she listened to one of the messages.

Sometimes she would rub Caitlyn's back and then other times, she would remind her she had to be strong.

Caitlyn had forgotten how great it felt just to have girl time.

Friday came, and Melinda and her boyfriend were heading out of town for the weekend to join his family for a nephew's birthday party.

"Caitlyn. Come with us. You can hang out and relax with no worries. It'll be fun. We can even go hiking if you want. The mountains are gorgeous and I bet we can find a great trail."

Caitlyn appreciated Melinda's concern but felt bad about monopolizing all of her time. Melinda was really excited about spending time with her boyfriend's family and Caitlyn didn't want to feel like a third wheel. She also knew she needed to come to grips with her own thoughts and feelings. Melinda was great, but Caitlyn knew she couldn't depend on her forever.

"Melinda. You have been so great. I love you for all your support, but go and have fun. I'll be all right. I promise. I'm just going to hang out here, watch some movies and do homework." assured Caitlyn. "No worries. I can't get into trouble by myself."

"Are you sure?" Melinda looked worried about Caitlyn, but excited at the same time. She couldn't wait to hit the road. She was throwing last minute items into a bag the whole time she kept asking Caitlyn if she was sure.

"Yes. Go. Have fun. Besides, Tanya said she would be around later if I want to watch a movie," smiled Caitlyn.

After Melinda left, time seemed to drag as Caitlyn tried to occupy herself. She picked up books to read for class but closed them over and over, unable to concentrate. She flipped through channels on the television, but nothing captured her attention.

How come I feel so alone?

Her chest felt heavy and her stomach hurt every time she thought about Justin. Tears came to the surface easily when she forgot to keep a clamp of control locked in place. She still felt numb knew that cocoon of protection wouldn't last forever. No matter how hard she tried, she couldn't come up with the words to make herself feel better. The ability to bring comfort to her soul wasn't coming from within.

* * *

Later, heading over to The Union for dinner, Caitlyn found herself looking over her shoulder, wondering if Justin was lurking nearby, waiting for a chance to pounce. When she made it to the door without incident, she breathed a sigh of relief. She walked in and stopped dead in her tracks. There, in a chair facing the door, was Justin. He stood up as soon as he saw her.

"Caitlyn. I'm so glad to see you. I've been here every day, waiting to see you. Please give me a chance to talk to you."

He looked tired, like he hadn't slept much. His clothes were rumpled and there were dark circles under his eyes.

"What do you want?"

"Let's eat and then talk." Justin looked into Caitlyn's eyes and waited for her response.

He stretched out his hand and attempted to touch her check.

Caitlyn flinched away and shook her head.

"No. Say whatever it is you have on your mind right now." Food became the last thing on her mind. Part of her wanted to scream and run away. Her wrists began to throb just from the memory of his tight grip. People always say, confront bullies, but all she wanted was to feel safe.

"Caitlyn. I love you so much. Please eat with me. That's all I ask. Just hear me out and give me a chance to tell you what you mean to me." Head down, he shuffled his feet and jammed his hands into his front pockets while he waited for Caitlyn's reply. He didn't attempt to touch her again as he peeked at her and waited.

Caitlyn sighed and nodded her head and Justin's face broke into a huge smile as he grabbed her arm and led her to the dining area. After they purchased their food, they sat down. Justin made sure to steer her to a table near the back, away from other diners.

Caitlyn felt her stomach twist into a knot of anxiety and stared at Justin while he wolfed down his food. She felt nauseous.

Finished with his meal, Justin leaned his elbows on the table and studied Caitlyn's face. "Caitlyn. You know I didn't force you to be with me. I wouldn't do that. I just don't understand how you can kiss me and touch me and then say 'stop' all the time. It isn't right because it seems like you want me, too. It's torture to be close to you all the time and not be with you. I love you so much and I want us to be together, forever. I'll never quit on you and I'll always want you. Every part of me belongs to you. Please. Please give me another chance. Just let me show you how much you mean to me."

Caitlyn felt her eyes well up with tears as Justin spoke. "I don't know Justin. You were really rough and it didn't feel like you were in control. I told you, I'm not ready for that level of commitment. How do I know you won't act like that again? I need more time to think," Caitlyn whispered.

"You can have all the time you need. Just please don't keep me away. I go crazy when I don't see you and I can't stand being away from you. I need you. I miss everything about you. I miss the way you smell and feel. I miss holding you. My arms feel empty when they're not wrapped around you. I feel like I can't breathe when we aren't together. I'm not complete when we're not together."

Justin's voice always became low and raspy as he pleaded his case and Caitlyn found herself drawn to his magnetism.

She sighed and nodded.

"Okay. But, if you ever do that again, I swear you won't be able to say sorry enough."

"Sure. No sweat babe. Just let me back in and I promise you won't be sorry. Are we good?" He looked like a little boy. It was amazing how quickly he went from low to high.

Caitlyn smiled at his boyish charm and nodded. She hoped she wouldn't regret this decision. It was easier to hold fast to her convictions when she wasn't close to him. When they weren't together, it was easy to hold onto the hurt, shock, and disillusionment. When she was with him, he made it hard to feel anything except desired, beautiful, and most importantly, cherished.

Justin grabbed her hand and raised it to his lips. He sighed as he held her hand and gazed into her eyes, then rubbed her palm against his cheek, sighed again and turned her hand so he could kiss her palm. He was very good at letting Caitlyn know how much he desired her. It was there with every look and touch.

After being forgiven, Justin walked Caitlyn back to her room. Of course, he spent the rest of the evening lounging on the floor in her room. He was so eager to be close to Caitlyn that he ended up staying and sleeping on the floor in her room.

"I just want to be close to you. I'll stay down here, I promise." Justin acted as if this reprieve would vanish if he left Caitlyn's side, so he stayed.

Saturday turned out to be low key. Justin left long enough to get his accounting materials and spent some time studying for an upcoming quiz. Caitlyn spent some time doing laundry, revising an article and a paper she had started for submission. Justin worked hard to keep the atmosphere casual and low key. They ended the evening lounging on Caitlyn's bed watching comedies.

They spent Sunday on a hike, in the snow, after Justin came back from going to shower and change. He loved hiking and always found trials that provided fun with just a little bit of challenge thrown in. After hiking for half an hour, Caitlyn decided enough was enough without a break.

"Come on Caitlyn. We only have a little bit further to go. Pick up the pace, babe or we're never going to get there."

"Where in the world are we going anyway? We didn't bring any food and my water is gone." Caitlyn crossed her arms and tapped her toe while she glared at Justin with a scowl on her face.

"I promise. It'll be worth it and it's not much further. Come on."

Justin took her hand and off they went. The trail was barely visible. Snow covered banks showed evidence of animal activity in places, while undisturbed areas shimmered with pristine smoothness and tree branches sagged from the weight of their heavy burden. Caitlyn felt thankful for her vegan snow boots, scarves, and gloves.

Another 10 minutes or so, they rounded a curve in the trail and Caitlyn's breath caught in her throat as she gazed upon the lovely scene of small sloping hills that led to a wide open valley. Caitlyn looked over at the closest tree and saw two snow sleds.

"Are those for us to use? When did you do this?" Caitlyn looked at Justin in amazement, her eyes wide.

He nodded and laughed, a huge smile showing sparkling white teeth. His enthusiasm was infectious and Caitlyn couldn't help laughing at his expression.

"When I left to go shower and change, I came out here before I came back to pick you up. Not many people come here so I figured no one would bother them. I even have food in my backpack. Did I make you happy?" Justin shuffled his feet and waited for approval, his eyes never leaving Caitlyn's face.

Caitlyn felt the last of her doubts melt away. She couldn't believe he had worked so hard just to surprise her.

A monster wouldn't go through all this trouble. He wants my approval.

With tears in her eyes, she nodded her head and leaned over to give Justin a soft kiss. He smiled, let out a sigh, and then led her over to the sleds.

They pulled the sleds to the top of the hill and raced to the bottom. Caitlyn's face felt frozen from the cold chill wind but her body glowed from the warmth of her excitement. She beat Justin three times and reveled in the exhilaration of her victories. She jumped circles around Justin, pumping her fists in the air while chanting, "I won, I won, I won."

"I get a consolation kiss." Justin wrapped her in his arms and gave her a long, slow kiss.

Lunch consisted of sandwiches and chips from the Union and a couple of bottles of water. Caitlyn was amazed this was the same Justin who had attacked her.

Did I do something to bring on his attack? He is being so kind and thoughtful now. What happened before?

Justin made up cute, silly stories about animals that might or might not be watching just to keep her entertained while they ate. The afternoon was a perfect blend of lighthearted fun, mild flirting, and peaceful friendship. Relaxing, Caitlyn gave herself up to the moment and enjoyed the happiness that came with a sense of peace.

This is the Justin I think I'm falling for. Things will be better, I just know it.

* * *

Melinda became incensed when she returned from her weekend trip to find Justin lounging on Caitlyn's bed.

"You have got to be kidding me!" she yelled. "Are you so weak you just have to be with a male, even one who treats you like crap? Why are you so afraid of being alone? What is with you and your penchant for misery and pain? This guy is a loser!" Melinda placed her hands on her hips, her eyes narrowed and her cheeks had a hint of pink.

"Melinda, please don't do this. I can explain." Caitlyn grabbed her torso as she felt her stomach clench into knots.

Melinda wouldn't listen. She kept pacing, pointing, and yelling.

"You don't have to tell her anything. What we do is none of her business anyway. Let's go. Listening to shrews isn't my idea of fun anyway."

Justin grabbed Caitlyn by the hand, pulled her out of the room and down the hall to one of his friend's room. The evening started out relaxing but quickly turned into one of tension and dread.

Caitlyn did not want to face Melinda. Part of her knew Melinda might be right.

Am I weak? Justin has been so great. He went to all that trouble to set up the picnic. He wouldn't do that if he was an awful person. I don't think he'll treat me that way again. He knows I didn't like it and that he hurt me. He must care and someone who cares won't hurt me again.

Doesn't he deserve another chance? People make mistakes. It doesn't mean they can't change. Melinda doesn't know him like I do. She just doesn't understand.

The silent conversation in her head continued to play, a never-ending loop.

She and Justin lounged in his friend's room until close to 3am. Justin was loath to leave but Caitlyn convinced him she was tired and it would be best for him to go home and sleep.

She went back to her room long after Melinda usually went to bed to avoid the inevitable confrontation. She opened the door and breathed a sigh of relief when she saw the lights off.

"I'm still awake, still mad and I'm not going anywhere. Tell me what happened. You said you were going to stay in the room and do homework. Did you let him back in the moment I left? I thought you wanted to get away from his crappy treatment."

Listening to Melinda's tirade made Caitlyn's head hurt. The words coming at her were all too true and she knew she didn't have any answers that would satisfy Melinda. Melinda, who never backed down from anything, would never understand.

How can I admit that I fell for Justin's apology again?

"Please Melinda, I just like him. I don't know what else to do. He said sorry and I think he really means it. He took me on a picnic and we had a lot of fun sledding. He was gentle and funny and he didn't do anything to make me feel uncomfortable at all. It was as if the other night never happened. Maybe I was wrong or jumped to the wrong conclusions. Maybe it was me. I don't know. I have to give him a chance."

"I think you're nuts. Don't come crying to me the next time he smacks you around. Guys like him don't change. As long as you keep taking him back, he doesn't have to." The words came out with the sting of a venomous bite.

"Sorry. I know."

"Quit saying you're sorry and grow some guts. You better have a plan about what to do the next time he man-handles you because there will be a next time. With guys like him, there is always a next time and the treatment gets worse over time, not better. Zebras don't change their stripes."

"I hope you're wrong," whispered Caitlyn with a voice that cracked as she tried to choke back tears.

"Humph. I'm not. I knew I shouldn't have left you here alone. But I can't be strong for you. You have to be strong for yourself." Melinda kept tossing and turning and punching her pillow.

As tears slid down her cheeks, Caitlyn gathered her nightclothes and began to get ready for bed. Her mind felt tired and her brain hurt with the effort to think. Still, she couldn't keep her mind from replaying the words and actions of the past week. It was like there was a switch that she couldn't shut off. Her heart ached along with her head.

The days settled into a familiar routine again. Justin spent most of his time hanging out in Caitlyn's room, arguing with Melinda, and touching and kissing Caitlyn at every opportunity.

Caitlyn thought he had learned his lesson because he didn't push as hard to be intimate as he had before their time apart, except when Melinda was in the room, then explosions followed.

Tanya never said anything about Justin's return to Caitlyn's good graces. As always, she offered an open door and a listening ear whenever a break was needed from the caustic atmosphere that erupted whenever Justin and Melinda spent more than a few moments in the same room. The peace Tanya offered gave Caitlyn a much needed break.

9

Caitlyn jumped, back in the moment. The phone was ringing. She looked at the clock, shocked and alarmed that her thoughts about Justin had taken over for more than an hour.

Breathing hard and feeling somewhat shaky, she jumped off the couch and grabbed her cell phone off the table by the door. Who could be calling so late?

"Hello?" She hoped that her voice didn't sound as breathless as she felt.

"Caitlyn, I wanted to let you know I had a really great time with you today and to wish you good night. Think about me, okay?" whispered Victor quietly.

"I had a really good time, too." Caitlyn smiled as she sat back down.

"Can I see you tomorrow?" She heard the wistfulness in his voice and smiled.

"I'm not sure. I have some errands to run and I have dinner plans with my parents."

"Want some company with your errands? We don't have to do anything specific, just hanging out would be fun."

"Okay. Should we meet somewhere?"

"How about if I come over and share that egg-foo young you bought? Then we can head out and take care of your errands. Just name the time and I'll be there."

"Um, how about 9:00? Is that too early?"

"9:00 it is. I'll see you in the morning. Should I bring anything to go with the egg-foo young? What do you eat with that anyway?"

"You don't need to bring anything unless you want something specific. I always prepare rice as a side."

"Rice it is. No stress, just you and me being together. That's all I want."

"Okay. Sounds like a plan."

"I'll see you in the morning, Caitlyn. Goodnight."

"Goodnight."

That's it, no more thoughts about Justin for now, not tonight. He is not going to steal any more of my time and energy.

* * *

Caitlyn forgot to close the blinds completely and the sun managed to find every single, minute opening and came streaming in. Looking at the clock Caitlyn groaned, unable to believe it was only 6:30.

Why does it have to be so blasted bright? Just a little while longer.

She rolled over and tried to ignore the cheerful sunshine that insisted on piercing through her eyelids. Sighing, she got up to close the blinds and decided to lie back down, just for another minute. Memories of Justin had her tossing and turning for hours before she managed to fall back into a heavy slumber.

* * *

Caitlyn sat up quickly. Heart pounding from being startled awake, she looked around and tried to figure out what jerked her out of a deep sleep. The dream was still fresh in her head and it took a moment to clear the cobwebs away and realize it was the ring of her phone that had pierced through the stranglehold of her nightmare. Still groggy, she stumbled over to the dresser and grabbed the phone so she could put an end to the insistent ringing. With a husky, sleep filled voice, she answered the phone.

"Hello?" Trying not to yawn, she cleared her throat and tried to concentrate on the voice on the other end of the line.

"Caitlin, are you okay? I've been knocking on your door for about five minutes. Did you forget about me already?" teased Victor.

"Oh, no. I mean yes, but not on purpose. I'll come get the door. Bye."

She hung up the phone, pulled on a robe, ran her fingers through her hair, went to the bathroom, swished some water around in her mouth and went to open the door.

"Sorry Victor. I tossed and turned all night. I finally fell asleep this morning and overslept. Come on in. I'll just be a moment. Have a seat."

"Are you okay?" Victor sounded concerned as he saw the circles beneath Caitlyn's tired eyes. Her difficult night showed and he noticed that she averted her eyes.

"Yeah. I'm just a little tired. I'll be right back. Breakfast won't take long. I just need to start the rice." Turning away, Caitlyn started towards the kitchen.

Victor caught her hand and steered her away from the direction of the kitchen. "You go ahead and get ready while I start the rice. I'm here to be your partner for the day, so don't worry about a thing. I've got the rice covered."

"Really?" Looking up at Victor, Caitlyn couldn't help smiling.

Here come those good feelings again.

"Yes, really. I can do some cooking. It's not all take out and restaurants, you know."

"Okay. Great. I'll be right back. The rice is in the cabinet furthest from the fridge, second shelf." With a lighter step, Caitlyn headed for the bathroom.

Catching her wrist as she turned away, Victor pulled her back for a quick kiss. Just as he was about to kiss her, he felt her stiffen and pull back. When he saw a grimace on her face, he paused.

"Caitlyn? What's wrong? I hope I didn't scare you. I was just going to give you a good morning kiss. That's all. You're in control, remember? I'm a good guy. You can trust me."

"Sorry. You grabbed my wrist."

"Did I hurt you?" Holding her wrist, Victor looked down and saw the discoloration that circled her wrist. Gently catching her other wrist, he looked at the matching bruises and took a deep breath.

He gently stroked the marks with his thumbs, then brought each wrist up to his lips for a gentle kiss before releasing her so she could go and take a shower.

Caitlyn watched the changing expressions cross Victor's face as he looked at her wrists.

Will he blame me for their presence? Will he think I asked for that kind of treatment?

When she felt him gently kiss her wrists, tears filled her eyes.

How is it that he is so kind? Is there a limit to his kindness?

After Caitlyn walked away, Victor clenched his fists and took several deep breaths, as he thought about the evidence of mistreatment on Caitlyn's wrists.

Caitlyn showered and got ready in record time. The warm water had done a great job of washing away the cobwebs of her restless night. Today promised to be a great day after all and she was determined to take one day at a time. She didn't need all the answers about Victor's feelings today and she was determined not to look for motives behind every move, look, or word. He deserved better than that and she would take him at his word. He wasn't Justin and she would not treat him with suspicion.

I can do that, can't I?

Victor had cooked the rice, warmed the egg-foo young, and poured orange juice for both of them. He had even sliced a couple of pears as dessert.

"Feel better?" Victor kept his voice casual as he turned to look at Caitlyn. He placed some food on their plates and waited for her reply.

"Much better. Thanks for doing all the cooking. I haven't had anyone cook breakfast for me in a long time. Not since I lived at home. This is great." Caitlyn smiled as she eyed his work with appreciation and tried to stop her nervous chatter.

"Anytime. So, what's on the agenda for today?" Victor breathed a sigh. They sat down at Caitlyn's small, round table and started eating.

"My nephew's birthday is in two weeks and I have to shop for his present. He gave me a list of choices so I have a couple of stores to hit. The first present I find is the one I buy."

"He gave you a list? That's funny. Why shop two weeks early?"

"Well, if I can't find anything locally, then I have time to order it online. My family always gives lists of possible gifts. I guess I could give money, but he always puts a challenge on the list just to see if I can find it. So far, I haven't disappointed him. He's still young so he hasn't been able to ask for anything too extravagant."

"Sounds like a fun game. My family doesn't do anything like that. My mom asks us what we want through-out the year and picks things up here and there. We never know what we're going to get because it could be something we mentioned six months or six years ago. She keeps things stashed away in what she calls her present closet. When a holiday or birthday rolls, around, she goes shopping in her very own store." Victor showed a small, crooked smile as he talked about his mom.

Caitlyn thought it sounded adorable. It was fun to hear about Victor's family. Justin never talked about his family except to say he was glad to be away from them.

Stop it. No comparisons.

Caitlyn looked at Victor's face and felt herself smile as she took in the soft expression on his face.

She heard the phone ring and excused herself to answer it. "Hello?"

"Caitlyn, are you okay? I was so freaked out about the way you left with Victor. What happened?" asked Penny. She was speaking rapidly, with animated concern.

"I'm okay. Thanks for calling. Listen. Victor is here and we're going shopping for Larry's birthday. Talk about freaked out, I was totally blown away when I saw 'the friend' you brought along. Do you remember when I talked about the guy I went out with in college? Well, Justin is that guy. Of all the people in the world for you to bring, I still can't believe he's your new friend. You didn't tell him where I live, did you?" Caitlyn crossed her fingers and waited anxiously for Penny's answer.

"No. He does know where we work, but that's it. I swear. I didn't even give him your number. You never told me what really happened at school. Hey, wait a minute. Victor again? What's up with that? Are you two dating?" Caitlyn heard the excitement in Penny's voice.

Penny's enthusiasm was infectious and Caitlyn looked forward to sharing the budding feelings that were starting to grow about Victor. It felt so good to have a girlfriend to talk to, but Victor was waiting.

"Well, I guess so. He's been here most of the weekend. He's so great. But listen, I can't talk now. Come over for dinner tomorrow after work and I'll fill you in. Okay?" Caitlyn bit her lip, head tilted as she waited for Penny's response, her mind distracted by Victor waiting in the other room.

"All right, but you have to fill me in. I just can't believe it. You and Victor! Awww. This is so awesome, I can't stand it! Promise you'll tell me everything."

"I promise. Bye." Caitlyn smiled, hung up the phone and went to join Victor.

"Everything okay?"

"Yes. That was Penny. I left her a message yesterday but didn't talk to her. She called to check on me. She was worried because of the way Friday night ended."

"She seems like a good friend. Is she friends with the guy from the club?"

"I don't know how close they are. They met and she thought it was high time for me to go out and have fun. She thinks I spend too much time alone in my apartment. I just can't help thinking that of all the people in the world to meet, it's just my luck that it had to be him." Grimacing, Caitlyn looked down. It was clear her thoughts had taken her away.

"Does this 'him' have a name?" Victor watched Caitlyn's face closely.

"It's Justin." Head down, eyes, averted, Caitlyn whispered the name. Her gaze still seemed unfocused, as if she was unaware of this current time and place.

"So, Justin had a pretty good grip on you. Has he left bruises before? I'm sure there's quite a story there. Just for the record, I also hope you know I'm not a man who would ever leave bruises of any kind, anywhere."

Caitlyn felt herself tighten up inside and looked at Victor with wide eyes. She shook her head and she whispered, "No. I can't talk about it yet. I need some time to think first."

"Okay. But remember, you're safe with me. I won't hurt you physically and I'll try my best not to hurt you emotionally. You don't have to tell me anything that makes you uncomfortable. I just want to know you. I want to know what makes you tick. What makes you happy and what makes you sad. I'll give you the time you need. Just don't push me away while you sort things out. Don't take away the chance for us to continue getting to know each other, okay?"

"Trust is something that doesn't come easily for me, but I will try. I enjoy my time with you and I don't want to push you away."

"That's all I ask. Now, let's tackle those dishes, and then, shopping. By the way, do I get to meet your family?"

"Do you want to? Why?" The surprise in her voice made Victor smile.

"Well, for starters, if I go with you to dinner, then I get to spend the whole day with you. Then there's the added bonus of finding out more about you. Moms always tell something fun and juicy about their kids. You know, something cute you did as a baby or something."

"Hmm. That's probably a good reason to forgo dinner and grab a bite somewhere else. I don't know if I can take any stories today." Caitlyn laughed and shook her head as she imagined some of the stories her mom loved to tell anyone who would listen. Thinking about some of those stories brought a slight grimace to Caitlyn's face.

Justin had willingly listened to way too many stories and that was one reason her mother had loved him. He never acted as if he was uncomfortable around her family. He lounged around on the couch as if he had done it for years. Caitlyn wondered how her mom would react to Victor. She hadn't brought anyone home since Justin.

Victor watched the play of emotions flit across Caitlyn's face and could tell she was just about to change her mind about his self-invitation to join her for dinner.

"Hey. I do great with families. I even have one of my own. My mom does the whole story thing, too. Every time she gets a chance to tell someone what a cute kid I was, she takes full advantage. I'll give you your turn to laugh at my childhood antics when my parents come to visit. No stress, remember? I just want to hang out and enjoy the day with you. No pressure, just two friends enjoying the day." He put a finger under her chin and gently tilted her head up so he could look into her eyes.

Caitlyn met his gaze and felt herself relax.

Okay, no stress. It's time for mom to get over her notion that I'm going to 'patch things up' with Justin.

"Victor, before we go, I have a question. How did you know where I live? After you helped me with Justin, you drove me straight here and I didn't tell you where to go. How did you know?"

"Easy answer. I asked Penny while we gave you some privacy. I knew you weren't in any shape to drive yourself and there was no way I was going to walk away after what I saw inside Palisades. I'm glad she trusted me enough to tell me. I was seriously ticked off and knew I wouldn't calm down if I didn't know you were okay."

"The way you stayed with me was great. I appreciate the way you didn't make me feel uncomfortable or weird. Speaking of great, I never did thank you for the wonderful treats you sent to my office. You know, you certainly drove everyone crazy wondering what was going to be delivered next. I couldn't believe it and I kept wondering how you were doing it since you weren't even around." She smiled as she thought about those baskets and his notes. She had kept every single one and read them over and over.

You don't need to know that little detail.

Victor laughed as he watched Caitlyn's eyes sparkle while she recounted her joy with the gift baskets.

"I don't know how I'm ever going to top it. I'm glad you liked everything, though. What did you think of the notes?"

Victor smiled as Caitlyn dropped her head and changed the subject, asking him to get the dish soap under the cabinet.

"Yeah. The notes were great. You sir, are quite the writer, and here I thought you were a photographer all this time. Is writing a hobby or is that something else you're good at doing?"

"You're trying to get out of answering, I can tell. Those notes were just for you. Did they make you think about me? Hmm?" Victor wiggled his eyebrows comically and smirked as he gauged Caitlyn's response.

"Isn't that what you intended? I found myself very distracted because I kept thinking about them even when I had to concentrate on some not too interesting interview. By the way, when I saw you outside my office, you said you wanted to give me your latest gift in person. What was it?" Caitlyn put her hands behind her back and rocked back onto her heels, then toes, then heels again as she waited for Victor to respond.

"I already gave it to you." All signs of humor left Victor's face and he became motionless, looking intently at Caitlyn.

"Really? I don't remember seeing anything. I hope I haven't lost it already."

"Trust me, you haven't lost it. You'll know it when you find it or should I say, when you see it."

"Okay, you're talking in code. You do realize that, don't you?"

"Yep. Deal with it. Come on. Daylights burning and we have a present to find. We can't disappoint Larry now, can we?" Victor crooked his finger to beckon Caitlyn with a smile to follow him and headed out the door.

* * *

They traipsed through store after store. The October heat outside made the coolness of the stores a welcome treat Caitlyn relished. Running from one air-conditioned building to the next became the only way to endure the ever-present heat. Despite the heat, though, Caitlyn found she was enjoying the day of shopping. For once, she was able to concentrate on more than just the heat, the long lines, crowds, and the thirst brought on by browsing from store to store.

Victor seemed to enjoy the stores. They'd be looking at something and the next thing Caitlyn knew, his attention had been captured by something and off he went. Keeping up with him became the task of the day. He always managed to look surprised when she finally caught up to him.

Victor smiled and said, "keep up," and then he was off again. They took a break and went to a local Cross Over coffee shop, located inside the food court.

"I usually feel frustrated after two stores but it's fun shopping with you. I can't believe you're so patient. I get crabby with rude people who jump in front of me, cut me off, or pretend they don't see me. You don't seem to let anything get to you," observed Caitlyn.

"When I look at people, I don't look at the surface. I look at their eyes. You can read a lot when you look into someone's eyes. Have you ever noticed how some people refuse to make eye contact with you? When I notice that, I find myself wondering what happened to make them so fearful of having a brief, cordial moment of contact with another person. Then there are people who go around with an angry look all the time. It makes me wonder what they have going on inside. I wonder if that look is a defense mechanism to keep people away so they can't be hurt anymore. Sometimes, I take my camera with me. It's amazing how people open up when someone takes their picture. Even people who look really tough will act a little goofy when they stare into the lens of a camera."

"I guess I never thought about what might be going on with the other person. My thoughts are usually that I'm in a hurry and could you please just get out of my way. Have you always thought of things from the other person's perspective?" Caitlyn fiddled with a napkin as she waited for his reply.

Victor looked down and played with the water condensation that had pooled on the table. "No, I do have moments when it's all about me. Remember when you told me you were going out with Penny? I was disappointed and a little angry I couldn't spend my first night back in town with you. I had built up this whole picture about how I wanted the night to go and having you go out with someone else wasn't it. Friday night was supposed to be all about me being with you. Then, yesterday and last night was awesome. I was right where I wanted to be and here I am today, with you again. I have to admit, I tried every way I could think of just to spend the day with you. If that meant shopping for birthday presents or doing laundry or whatever, I was going to do it, just so I could spend more time with you. Remem-

ber when I said I wanted more of everything? That still holds true."
Victor flashed a small, crooked smile and met Caitlyn's eyes.

Caitlyn felt her body flood with warmth and her mind reeled from
the strength of Victor's words. She gave herself over to the burning intensity in his eyes.

"I hope you like the 'more' that you're getting," she whispered.

"I like it just fine. The more the better and I'll take all I can get.
Bring it on."

Victor lifted her hand to his lips and gently kissed her palm, then
laid her hand against his cheek. He turned his head and nuzzled his
face into the palm of her hand, closed his eyes for a moment and
sighed against her wrist. Then he smiled, looked into her eyes and deliberately kissed the bruises that encircled her wrist.

"Come on. As much as I could sit here kissing you forever, we do
have a present to buy before heading off to dinner with your folks. Do
we need to stop and buy anything to go with dinner? How about
dessert? Should we pick something up?" Victor tried to lighten the
moment.

"No. If I know my mom, she'll have dessert prepared. She tries to
stuff me whenever she can talk me into staying long enough to eat. I
stop by every chance I get but it's never enough. She loves it even
though I hear the same stories every time we talk. I call her every couple of days. She's so funny. When I talk to her on the phone, she always tries to think of new topics just so she can keep me on the phone
longer. "

"She must love the sound of your voice. I imagine most parents live
to hear the sound of their child's voice, no matter how old that child
might be. What about your dad? You don't talk about him very much.
Is he a good guy?"

"My parents are divorced, but my mom's husband is Darius and
he's a nice guy. He and my mom are perfect. She's flighty and somewhat scattered. He's patient and just lets her be who she is. My mom's
whole mission in life is to make sure everyone around her knows

they're loved. Sometimes she goes to the extreme of neglecting her own desires just to please the rest of us. Darius has to put the brakes on her ideas every now and then, but his mission in life seems to be creating a world of contentment for my mom. She doesn't always get her way, but his patience with her is amazing. And he truly loves her. He laughs at her silly jokes, fusses at her to eat, rubs her feet and still holds her hand. After all these years, he still looks at her like she is the most beautiful woman in the world." Caitlyn's eyes had taken on a dreamy look.

"He sounds like a lucky guy. I don't think everyone is lucky enough to find a once in a lifetime love."

"What do you mean?" Caitlyn paused before entering the next store to look back at Victor.

"Well, I think everyone wants to find someone who will still look at them as if they are still beautiful or handsome after life has erased away the bloom of youth. It sounds like your mom and Darius have found that kind of love, an enduring love that lasts in spite of the trials life throws. I would love to get a picture of them and see what the lens captures. Sometimes, the eyes tell the story better than words." Victor placed his hand on the small of Caitlyn's back and guided her toward the back of the store.

"Maybe you can take their picture sometime. I bet they would love to have photographs taken by you. After all, you are the famous Victor Knoble," teased Caitlyn with a small laugh.

Victor smiled back, winked, and smugly answered back, "You know it."

They never found the shoes Larry wanted so Caitlyn moved to the next item on his list. Two stores later, they found a game Larry was dying to add to his collection. It was amazing how seriously he took his video games. She paid for the purchase and they headed to Victor's car.

Caitlyn wondered how Victor would fit in with her family, bit her lip and looked at Victor as she tried to find a way to prepare him for the possible onslaught of questions.

Victor caught her hand and stopped her from getting in the car. He looked into her eyes and smiled before bending his head to give her a gentle kiss.

"Listen, I'm looking forward to meeting your family. I promise I won't embarrass you and I won't make your family uncomfortable. This might be my last chance to kiss you for a while so I think I better make the best of this moment."

"I'm not nervous that you might embarrass me. I do know my family, though. They might ask you some personal questions."

"Like what? Are they going to ask how much money I make or what my blood type is? No problem. I might fudge the money part but most everything else is fine. With me, what you see is what you get. I'm pretty much an open book. I don't lie and I don't play games. I can handle it. What are you really worried about?" Victor waited for Caitlyn to respond.

Caitlyn felt her breathing accelerate and tried to find the right words. She didn't want to hurt Victor, but she hadn't prepared her family for this change.

Victor observed Caitlyn's furrowed brow and worried expression for a moment, then placed his forehead against her's, closed his eyes and sighed, then held open the door for her. After getting in, he looked over at her and smiled.

"It's okay. I need to do some work I've been putting off. Maybe next time you'll be ready to take me along. Do you want me to drop you off or would you prefer to go back to your place and get your car?"

Caitlyn felt tears form and couldn't answer right away.

He's hurt. How can I let him know it's my ambivalence getting in the way? I'm the one who isn't ready.

"Victor..."

"No. It's okay. You had plans. You told me that and I talked my way into being a part of your day."

"No. I need to tell you why I'm nervous. It's just that my mom was crazy about Justin. They used to talk on the phone a lot. Sometimes, he would call just to talk to her. She still thinks we'll patch things up someday and get back together. I haven't brought anyone home since him. I didn't prepare her for you and I don't know how she'll react. I don't want her to talk about Justin or compare you to him. She could do that and hurt you without realizing how her words might affect you."

Caitlyn twisted her hands together and tried to picture her mother's reaction. Her mother had been disappointed when Caitlyn told her she and Justin were through. She hated disappointing her mom, and now here she was, disappointing and hurting Victor.

How come things can't be simple?

"Are you afraid she won't like me?" asked Victor.

"I don't know if she'll give herself a chance to like you. She might make up her mind as soon as you walk in the door and keep comparing you to him. If she does, changing her mind could be difficult. That's what I'm worried about. It's not you."

"Earlier, you said your mom's greatest desire was to make sure her family feels loved and taken care of. It sounds like she loves you enough to want you to be happy. Do you think her feelings for Justin will overshadow her feelings for you?"

"She does want me to be happy and I know she would like you. Maybe not right away, but it wouldn't take long. I just think it would be easier if I had time to prepare her and to make sure she knows Justin and I are finished for good."

"Okay. Do I drop you off or do you drive yourself?"

"You can drop me off. My mom won't mind giving me a ride back home. Are you okay? I hope you understand I'm not trying to hurt you or brush you off."

Victor smiled and replied, "It's okay. If you were trying to brush me off you wouldn't have me drop you off at your parent's house. You would make sure I knew as little as possible about you. Besides, you said you needed to tell your mom that you and Justin are finished. I think that means you like me a little, right?"

"I suppose you could look at it that way, if you want to," replied Caitlyn with a slight smile.

"Oh yeah. That's how I'm looking at it all right." Victor caught Caitlyn's hand, raised her hand to his lips and kissed her palm softly then folded her fingers over with his kiss inside.

"Tell me where to go."

The drive to Caitlyn's parents flew by. Victor kept the atmosphere light by talking about the work he had waiting for him and his next assignment.

Victor stopped outside her mother's house but kept the car running.

"Give me a call sometime soon, okay?" asked Victor as Caitlyn prepared to climb out of the car. "Have fun."

Caitlyn nodded, smiled at Victor, gathered her packages and prepared to get out of the car. She hesitated, then leaned over to kiss Victor softly on the lips first.

As he watched her walk away, Victor smiled and touched his lips.

10

The cars in the driveway told Caitlyn that everyone was already inside. She stopped a few minutes to compose her thoughts before grabbing the doorknob to go inside, then turned to watch Victor drive away and smiled.

He is so thoughtful.

She was glad he didn't feel the need to be glued to her side every second of the day. She enjoyed being with him, but she also wanted to be able to enjoy herself away from him. That was a nice change from the intensity of being with Justin during every bit of her spare time.

Everywhere she went was where Justin felt he needed to be. Sometimes when she worked in the dining hall, she looked around and found him sitting at one of the tables watching her. He would smile and wave as if his presence was the most natural thing in the world. She asked him about it once.

"Why do you sit around while I'm working? I don't mind if you go out and have fun with your friends."

Justin rejected the offer.

"I'm good. I just thought I would wait until you're done and then we can go hang out or something. I wish you didn't have to work. That sucks."

Of course he thought working sucked. His step-dad paid all of his expenses and gave him spending money to boot. Justin liked that part of his relationship with his family, if you could call what they had a relationship.

His step-dad, Denny, owned a very successful construction company. He met Justin's mother, Karen, at the bar where he and the crew hung out after work.

Both Denny and Karen loved hanging out with their friends after work when they were younger. They believed in working hard and playing hard. Getting together seemed inevitable, and then, bam. Out of the blue, Karen found herself pregnant. Justin was sixteen at the time and soon learned that he was not her priority.

Justin and his mom had an easygoing relationship, but she never seemed truly happy or content with their life. She acted as if she and Justin weren't a real family as long as it was just the two of them. Karen had tried dating many times; often going out with men she met on internet dating sites, at this bar or that sports bar, in restaurants, or in stores when shopping. It wasn't unusual for her to give her phone number to a stranger with a wink and a smile.

"Call me, I think you're cute."

Justin complained when she handed out her number in his presence. He never understood her need to constantly look for a man to join their life. He asked her about it once and she said she was a good person and deserved to be happy.

"Things didn't work out with your father, but I know there's a man out there waiting for me, I just have to find him."

Her quest Justin left to his own devices a lot. He learned to fix his own food, fend for himself, and decide how he was going to spend his time. He spent a short span of time experimenting with alcohol. Getting the alcohol was easy. Karen always kept something on hand. She never knew what her date might like so she kept a variety of choices on hand. She didn't really care how Justin spent his time as long as his activities didn't interfere with her plans.

After Karen got pregnant and married Denny, life became more complicated. On the surface, Denny seemed like a pretty good guy. He loved having fun and wanted his fun to continue. He got irritated with Karen when she complained of being tired or sick.

"Here we go. It's always something with you, isn't it? If it isn't a headache, then your back hurts or your feet are swollen. You weren't like this when I met you." Denny ended his complaint by popping open another beer.

Karen practically killed herself trying to continue being the fun-loving woman Denny met in the bar.

Justin hated it when he found her crying from exhaustion and begged her to leave Denny. He promised her he would take care of her and tried to convince her he was a man and she didn't need Denny. The first time Justin called him a jerk, Karen took Denny's side and told Justin he should be thankful she had found such a good man. Denny overheard Justin and shoved him against the wall. He grabbed a handful of Justin's tee-shirt in a fist.

"I'm the man around here and you're lucky I let you live in my house, 'boy' and don't you forget it. Anytime you think you're grown enough to take me on you just go ahead and try. Better yet, you can leave any time you want, all you have to do is walk out the door. I promise you, nobody is going to stop you."

He hit Justin in the stomach for good measure, doubling him over and left him gasping for breath. That was the first time he hit Justin. Karen ran over, holding her stomach and screaming at Denny not to hurt her 'baby'.

After that, Denny never hit Justin in the face or on any part of his arms where people could see marks. He established his authority in several ways: a punch in the back or the sides always made good targets. Thighs also made good targets for bruises that wouldn't show. Justin found it hard to defend himself when he didn't see the punch coming.

Karen tried, for a while, to defend Justin. She would cry and tell Denny that Justin was her first baby and she would ask him to calm down, that she would 'fix' whatever it was that was making him so up-set. Denny would remind her that she only had one baby now and it wasn't Justin.

After awhile, Karen gave up trying to get between Justin and Denny. Then, she would give Justin money and tell him, 'just stay out of Denny's way'. Since Denny had his own son now, he made sure Justin knew his time in the house was running out. Yep, the gravy train for Justin was coming to an end.

The next couple of years were hard. Denny seemed determined to make life miserable for Justin. In order to 'toughen' Justin up for the real world, Denny started making him go to work at some of the com-pany's construction sites. Justin was required to learn the ins and outs of putting buildings together from the ground up. As far as Denny was concerned, there was no task too hard or dirty and no day that started too early. Some of the guys knew Justin was being pushed hard, but they also told him that by learning the trade, he would be able to walk away from the 'old man' any time he wanted to and be able to take care of himself. Heck, if he played his cards right, he could even build a bigger/better company than Denny someday.

To his credit, Denny did pay Justin for his work on the construc-tion sites. The only problem was that he started charging him for room and board at the same time. Justin was required to start paying for his own clothing and recreation and had to pitch in for household groceries. Saving money was difficult. Even if he wanted to leave, he couldn't because it took most of every paycheck just to pay for all the charges Denny said he owed.

By the time Justin became a senior, the bloom of early, passionate, love had completely faded from the relationship between Karen and Denny. They didn't even pretend to feel passion for each other any-more. There was no handholding, stolen smooches, cuddling, or soft glances between them. All physical contact had ceased to exist and they both seemed too tired and fed up to try keeping up pretenses. Denny wanted more children but Karen said she was too old to keep having babies and if he wanted more, he better go and find someone else because she was done.

Shortly after that, Denny started hanging out at the bar again with the guys from the crew. Karen started drinking again and hanging out with some of the women she became friends with at the gym she attended. She and Denny started arguing more and more so Justin was left to take care of Robert. That suited him just fine, but he was worried about leaving for college. Who was going to take care of Robert if he left?

Karen caught Denny doing a bit more than flirting one evening when she made a surprise stop at the bar and saw him tickling a giggling young woman sitting on his lap.

Denny looked up and saw Karen watching him from across the room. He quickly joined her and started to explain that it wasn't what it looked like. It didn't mean anything because he was just having a bit of fun with the boys. Karen slapped him and walked out.

* * *

That encounter was a sweet turning point for Justin. Karen used Denny's guilt to make him ease up on Justin, pay for his college, and give him money when he needed it or else she was going to leave and take Robert away. Denny wouldn't be able to see him except through a visitation schedule. Karen also demanded they see a counselor together and she used the opportunity to make Denny do the whole church thing.

He did, but Justin could tell he only went through the motions. Denny was still the same flawed man and continued to take every opportunity available to use Justin as his personal punching bag. Denny decided the cost of the college expenses was worth it to get Justin out of the house and away from Karen. Justin learned to be tough and take anything Denny could dish out without crying.

11

Thoughts about Justin continued to haunt Caitlyn as she entered the house and she had to admit she felt a little bit bad for him. He wanted so badly to be loved, but he didn't know how to be part of someone's life without dominating the other person. His gift of gab had thoroughly charmed her mother. Caitlyn wondered if her mom would be able to let go of her feelings for Justin long enough to give Victor a fair chance. She desperately hoped so.

* * *

Caitlyn entered the front room and saw that the kids had taken over the television, the floor, and the couch. The kids were playing a board game, texting with friends and watching television, all at the same time. Caitlyn stepped over them and headed for the kitchen where she heard laughter and loud voices.

"Caitlyn! I'm so glad you finally made it. Come on in, honey. Can you help me finish the salad? I just don't know where the time went. Darius and I came home from church and I started cooking and before I knew it, everyone was walking in the door."

Caitlyn smiled as her mom talked a mile a minute and didn't wait for her or anyone else to reply or comment. She just kept right on talking as if everyone knew when to jump into the conversation. The rest of the family always teased her about it and Rosie would laugh and reply that there was no need to worry about it unless she started answering herself.

Mike, her brother, used her entrance as an excuse to slip away from the hustle and bustle of the kitchen to join the kids out in the front room. Rosie directed Darius to make sure everything ended up in serving dishes. Caitlyn's sister had already come and gone, her usual way of operating. Her boyfriend was always in a hurry so they never stayed long enough to eat with the family. They worked hard at keeping the rest of the family on the outside of their world.

Caitlyn noticed a beautiful bouquet of fresh cut flowers in a vase on the counter. The colors were bright and colorful, just the kind Rosie loved. She always said that fresh flowers had a way of bringing sunshine into a room and she welcomed any chance to have them in the house. Her motto was, one could never be too gloomy as long as there were fresh flowers in the house. She also believed in enjoying flowers now. She told them not to wait until after she was dead to bring flowers.

"Mom, those are beautiful flowers. I love the yellow and orange color combination. It's so bright and cheery."

Still a little distracted with setting out the food, plates, and utensils, Rosie gave a distracted reply.

"Thanks honey. They are beautiful, aren't they? I couldn't believe it when Justin came by yesterday and dropped them off. It was so good seeing him again. He looks good and we had a real nice visit."

Rosie continued to rattle on, but Caitlyn missed most of the words as she froze in horror. She frowned and her mouth dropped open. She couldn't believe what she was hearing. Justin had some nerve to come here, to invade her safe place.

Suddenly sweltering hot, Caitlyn found it a little hard to breathe.

What the crap? I can't believe he came here.

Her hands were shaking so hard she had to set the knife down and stop cutting tomatoes.

She looked at her mom and felt tears prick her eyes. She saw the little smile that came to her mom's face as she talked about Justin.

Why do you like him so much? Can't you see that he's a hurtful, lying controller?

"Caitlyn honey, what's wrong? You look like you don't feel good. Are you okay? Sit down love. I'll finish the salad." Rosie took the tomatoes and ushered her into the nearest chair. The commotion of preparing for dinner continued but Caitlyn found it difficult to focus.

"Hey sis, what's up with you? Larry thinks you didn't find a present for him. He said he knew this one would be hard and he doesn't hold it against you. You had to fail sometime. Hey, you in there?" Mike waved his hand in Caitlyn's face and then snapped his fingers to get her attention.

"His gift is in my purse. He's going to have to make it harder than that if he thinks his lists will defeat me. Hey Mike, I'm not feeling so good. Can you drive me home?" Caitlyn tried to smile, bit the inside of her lip and dabbed at her tears.

"What? But honey, you just got here. Maybe you can go lie down on the couch for a minute to see if you feel better." Rosie rubbed her back and felt her cheek with the back of her hand.

"Mom, I really feel sick. I need to go home and lie down. I'll call you tomorrow, okay?"

"I hate to have you leave so soon. Let me fix you a plate to take so you can eat later, okay?" Not waiting for an answer, Rosie set off to pile a container full of food for her to take home. The amount was enough to feed two people for several days.

Larry loved his gift, of course, and Mike drove her home. Still, Caitlyn couldn't get those flowers out of her head and squeezed her fingers into fists.

How am I going to get her to see him the way I know him? I can't disappoint her by telling her everything, can I?

Caitlyn remained quiet on the ride back to her apartment. Mike tried to talk but gave up after receiving one-word responses. Caitlyn put the food away, poured a glass of Sangria, and settled herself on the sofa. Mentally exhausted, she leaned her head back and closed her eyes.

She thought about her relationship with her mother and knew beyond a shadow of doubt they were close, but realized they hardly ever talked about anything serious or personal. They seemed to get along best when the conversations stayed lighthearted and superficial. Caitlyn felt sad at the reality that even though she loved being around her mom, they avoided discussions about feelings, situations, or thoughts that might be uncomfortable.

Rosie taught Caitlyn that being disagreeable was not in anyone's best interest and Caitlyn had learned at a young age how to put the feelings of others above her own so everyone would feel good and get along.

But, how can I go on letting Justin sweet talk her, give her flowers and try to squirm his way back into my life without getting the truth out in the open?

Caitlyn didn't know what the future might hold or how big a part Victor might play in it, but she wanted to give her feelings for him a chance. Since her mother was important to her, she knew she would have to find a way to let Rosie know it was time to move on. Both of them needed to let Justin go. As she crawled into bed, she willed herself to sleep, determined that just for a little while, Justin would stay where he belonged, in her the past.

* * *

Caitlyn found that sleep did not come easy. No matter how many times she flipped from one side to the other, Justin's face continued to find its way into the dreams her mind managed to weave. With a start, she realized it was morning. The drone of the alarm caused a piercing sensation inside her head that refused to go away. Dragging herself out of bed, she made her way to the bathroom so she could prepare to meet the demands of the day.

Penny pounced as soon as she noticed Caitlyn had arrived at work on Monday. "Hey you. What gives? What happened between you and Justin? I did talk to him yesterday. He said you just walked off and he didn't know what he did wrong and I was totally blown away when I saw Victor. Did you brush Justin off for Victor? I thought you would find Justin a delicious slice of no calorie pie." Penny continued to rattle on about how Justin wanted to try another get together.

Caitlyn closed her eyes, took a deep breath and rubbed the bridge of her nose as she tried to block out the constant prattling. As Penny continued, Caitlyn opened her eyes and glared.

"Penny, I told you Justin was the guy I dated for a while at NAU. I know more about him than I want to know and I will not see him again. I don't know how you met him, but if you're my friend, you won't bring him around me ever again."

"Hey. Are you all right? I mean, what's the story here?" asked Penny with a puzzled look on her face.

"I can't tell you about it right now. Things happened a long time ago and I know I don't want to be anywhere near him *ever again*."

She waited a moment and then continued.

"Please understand that I just need, no, I will keep him where he belongs, in my past and out of the present, with no chance of being in my future. I've moved on and it feels really good."

Penny looked at Caitlyn without speaking, gave her a hug, nodded her head and walked away.

She picked up the phone to call her current boyfriend, Len and told tell him that all the plans they had made to get Caitlyn together with Justin were now plans of the past.

Concentrating on work was difficult. Caitlyn felt a sense of panic start to choke her as she pictured Justin finding new ways to invade the life she had worked so hard to build.

Being with Justin was the mistake of a lifetime. She sounded brave when she told Penny he was part of her past, but she had to admit that inside, she didn't feel as confident as she sounded. Caitlyn tried to recall the words from her counseling sessions. They had given her the strength to face another day and she needed them now.

I am strong. There is nothing that can happen to me today that I can't handle. I am capable of great love. I can accept the love of others. I can achieve my dreams. My past is behind me and my future is looking bright.

Great words, but today they felt a little empty. They were easy to say, but harder to make her heart and mind believe in the face of Justin's untimely and unwelcome reappearance in her life.

Caitlyn waited all day for a call from Victor. She wanted to call him but still felt a little uneasy about what he might be thinking since they had come so close to being together, only to stop. Even though Victor was the one to stop and hold back, Caitlyn knew that for some men, that would be the death blow to continuing a relationship.

Relationship? Do I want a relationship that hinges on sex? What does Victor think and feel about me?

Caitlyn's heart skipped a beat as she thought about times with Victor. First, there was the sharing of her fantasy in the restaurant, the wonderful daily surprises while he was away, his disappointment over her plans for Friday night, their day together Saturday, and then there was Saturday night. Sunday had proven to be an added bonus. Just thinking about the passion, the touching, the kisses, and the proof of Victor's desire, made her flush.

Am I in a relationship with Victor?

Caitlyn headed to the washroom in order to cool her flushed face. She felt a little smile form on her face as she continued to think about the possibility of being in a relationship with Victor Knoble.

I like him, but I want him to like the person I have inside, the one I don't always share with other people. I want him to like the me that isn't so confident and held together all the time.

Caitlyn headed back to her desk and picked up her messages. She was pleased to note that Victor had called to invite her to lunch. She called his office and told Sheila she would meet him at Avino's, a little place located between both of their offices.

12

Victor waited for Caitlyn in the reception area of Avino's and she caught her breath when she saw him. He smiled softly when Caitlyn walked in the door and held out his hand to her.

She slid her hand into his and they interlocked fingers.

"I'm glad you could make it on short notice. I had fun yesterday and couldn't wait to see you again." He looked down, cocked his head toward his right shoulder and smiled.

As he spoke, Caitlyn looked into his eyes and felt her heart leap. "You made shopping a lot of fun. What did you do later?"

"I developed the shots from Saturday and planned out some upcoming shoots. I like to have an idea of possible shoot locations and shots that might work ahead of time. Things are likely to change once I'm in the thick of it but I like to have some scenarios played out in advance."

Victor rubbed his thumb back and forth across the back of Caitlyn's hand as he spoke. "Your table's ready, Mr. Knoble. Right this way." The hostess led them to a table near a window and Victor held the back of Caitlyn's chair.

As she slid into the chair, Victor brushed her hair off her shoulder and tucked a lock behind her ear. Caitlyn shivered as goose bumps appeared on her arms.

Victor ordered jerk salmon over rice with broccoli and Caitlyn ordered pasta primavera. They ate thick slices of fresh Italian bread dipped in olive oil and fig balsamic vinegar as they waited for their meal.

"So how was dinner?" Victor waited for Caitlyn to answer and saw her expression change as she lowered her eyes, avoiding his gaze.

"It was okay. I ended up leaving a little early. My brother, Mike took me home."

Caitlyn's voice was low and husky, her facial expression serious.

"Are you okay? I didn't know you weren't feeling well." Victor had a slight frown on his face.

"No, I'm fine. It's just that Justin stopped by my mom's house a couple of days ago and gave her some flowers. I was pretty upset when she told me."

Victor sat, silent for a moment.

"So, does he go to your mom's house very often?"

Caitlyn heard a change in his voice and looked up. His eyes looked narrow and he watched her intently.

"I don't think so. This is the first I've heard of him going to the house. I hate that he thinks he can just waltz in and establish himself again."

"Did you tell your mom about me?"

Caitlyn sighed as she shook her head and met Victor's gaze.

"Not yet. I will, I just need to think about the actual words. I haven't worked out my approach yet."

"Why can't you just tell her Justin's history and you've met a really awesome man?" Victor smiled and lifted his left eyebrow into an exaggerated arch.

"I will." Caitlyn looked at Victor and smiled.

Lunch flew by, punctuated with shared laughter. Victor talked Caitlyn into going hiking in two weeks. She groaned at the thought of the work needed to make it to the top of a mountain.

* * *

Victor arrived at Caitlyn's apartment bright and early the last Saturday in October. He rang the doorbell and waited, two coffees and a couple of bagels in hand.

Caitlyn opened the door, yawned and placed her hand over her mouth as she beckoned for Victor to enter.

"Come on in. I'm almost ready. I'll be right back." She spied the coffee and smiled. "Mmmm. That smells awesome. Thank you." She took the cup he offered and lifted it to her nose and inhaled deeply as she closed her eyes and smiled.

"You're welcome. Now shake a leg. We need to start the hike before it gets too warm."

"Yeah, yeah. I still can't believe I let you talk me into hiking." Caitlyn muttered as she walked into her bedroom to put on her shoes.

* * *

The drive out to the park flew by. Caitlyn ate her bagel while Victor drove and talked about the beauty of the trail and the views it offered. After parking, Victor pulled a backpack out of the trunk, slung it onto his back, pulled on a hat and offered a wide brim hat to Caitlyn.

"No thanks. I don't want to wear a hat."

"Okay, let's go." He led the way over to the start of the trail and started walking the rocky path.

"So, how long is this trail?"

"Just a little over two miles. It's an easy hike."

"Easy for people who hike a lot or easy for people who don't hike a lot?" Victor chuckled.

"It should be easy for you. I told you I would pick a trail you would like."

The rocky path transitioned into a smoother dirt path as the slope began to elevate. "Okay, so tell me this; is it all going to be uphill because I swear I'm going to need some oxygen soon."

Victor slowed to a stop and turned to look at Caitlyn. She was a few feet behind, bent over, hands on her thighs and breathing hard.

He took the backpack off, pulled out some cold water and handed it to Caitlyn.

"Here, have some water. We can go as slow as you want. Hiking can be hard if you aren't used to it. Let's rest a moment." Victor took a pull on the water bottle, offered it to Caitlyn again, then capped it and put it away.

"Okay. I guess I'm ready. Let's commence with the torture."

"That's my girl." Victor smiled, gave Caitlyn a quick kiss and turned to lead the way again.

As they started up the next incline, Caitlyn looked around the landscape. The scarcity of trees gave an uninterrupted view of the park below. There were desert shrubs, cacti, and a lot of dirt, but the varying shades of greens and brown blended to form a beautiful tapestry unique to the Arizona desert.

"My legs want to know how much further."

"Trust me, it'll all be worth it. The hard part is just about done."

"I need more water. I hope we have enough to make it to the end or someone is going to find my dried, withered bones lying on the trail."

"Okay, drama queen, let's stop for some water."

Victor coaxed Caitlyn to the top of the slope where they sat down to take a break.

"I thought I was in better physical shape than this since I exercise, but this is kind of kicking my butt." Caitlyn took several gulps of water and attempted to slow her breathing by forcing air in and out of her nose.

"I think the body can get used to the movements and energy required when you do the same thing over and over, then when you do something different the energy needs can be higher or lower. Just a thought. So, are you hating the hike too much to continue?" Victor took the empty water bottle from Caitlyn and placed it in his backpack, then pulled out a second one and offered it to her.

"I'm good, thanks. I can keep going and I promise to try and keep my grumbling to a minimum even though I think my thighs hate me." Caitlyn smiled and looked around. To her right, she could see a descending trail that led to a small valley on the right and a dome on the left. Looking back to the west, she was surprised to see how high they had hiked, evidenced by the zigzag paths.

"It really is pretty out here. If I live through this hike, I think I might be willing to do it again." Caitlyn stood up and motioned to tell Victor to take the lead.

"I won't let the hike kill you and if you go down I'll figure something out. I have a no man left behind policy."

"I will hold you to that because you don't want me coming back to haunt you."

Victor laughed and shook his head as he began to follow the south trail. Caitlyn fell in behind but caught up so they could walk together as often as the trail allowed.

They followed the trail to the northern side of the hill and sat down on a large boulder.

Victor pulled out a water bottle for each of them and offered Caitlyn a snack.

"So, what do you think? Are you going to make it?" Victor looked over at Caitlyn and waited for her reply.

"I will. I thought I would hate this but it isn't that bad now. My legs have stopped screaming and my lungs figured out how to work so it's all good." Caitlyn's mouth tilted up in a lopsided smile.

"This is one of my favorite places to hike. I love it here."

Victor packed away the water bottles and wrappers from their snacks and they set off to finish the hike.

They had breakfast at a local restaurant and spent the rest of the day lounging at Caitlyn's apartment watching movies.

* * *

During the next few months, Victor and Caitlyn hiked, explored the zoo's and other Phoenix attractions. When Victor was in Phoenix, they spent one evening a week watching movies and sharing pizza from Submarinos, a Glendale pizzeria.

Victor spent most of December away on assignments but called Caitlyn on Christmas day.

"I miss you."

"I miss you, too. What are you doing?"

"My parents invited some friends over for dinner so I'm on potato peeling duty. We're going out on the boat before dinner and my mom is anxious to have everything ready before people show up."

"That sounds like fun except for the potato peeling part." Caitlyn laughed and grimaced.

"What are your plans for today?"

"My parents decided to make Ethiopian food this year for Christmas. My job is to come up with a dessert and I'm totally stuck for ideas about things that would complement the menu. I should have figured this out sooner."

"Time for plan B."

"I was all set to make vanilla cheesecake but they changed the menu after I had purchased ingredients." Caitlyn sighed and ran her fingers through her hair, brushing errant wisps off her forehead.

"If your family likes cheesecake then just go with it. It'll still taste great."

Caitlyn bit the right side of her lower lip and tapped her fingers on the arm of the sofa. "Yeah, I think I will. They'll love it. Thanks." Smiling, she got up off the couch and went to the kitchen. Taking out her ingredients, she began to make her dessert while talking to Victor. They stayed on the phone until Victor had to join his family.

* * *

January and February passed with continued moments of shared tenderness. On Valentine's Day, Victor took Caitlyn out to dinner.

"I know we said we weren't going to do the whole gift thing, but I really wanted to do something to celebrate our first Valentine's Day together."

"Victor..."

"Just open this before you say anything."

He handed her a plain white envelope and watched her face.

She pulled out a receipt and read in silence, then looked up at Victor without a smile, a blank expression on her face.

"Tell me what you're thinking."

"I think this is the most interesting gift I've ever received. What made you think of it?" Caitlyn had a slight smile on her face as she spoke.

"Well, you tear up every time you see a commercial talking about the plight of homeless or hurt animals and you talk about wishing you could save every stray you see, so I thought I would help you save a few." Victor spoke rapidly and fidgeted in his chair.

"I know some women want chocolate and flowers, but I wanted something unique. I wanted something to show you I care about the things you care about."

Caitlyn watched him speak, reached over, caught his hand, and squeezed his fingers. "I love it. Chocolates are great and flowers are pretty and smell awesome, but their beauty fades when they wither and die. This gift will last a lifetime for some animals. No kill shelters always need donations. Thank you" She smiled, raised his hand up and kissed his fingers.

Victor smiled widely at her words and exhaled. They laughed and talked during the rest of dinner, then Caitlyn dropped him off at the airport for his flight to Costa Rica.

She pulled up to the curb and waited while Victor grabbed his bag from the back seat, then she joined him on the sidewalk.

"I'm sorry about leaving on Valentine's Day." He wrapped his arms around Caitlyn and kissed the top of her head.

"It's okay. I had fun." She laid her head against his chest and closed her eyes for a moment.

"Maybe you can tell your mom about me while I'm gone and then I can meet her when I get back."

"Yeah. That should work. Do you think you'll really be back in two weeks?"

"I should be as long as the weather cooperates and I get all the shots I need."

"All right. Call me, okay?" Caitlyn looked up into Victor's eyes and stood on her tiptoes to give Victor a kiss.

"You know it. I'll call you every night if I can." Victor tucked some of Caitlyn's hair behind her ear and stroked her cheek.

"No worries. Have fun."

An attendant walked up and offered to help Victor with his bag and silently pointed to the airport security guard slowly walking toward them and tapped his watch. Victor looked at the guard, handed his bag to the attendant and whispered, "Thank you." The attendant took the bag and nodded his head.

"I have to go. I'll miss you."

"I'm going to miss you, too." Caitlyn gave him another quick kiss, then got into her car and drove away while Victor stood and watched her leave.

* * *

The days merged into a comforting routine of work, hanging out with Penny and her parents, followed by long nightly phone conversations with Victor. She laughed and commented as he told her about the locals he had the opportunity to interact with, the dishes he tried and the beautiful countryside. She smiled with the memory of his voice inside her head as she drifted off to sleep.

* * *

"You're flying in tomorrow evening at 5:30, right?" Caitlyn yawned the question into the phone and fought to keep her eyes open as she waited for Victor's reply. "Sorry about that. I'm a little tired."

"It's okay. Yes, my flight is due to arrive at 5:30. Can you still pick me up?"

"Yes. We do have meetings that last most of the day the 1st of every month and March is going to be busy, but it shouldn't be a problem. I already told Janice I need to leave by 4:45. I'll park and meet you upstairs."

"Sounds great. I know you're tired so I'll let you go to sleep. I'll see you tomorrow."

"Okay, goodnight."

* * *

Caitlyn found a spot near the international arrival gate and shifted from foot to foot while she waited for Victor to come through the doors.

He looked tired. His curls were going in different directions, as if he had run his fingers through his hair multiple times. As soon as he spotted Caitlyn his face broke into a huge smile and his eyes lit up. He walked over, wrapped an arm around her and moved with her to a nearby wall where he gave her a long kiss, then wrapped her in his arms and gave her tight squeeze.

"You are a sight for sore eyes. It is so good to see you. I can't believe how much I missed you." He pulled back to gaze down into Caitlyn's eyes and was pleased to see a soft smile and dreamy half-closed eyes. He gave her another kiss, gently massaging her lips with his.

"Can I spend the evening on your couch, wrapped around you?" His whispered voice caused tingles to race up and down Caitlyn's arms and her stomach lurched in response.

"That sounds wonderful. Do you want to come over now or go home first?"

"I should probably go home and get cleaned up. Then I can drive over."

"Are you glad to be back?" Caitlyn cleared her throat after she heard the husky, breathless sound of her voice.

Victor reached over and began to lightly stroke the side of her neck. Up and down and around her ear, playing with the fine, silky hair.

The quivering in Caitlyn's stomach increased and her breathing became more erratic. She gripped the steering wheel and tried to concentrate on the road.

"Yes, I am glad to be back. I'm really glad I get to hold and kiss you again." Victor watched Caitlyn as he spoke, a little smile tilting up the left corner of his mouth.

"You sir, are making it difficult for me to concentrate on driving."

"Am I? That's good to know. I've been thinking about doing this for days." Caitlyn sighed and repositioned her hands on the steering wheel, her palms sweaty.

She cleared her throat again. "So, tell me more about your trip. Did you get everything accomplished?"

"All right, I'll stop, for now. Yes, the trip was great but living in a hotel gets a little bit old. I'm looking forward to having some home cooked meals. Speaking of home cooked meals, my dad asked me to come home. My mom is depressed."

"What's wrong? Did something happen?" Caitlyn turned to look at Victor and saw that he was looking down, a frown between his brows.

"She lost two really good friends last week. They all met for lunch at one of their favorite restaurants and after the meal, the other two ladies wanted to go shopping but my mom had to go to a meeting for her gardening club. Her friends left together and a drunk driver struck their vehicle. They never even made it to the mall. They both died. My mom feels guilty and sad for not being with them." Victor ran his fingers through his hair and sighed as he looked out the car window.

"That is so sad. You have to go. Your mom needs you." Caitlyn wiped away a tear.

"I'm going just for a couple of days."

"When are you leaving?"

"Tomorrow morning. That leaves tonight free so I want every minute I can have with you."

Caitlyn dropped Victor off and hurried home. She had just enough time to make a vegetable stir-fry and take a shower before he arrived, clean-shaven and so handsome her knees felt weak at the sight of him. He wrapped her in his arms and gave her long, deep kiss as soon as he entered.

They ate dinner, then cuddled together on the couch. Victor stretched out along the length of the couch with Caitlyn stretched out in front of him. He wrapped one leg across her hip and pulled her back against his chest as he stroked her stomach and nuzzled her neck while she turned into a puddle of liquid desire.

"This is what I needed. You with me." His whispered words tickled her skin as she sighed with pleasure.

"Do you trust me?"

Caitlyn's eyes jerked open upon hearing those words. "What do you mean?"

"Just that. Do you trust me? I want you so much."

Caitlyn opened her mouth to respond, then pulled away from Victor and stood up. "What did I say?" He sat up and reached out his hand toward her but Caitlyn backed up and crossed her arms as she looked at Victor. Her eyes, large and round held tears that threatened to spill over.

Victor ran his fingers through his hair, took a deep breath and rested his chin on his hand as he gazed at Caitlyn.

"Caitlyn, what's going on? You look totally freaked out. Can we back up?"

"I need more time." Her voice came out as a quiet whisper.

"More time for what? Tell me what's on your mind."

"I'm not ready to be intimate with you. I really like you but I'm just not ready."

"I respect your feelings and I'm not going to push you before you're ready. Attraction is an important part of a relationship, so don't get jumpy every time I broach the subject, okay?"

Caitlyn nodded her head and gave a small smile. Victor patted the sofa cushion next to him and she came and sat back down, then sighed as she nestled her head on his shoulder. They leaned back on the couch quietly, his arm around her shoulders.

"So, did you tell your mom about me?" Victor rubbed her arm as he waited for her response. He felt her body tense up as she moved away.

"Not yet. The right time never came up." Caitlyn kept her eyes averted as she spoke.

"So she still doesn't know you've been seeing me? You haven't told her anything about me?"

Victor's voice rose in volume as he pulled his arm from around Caitlyn's shoulders and sat up.

"It's not like I'm trying to hide you or anything. We just had some casual conversations about her projects and she told me about how her days went. It's not a big deal. I'll tell her when the moment is right and it didn't seem like the right time." Caitlyn looked down at her clasped hands while she spoke and shrugged her shoulders.

"I know you're close to your mom so it's kind of a big deal to me." Victor stared at the side of Caitlyn's head with narrowed eyes and waited.

"Why does it matter?" Caitlyn looked up at the wall across from the couch.

"I told my parents about you. I told them I found someone I really like and that we've been seeing each other. They're looking forward to meeting you."

Caitlyn sighed and looked down, tucked some hair behind her right ear and looked over at Victor, no expression on her face.

"I don't know what to say. I don't want to answer any questions and I don't want her thinking that I'm getting all serious."

"So you're not serious about me, about us?" Victor stood up and walked over to the table, pulled out a chair and sat down facing Caitlyn.

"That's not what I mean. I just don't want her thinking I found Mr. Right or anything like that because we ..."

"I thought we were moving forward, toward something special. Now it sounds like we're in two different places and I don't know what to think. I need to go." Victor stood up again and strode to the door.

"I'll see you when I get back." He left and closed the door quietly behind him.

"Victor, wait...." Caitlyn leaned her head back against the cushions and closed her eyes.

13

Victor didn't call Caitlyn the entire time he was in Virginia. He finally called after he returned and left her a message, asking her to meet him for lunch.

Victor was just leaving his office to meet Caitlyn when Dawn, a childhood friend and now famous model/actress, entered the building. He couldn't believe she was back in town.

"Dawn! When did you get back? You look great," exclaimed Victor.

"I just arrived this morning. I was hoping we could get together for lunch. I'm doing a photo shoot over the next two weeks. By the way, can I stay at your place? I can't stand the thought of being in a hotel. Please? You know you love it when you have someone around to save you from all those lonely takeout meals." Dawn gave Victor a fake pouty face, knowing he would say yes. She stayed with him every time she came to Phoenix, whether it was for a day, a week, or even a month.

Victor shook his head at her antics and smiled. He draped an arm over her shoulders and they walked to his car while she continued to chat about her plans.

"Of course you can stay with me. You know I wouldn't have it any other way," he finally answered. "By the way. We'll be having lunch with someone special, so I want you to behave yourself. Her name is Caitlyn and she means a lot to me."

"Ooo, a lady-love at last. She must be special to have snared the interest of the great Victor Knoble," teased Dawn. She laughed and continued to go on about his reputation of being a ladies man.

Victor and Dawn laughed and talked during their wait at the restaurant. She showed him the latest pictures of herself and her husband, Steve.

"Victor, Steve and I are planning on starting a family when I finish this assignment. Can you believe it? Me, a mom. I'm so excited."

As he listened to her plans, he picked up her hand and kissed the back of it as he congratulated her on her decision to start a family.

"I look forward to meeting my niece or nephew. Even though I'm not really your brother, I expect those youngsters to call me Uncle Victor. You'll have to keep me informed so I can make sure I'm available to take pictures of the little one."

"Well, I have to get pregnant first, then we can talk about pictures. One step at a time my friend, one step at a time."

Victor looked at his watch and noted that Caitlyn should have joined them already. He and Dawn had been waiting for twenty minutes past the time when they had agreed to meet.

"Well, I guess Caitlyn ran into a situation and can't make it. We should probably go ahead and order," said Victor.

Dawn heard the change in his voice and frowned, then patted his hand.

* * *

Caitlyn called her office and told Janice she felt ill and would not make it back to the office. She sat in her car and recalled the easy smiles that had passed back and forth between Victor and the lovely woman with him. They seemed to laugh and talk so easily with each other. Seeing him with the other woman surprised her, but as she watched them, Caitlyn knew they had a history. She had told herself she could handle being around an old love of Victor's as long as she knew it was in the past. Their chumminess didn't look as if tender feelings had been put to rest.

Her insecurities began to grow large and ugly as she recalled stories about Victor being a ladies' man. She didn't want to be another notch on some egotistical rope of conquest. When she saw him pick up the woman's hand and kiss it she knew she had seen enough. She felt her heart begin to break so she turned around and left. Tears slipped down her cheeks as she started the drive home.

In order to pass the time and get her thoughts in order, Caitlyn began cleaning out closets, drawers, and every other area of her apartment in need of being straightened. This was the first time she had allowed herself to have feelings for anyone since Justin and here she was, feeling weak and uncertain.

I thought Victor really liked me. How am I supposed to know when a man is serious and when he just wants to have a good time? I don't want to be his good time. Is that what he wants?

Sighing, Caitlyn looked around the room and realized she had moved piles from one spot to another without getting anything accomplished.

A break, that's what I need. I don't want to think anymore. I need to get out of my head.

Caitlyn picked up the phone before she had a chance to change her mind and let Janice know she would be out the rest of the week. She got the okay and made plans to spend time at a quiet little cabin on the outskirts of Sedona in an area called Oak Creek Canyon.

How did you get inside my heart, Victor, and what do I do now?

* * *

Victor called Caitlyn's office as soon as he returned from lunch. There was no message from her letting him know what was going on.

He checked his calendar and saw he was due to shoot some preliminary photos for a story about the contributions of black soldiers who had been part of the early settling of the southwest. A local group ran an outfit that offered recreational outings to give tourists a glimpse of the trials and hardships the men had endured. Besides this job, his calendar showed several engagements for the next six weeks. He picked up the phone to call Caitlyn's apartment and left a message asking her to call him.

The shoot was set to last three days, with two of the days going through parts of the trail on horseback. Tonight offered an opportunity to work with the writer and get the outline of the story down, as well as some photos of the group prior to the start of the trail ride.

Victor stopped by Sheila's desk, equipment bag hanging off his shoulder.

"Sheila, can you go by Caitlyn's apartment to see if she is all right? She didn't meet me for lunch and I haven't heard from her. I have to do this shoot and I won't be back until sometime Friday or Saturday. I'll have my phone in case you, or Caitlyn, need to contact me while I'm out."

Sheila smiled and shook her head.

"I think you've got it bad, my boy. You've never asked me to check on any of the others. What am I supposed to say to her?" Sheila arched an eyebrow.

"Listen woman. I know you'll think of some way to let her know I'm concerned about her without being a nasty tease. Give her time to know you and love you like I do before showing her that wicked side of you. Just make sure she gets my hotel number. Oh. And let her know I'll be over on Sunday, please. Here's her number and address." finished Victor as he headed out the door.

Sheila smiled as she watched him leave. She picked up the phone to call Caitlyn's house when Victor came back in.

He smiled at Sheila, took the phone from her and dialed Caitlyn's number.

"I can't leave without calling her." He drummed his fingers on the desk while the phone rang.

Sheila shook her head and went out of the room for a moment.

"Caitlyn, it's Victor. I'm sorry you couldn't make it to lunch. I worried about you when you didn't show up. A family friend showed up as I was leaving and she wanted to meet you. I have to go on a shoot and I won't be back until sometime Friday or Saturday. I want to see you Sunday. No, I need to see you. Hope you're all right. Call me. Bye."

Victor hung up the phone and continued on his way to the photo shoot.

* * *

Caitlyn was walking out the door when her phone began to ring. Hearing Victor's voice brought goose bumps to her arms and her breathing increased in tempo. As she listened, tears trickled down her face. Caitlyn leaned her head against the wall and closed her eyes. She pictured Victor half sitting on his desk, one leg bent at the knee and the other one stretched out for balance as he cradled the phone against his ear. She was tempted to rush over and pick up the phone, but her heart still felt raw from all the emotions of the afternoon.

How do I tell the man who is the object of my dreams that I saw him kiss the hand of another woman? How do I tell him I spent the morning wrapped in warm memories of passion shared, only to end the day doubting I can make him realize I'm the only woman he needs? He's not the kind of man to waste time on some timid little miss who wavers and questions his feelings at every turn. No, I need time to think.

Caitlyn turned and walked out the door before listening to the whole message.

14

The room at the inn was a lovely, two-bedroom suite. The surrounding area had beautiful willow trees and a small creek that flowed through the back of the property. Caitlyn normally didn't indulge in this kind of opulence because of the cost, but decided just this once, why not? She quickly changed into a pair of walking shorts, a long sleeve top and a sleeveless vest, then set out for a walk beside the creek. There were couples strolling along, arm in arm, talking softly to each other and Caitlyn smiled as she watched them.

She continued along the path and felt the tension in her stomach ease as she enjoyed the warmth of the sun and the vibrant colors of the flowers. Slowly, her heart began to mend as an image grew in her mind. An image of herself and Victor strolling along this same path, arm in arm, formed and took root in Caitlyn's mind.

With each step, she became more determined than ever that she would not disappear like some vague dream that fades in the morning light.

I will not cower away from these newfound feelings for Victor like a timid little girl who can't handle a relationship.

Caitlyn headed back up to the inn to get changed. She walked with a confident stride, head held high and a determined glint in her eye.

* * *

Victor met with Ben Macke, the group's Trail Boss, and was pleased to find him both personable and entertaining. Ben was full of ideas to include in the story and he didn't hesitate to let Victor and Randy know the trail they would be taking over the next two days was going to be grueling and tough. He told them about how the men who helped settle the area were often cold, hungry, and required to live without the assistance of the good town folks who treated them as if they were less than human because of the color of their skin. The men had plenty of stories to share and Victor snapped images of Ben and his men as they sat laughing and talking.

Victor spent time prepping for the ride but stopped and checked his phone. No message.

No call. Sheila would have called him if she had found Caitlyn in need of his assistance.

* * *

Caitlyn felt rested and relaxed when she walked back into her apartment Sunday afternoon. Her time away had been well worth the money. All doubts about her feelings for Victor had eased as one peaceful day merged to the next and she felt confident she would be able to speak with him without losing her composure.

I will be open to accepting the feelings of someone else. My past is in the past and Victor is not Justin. The thoughtfulness and tenderness he has shown more than once has to count for something, doesn't it? My days of running away from my emotions are over.

She knew she would have to ask him about the beautiful woman in the restaurant, but now she was willing to listen.

After unpacking, Caitlyn checked her messages. There were the usual messages, Penny checking to make sure she was all right, her mom wondering why she hadn't called, and various telemarketers trying to sell her any number of unneeded items and plans. Then there was a message from Victor.

"Caitlyn. Where are you and why haven't I heard from you? If you don't want me around, I'm afraid you'll have to say it to my face. I won't let you walk away without telling me why. I told you I wanted more of everything with you, and from where I stand, more hasn't even begun. I need to hear from you."

As she listened to the nervousness in his voice, she smiled. Maybe, just maybe, the woman she saw him with didn't mean anything after all. She quickly dialed Victor's home number and left a message.

"Victor. It's me. I'm sorry I didn't call sooner. I don't know if you're in town or not. If you are, I would love to have you come over for dinner. Around 5:00 if you can make it. I'll wait for your call." Caitlyn hung up and went in search of something she could make for dinner.

Tonight's dinner was important. She did not plan on letting the evening end without some answers.

Victor arrived home at 4:15. Upon hearing Caitlyn's message, he quickly dialed her number while rushing to the bathroom to shower, clothes strewn along his path. Thankfully, Dawn wasn't around so there wouldn't be any possible chance that his time might be sucked away.

"Caitlyn. I'll see you at 5:00."

There was no time to pick up the phone. Caitlyn was in the middle of tossing a salad when she heard the phone ring, and by the time she put down the tongs and wiped her hands, Victor had already hung up. All the calm of the past week disappeared as she realized her moment of reckoning was soon at hand. Caitlyn gave the eggplant Parmesan a quick peek, looked over the table setting, and then rushed to the bathroom to finish getting ready. She wanted Victor to see a beautiful, desirable, put together woman who was confident within her own skin. She felt ready when she heard the ring of the doorbell. Right on time.

Caitlyn opened the door and caught her breath. Victor, freshly showered, hair still damp, looked gorgeous. She opened her mouth to speak but never got a word out because he leaned forward and captured her lips in a soft, lingering kiss. Slipping a hand behind her head, Victor deepened the kiss while gathering Caitlyn fully into his arms and backing her into the apartment.

Victor eased his lips from Caitlyn's, even though he refused to let her slip out of his arms. He kept her body molded to his and closed his eyes as he held Caitlyn in silence.

Caitlyn closed her eyes and smiled. She breathed in his wonderful scent and kissed the side of his neck.

"Dinner, kind sir, is served right over here. Allow me to satisfy your appetite with some filling cuisine."

Victor released her. "My appetite is fed when I hold you in my arms. They feel empty without you."

Caitlyn placed her hands on his shoulders and stretched up to give him another gentle kiss.

Caitlyn did not see the expression in Victor's eyes as he walked behind her and took everything in, from the swing of her hair to curve at the small of her back.

They worked together to place the food on the table. Caitlyn suddenly felt nervous after they sat down and fiddled with her utensils, sipped her wine and peeked at Victor. It was easy to feel brave and confident within her own head when he wasn't around, it was another thing to share her heart with the gorgeous man with beautiful eyes sitting across from her. She glanced up after placing some food on Victor's plate and felt her mouth become dry when she met his gaze.

He stared at her in silence with a burning intensity that made her stomach tighten while a tingling flush caused her to feel warm from head to toe. Victor pulled her into his arms again and tipped her face up for another soft kiss before releasing her to sit back down.

Caitlyn felt her legs go weak from Victor's kiss and had to use the edge of the table to feel her way back to her seat. She was breathless and felt her heart and mind soaring with pleasure.

"How was the photo shoot?" asked Caitlyn as she tried to find a way to make it through dinner.

Victor smiled and replied, "It was great. Ben, the group's Trail Boss is a great guy and the men he works with are all very knowledgeable. I have to admit though that I don't know how they can ride for days and weeks at a time. My backside began screaming after a couple of hours."

Caitlyn laughed as she pictured Victor bouncing along the trail with a grimace on his beautiful face. "So what was the shoot about?"

"My publicist was approached by a local writer who wanted to gain some background for a story about the role Buffalo Soldiers played in settling the west. The writer wanted photos to be included in his book. He could have hired anyone but this gave me a chance to capture some prints for archiving. I've never really thought about looking at how the west was settled from any other perspective before so the trip was interesting from an academic standpoint. Of course, I have to admit I was somewhat distracted. You see, there's this girl I'm crazy about and she disappeared on me without a word. Not hearing from her made me a little crazy. Any advice on how I should approach this situation with her? I don't want to scare her away, but I need to know what happened."

Caitlyn swallowed and looked down at her plate as she took a moment to compose her thoughts. The moment of reckoning had come, sooner than she wanted.

How can I tell him I saw him with a beautiful woman and ran away? What will he think?

Caitlyn looked up and tried to recall the resolve from her stay in Sedona.

Victor continued to stare at her with an intensity that never wavered. His steady calm gave her the courage to go forward.

"I was so glad when you called me for lunch. You don't know how excited I was. I was a little late getting there and you were already seated at a table. There was a beautiful woman with you and I stood there watching you two for a few minutes. I was surprised to see her because I thought it was going to be just the two of us. You seemed so happy while you were talking to her. Then, you kissed her hand and ..."

"You were there and you didn't let me know? Why would you do that?" asked Victor incredulously.

Caitlyn saw a change come over Victor. His eyes squinted and his posture seemed tensed and poised. She leaned back in her chair and waited for the explosion. Breathing shallowly, she waited to see what he would do next. She wanted to tell him how she felt but the words wouldn't come. How could they when her throat had locked all sound inside?

Victor looked at Caitlyn, slammed his hands down, pushed his chair away from the table and walked over to the couch. He sat down and put his head in his hands and took several deep breaths.

Caitlyn continued to sit in her chair, watching Victor.

What is he thinking? Is he getting ready to leave me?

Victor looked up and beckoned to Caitlyn to join him on the couch. She stood and slowly made her way over to the couch. As she stood in front of Victor, she waited. He took hold of her hand and pulled her down beside him on the couch. Then he put his arm around her and leaned back on the couch, pulling her with him.

"I wish I could make you understand how I felt, not hearing from you. It was really awful. I was out of my mind thinking you might be hurt or sick, and yet, you left the restaurant and didn't say anything just because you don't trust me. I don't know what I should do. You shut me out without giving me a chance to say anything just because you saw me sitting with a friend. A friend I was going to introduce to you."

The pain in Victor's voice brought tears to Caitlyn's eyes. She placed a hand on his chest and pushed herself back so she could look into his eyes.

"Victor, I'm so sorry. The way I feel about you is something I've never felt before. I don't want to push you away but I didn't know how to let you know I was there. I thought I would be able to handle seeing old girlfriends of yours, but when I saw just how beautiful that woman was, I couldn't stop my heart from breaking. How could I compete?"

Victor saw tears trickle down her cheeks. He reached out and let a finger follow the wet trail of one lonely tear. He caught the tear before it escaped from the edge of her chin. Then he sighed and looked into Caitlyn's eyes before leaning forward to capture her lips in a tender kiss. He pulled back, caught her face between his hands, and placed his forehead against hers.

"Caitlyn, there is no competition. The woman you saw me with is an old friend. We grew up together and she happens to be married to a really great guy. Her name is Dawn and she stays with me when she comes to town to work. She and her husband are going to start a family soon. I brought her to lunch to meet you since she was here. She's always bugging me about not having someone special in my life. Now I do and you go running off without a word. By the way, that's something that can't happen again. I can't stand not knowing you're all right. Promise?"

Victor pulled Caitlyn onto his lap and nuzzled his face into the side of her neck as they both began to relax and he cradled her in silence.

Caitlyn nodded her head and whispered, "I promise. I'm so sorry for not trusting you or letting you know I was at the restaurant. I will work on that, okay?"

He didn't grab me or try to push himself physically or emotionally on me against my will. He didn't call me names, berate me, or ridicule me.

Caitlyn looked down at her wrists and smiled. The days of having her wrists decorated with rings of bruises really were in the past.

Victor watched Caitlyn in silence as she looked at her wrists and ran a finger over her unmarred skin.

"Dinner was good. I'm sorry we didn't finish. Are you still hungry?" he whispered, "If you're not hungry, we can clean up later. Let's get comfortable and watch a movie, cuddle, or just talk. I need you to tell me what I can do to help you trust me. I still want you to meet Dawn, but you have to promise not to believe everything she tells you. If I know her, she'll try telling you stories about us growing up that might be a little over the top. What do you say?"

"Tonight?"

"No way. I want you all to myself tonight. Let's have dinner at my place tomorrow night and you can meet her then. I can call and see if she's available and we can hang out there for a while. You've never seen my apartment before and I want you to see it because it'll give you a chance to see a glimpse of me."

She met his gaze and nodded. "Okay."

"Now, what shall we do? Watch a movie?" asked Victor.

"I would love to watch a movie with you. Shall we clean up first? Then we won't have to worry about it later. How about it?"

"All right. Let's get it done then." Victor slid her off his lap and stood up. He pulled Caitlyn up and they headed to the table to clear away the meal. They made quick work of the dishes and Caitlyn found it oddly comforting to be doing such a mundane task with the gorgeous man beside her.

Victor smiled while he watched her continue to steal glances at him.

Victor settled himself on the couch and pulled Caitlyn down in front of him and stretched out along the length of her back.

He slid one leg between hers and began stroking her sides. Her body seemed to become softer with each passing second and every caress.

The feelings being aroused within her were pleasurable and growing stronger, but she was still hesitant.

"I'm not sure I'm ready for this," Caitlyn whispered. She pulled away from him and turned to place her hand on his chest. As she felt the rapid beat of his heart, she knew she needed to make a decision and make it fast.

What will happen if I don't go through with this? Will Victor change his mind about me and walk away? Will I lose my chance with him? Will he love me if I allow this?

She looked into Victor's sleepy, hooded eyes and felt like she couldn't breathe.

He's everything I want in a man. Why can't I feel good about this?

Victor read indecision and hesitation in Caitlyn's eyes.

Victor smiled softly. "It's okay. I need you to trust me. We won't go too far, I promise."

Caitlyn bit the side of her lip in uncertainty but forced herself to relax and allow Victor to ease her back down. She heard him sigh deeply and opened her eyes to find him staring at her body with an intensity she had never seen before.

He placed his hand on her stomach and began to knead her skin ever so gently. He trailed his fingers down the outside of her legs and then lightly back up the inside of her thighs. He placed a trail of kisses up the right side of her throat to her ear.

Caitlyn felt herself melting more and more each time Victor's fingers touched her. She didn't know how much longer she could take this delicious torment. Part of her wanted this moment to go on forever, but part of her started to feel like control was slipping away. Her breathing came in ragged gasps as she tried to control her feelings and she felt a moan slip past her lips. Caitlyn fought against her indecisive mind and heart.

I don't want to experience this only to have him leave me standing by on the sidelines while he moves on to someone else.

Victor felt a change in her and raised his head. His eyes widened when he saw tears streaming down her cheeks.

"Why are you crying? What's wrong? Please talk to me. What happened?"

"I want you to love me. I can do this, it's okay." Caitlyn sniffled and squeezed her eyes closed.

"What do you mean, 'it's okay'?"

He placed his hand under Caitlyn's chin and forced her to look at him.

"Caitlyn, I need you to tell me what's going on. I promise you we won't go any further than you want, so tell me what you meant when you said, 'it's okay.' What does that mean?"

"I won't try and stop you. I think I love you and I want you to love me, too. That's all." Caitlyn forced a smile and brushed the tears from her cheeks as she looked into Victor's eyes.

He pulled his hand away from Caitlyn's face and sat up. He turned and looked at her but didn't speak. Tears formed in his eyes and he took a quick breath.

"Victor, what's wrong? I said it was okay. Please look at me. I didn't mean to do anything wrong." She placed her hand on his arm.

"Tell me what he did to you. Why do you think the only way for me to love you is if you '*let me* do *this*'?" Victor pulled away from her hand and stood up.

"It doesn't matter. I don't want you to leave."

"Are you going to tell me what happened? Were you assaulted and told that he loved you after he was done?"

Caitlyn couldn't see Victor's face clearly. Her eyes were filled with tears that spilled down her face in an ever-increasing torrent of tears. *He's going to leave and there's nothing I can do about it.* She couldn't catch her breath.

Victor leaned over and kissed Caitlyn softly, then sighed.

"I can't be here right now. You have to decide if you can trust me. Don't make me pay for his mistakes because I don't deserve that. I'm here, I love you and I want to be with you. I'm not going to force you, now or ever. I don't know how you can think that the only way for me to love you is if we have sex. Having sex doesn't mean that someone loves you. Controlling someone or forcing them to do things your way doesn't mean they love you. I want to be with you more than anything in the world, but you have to be confident that I will love you even if things don't go my way all the time. If you can't tell me what happened, I can live with that.

What I can't live with is you questioning your worth and constantly doubting the strength of how I feel about you. You have to figure out what love really means and I can't do that for you.

Change your definition of what love is. Don't let anything that happened in your past determine what happens in your future."

"Victor, please don't go…" Caitlyn had her knees bent and her arms wrapped around her legs. Her forehead was down on her knees.

"I have to. I can't stay when you don't trust me."

"But I want you to love me…"

"I already love you! Having sex won't make me love you more. If you can't see that then there's nothing else I can do!" Victor stormed over to the door and turned for one last look at Caitlyn. He forced himself to walk out and quietly shut the door. He leaned against it and closed his eyes as he heard Caitlyn's moaning sobs.

* * *

Caitlyn couldn't believe he was gone. Just like that, she had lost him. Tears kept leaking out of her eyes. She put her hand over her mouth and tried to keep the pain inside. Rocking back and forth, she hunched lower, trying to draw within herself, into her safe place. She kept seeing Victor's face, filled with pain in front of her eyes.

How could I have hurt him like that? Why couldn't I keep quiet? He left. How could he say he loves me and still leave?

Holding the pain inside became impossible. She heard a high pitched keening sound from somewhere and tried covering her ears to block out the awful heart wrenching sound. Rocking faster and faster, Caitlyn tried to make the pain stop. Her mind became numb and her vision became a narrow tunnel. The long, narrow tunnel of darkness seemed to go on forever. How was she ever going to find her way back to the light?

15

Dawn became alarmed when she came in and found Victor sitting in the dark. After she turned on the light she saw the tears he hastily wiped away.

"Victor. Are you all right? What happened? Is Caitlyn okay?"

"She said she would, '*let me do it*'. She thought sex would make me love her and so she was willing to, '*let me do it*'. Can you believe that? What am I supposed to do now? The whole evening turned into a disaster." Victor pounded his fist against his thigh.

Dawn set her bag down and came over to sit next to Victor. She took a deep breath and gave herself a moment to think.

"Did you have sex with her?" she asked quietly.

"Yeah right. As if I could after she said she would, '*let me do it.*' I couldn't even if I had wanted to, not after that. I'm not a creep. I don't want her to feel like she has to have sex with me in order to get me to love her. I already love her but she's so messed up she doesn't even know what love is. I want her to want me because she loves me, not to secure my love. Doesn't she know what she means to me?" Victor's voice trailed off into a hoarse whisper and he caught his breath as fresh tears came to the surface again.

"What do you know about her past? Has she been hurt before?"

"Yeah, but I don't know the story. It's like she enjoys being touched one minute and the next she just freezes up and disappears right in front of me. The guy must have said he loved her, but I don't know if it was before, during, or after. She won't talk to me about it. What am I going to do? Help me, please." Victor turned to look at Dawn, eyes red-rimmed.

"If it was a boyfriend, then she may not understand what real love is. You have to show her your love for her isn't dependent on having sex with her. You also have to know what you really want. If this is just a momentary affection then you should walk away now. You could hurt her without even realizing what's happening. I suspect she's been hurt really bad in her past." Dawn watched his face closely to gauge his reaction to her words.

"I'm not walking away. I think I want to marry her, have babies with her and grow old with her. But how can I have any of that if she won't trust me? She won't even tell me what happened with the guy from her past. I met him you know. He bruised her wrists. I should find him and beat him to a bloody pulp for what he did." Victor stood up and began to pace back and forth.

"Victor, what she needs doesn't include you getting into a fight with anyone, especially not the man who hurt her. She needs you to tell her about the future you want with her, don't be afraid to share your heart. She needs to know she isn't some temporary attraction, especially since you are a high profile person. It is going to be very easy for her to feel insignificant in your life because of what you do and the people you interact with. She also needs lots of time with you in a lot of different settings. Pay attention to her, romance her, and for Pete's sake, don't try to be intimate with her. She needs to know your attraction and love for her isn't dependent on sex. That's the ticket my friend. Smooching, hugging, and touching are all great, but make sure you stop there. If you can get her used to being physical with you and maintain control, she'll learn to trust you."

"I've been doing that already and she still doesn't trust me."

"So don't stop. If you truly love her, it shouldn't be much of an effort. She needs your affection without the sex. She needs security."

"Do you think it's too late? Did I screw up by leaving?"

"I hope not. All you can do is keep trying to show her you aren't like anyone else she has ever trusted before. Give her a call and tell her you love her and you'll see her soon."

"I don't know." Sighing, Victor ran his fingers through his hair and massaged the back of his neck. Victor sat back down, leaned his head back and closed his eyes.

* * *

Caitlyn heard the doorbell and tried to stop the sounds that were escaping. She rocked faster and put her hands over her mouth again and squeezed her eyes closed.

If I can stop the sounds no one will hear. No one will know.

Penny heard sobbing coming from inside and felt alarmed. She started pounding on the door and calling Caitlyn's name.

"Caitlyn. I know you're in there. Honey, please open the door. Let me in." Penny waited a moment so that she could get to the door. The sobbing stopped momentarily, then started again with more intensity. Penny pounded on the door again.

"Caitlin. Please let me in. If I stand out here much longer people are going to think I'm some looney stalker. Open the door and let me in. I am not going away so don't even think you can wait me out. I have brothers. I can out wait anyone."

It was obvious Penny wasn't going away so Caitlyn got up and trudged over to the door. She opened it, then turned and staggered back over to the couch while Penny came in behind her.

Penny locked the door and followed her over to the couch. She sat down and gathered Caitlyn into her arms. They rocked back and forth, for what seemed like hours. Penny held her in silence until Caitlyn seemed to run out of tears.

She took a few shuddering breaths and slumped fully against Penny. She relished the comfort and familiarity of pain and numbness that threatened to swallow her whole.

I've been here before, inside this solitary abyss of darkness.

She didn't have the strength to fight it this time and welcomed the brain fog that stopped her from feeling and thinking about her bruised and disillusioned heart.

Penny looked at Caitlyn's face and knew her friend needed help. She wasn't sure what to do but she knew she had to do something.

"Caitlyn, is there someone I can call for you? Have you been hurt?"

"I'll be okay," answered Caitlyn in a monotone voice. "Victor was here and said he loved me, but he left. I guess he doesn't love me after all." She choked off a hoarse, "ha."

Tears started to leak again and she wiped them away as she tried to close off her mind.

She couldn't talk about it. Talking would bring the pain back. She had to lock it away and bury it deep down inside or she wouldn't be able to make it through the days ahead.

"I'm so sorry, Caitlyn. I'm glad I stopped by. How about if I stay over? We can hang out, talk, not talk, whatever. I'll even drive us to work in the morning if you feel like going."

"No. You don't have to do that." Caitlyn looked down and refused to meet Penny's eyes.

"Caitlyn, I don't think you should be alone tonight. You don't have to tell me what happened if you don't want to, but I would feel a whole lot better if I could stay."

"Okay, whatever," answered Caitlyn in a tired voice. "What are you going to do about clothes?"

"I'll wear yours. Now, can I fix you anything, maybe something to eat or drink? My mom always gives me her special hot chocolate when I'm sad. She tried to keep the ingredients a secret so it was the one thing she could give us that we couldn't give ourselves, but I found out the secret. She left everything on the counter one day and it was easy to put two and two together. I'll make us both a cup."

Penny walked into the kitchen to make the hot chocolate and kept up a lighthearted stream of chatter about her family and their traditions. Nothing required a response so Caitlyn was free to sit and let the sounds of Penny's words bounce around the room.

"... and I told him that you didn't want to see him again. He kept insisting that he had to see you to '*make things right*', whatever that means. So I told him ..."

"Wait. What are you talking about?" Part of Penny's chatter caught her attention.

"Justin. He came to the office on Thursday and said he really needed to talk to you."

"He was at the office?" Caitlyn's eyes were huge as she stared at Penny in horror.

Suddenly, her whole world was crashing down around her. Victor left, even though she wanted him to stay. Justin wouldn't leave, even though she didn't want him around.

How am I going to be able to go back to work without feeling like I have to look over my shoulder or check doorways? This is Penny's fault.

"Why did you have to tell him where we work? Why did you have to bring him back into my life?"

"I told Mr. Wingate he was an unwelcome visitor. I didn't go into details because I don't know any, but Justin has been put on the list of people who don't have clearance to come upstairs. I also told Justin that if he cared about you at all, then he would just leave you alone so you could have peace and a life with someone else. Then I told him you were in love with someone else and you deserved to have the chance to see where it goes."

It was obvious Penny was trying to make amends for her actions.

"Well, I hope that having his name on a list of people not to admit does the trick. I know Justin though; he can talk the sugar off a doughnut if he wants to. I hope he doesn't charm his way in. Thanks for try-ing. If it works, I owe you big time."

"Honey, do you think maybe you should talk to someone about Justin? Like a counselor or something?"

Caitlyn shook her head as she got up from the couch and crossed over to the table where Penny had set two steaming mugs of hot chocolate. It smelled delicious and she found she was thirstier than she realized. She took a tiny sip and felt the warmth slide down her raw, parched throat.

"No, I saw a counselor when I was at NAU. The counselor had a downtown office.

Counseling helped then, but I don't think it will this time. I just don't know what I need because it feels different this time. I needed to see a counselor because I didn't feel strong. I may not be explaining this well, but I felt like Justin had taken away a part of me. I felt like I would never be myself again. It's like, everyday, I would get up and force myself to go through the motions to feel and act normal. But inside, I was quaking and ready to cry over everything, or else I felt like a walking zombie. I had a hard time finding happiness in anything. The counsel-ing helped me to see that no matter what I had been through, the essence of who I was, the real me, was still in there. They even gave me some words, phrases really, that I said every day, sort of like a mantra that gave me a sense of calm. I was able to focus on the chants and move forward without dwelling all the time on what had happened. Now I feel like I've taken ten steps backward. I need to find strength again."

Her brain fog began to clear. It was comforting to have Penny chat-ter about this and that because trying to concentrate on her words helped to keep the pain in check.

"What happened with you and Justin? Can you tell me?" whis-pered Penny.

Caitlyn looked at her, but her gaze didn't seem focused on Penny at all. As Caitlyn began to drift back to those painful memories, Penny silently waited for the story to begin.

16

Complete mid-terms? Done. Caitlyn looked forward to dinner and the party with Justin and a few of their friends. He came over to her dorm room early and lounged on the bed while she got ready. They planned to eat before heading over to Steven's house for a party. Justin kept pacing and fidgeting. He seemed edgy.

"Come on babe, hurry up. Why do you take forever to get ready?"

She had taken extra care with her hair, clothes and make-up so that she looked as cheerful on the outside as she felt on the inside.

"Why don't you wear that pink dress? You look hot in that one." Justin didn't like the dress she had chosen.

Dancing in-front of her mirror, Caitlyn knew she looked awesome and felt vibrant, alive, and beautiful.

"Well, I like this dress and I'm not changing." For once, she refused to be bullied into changing just for him.

Finally ready, Justin rushed her out the door.

The restaurant was crowded and noisy as usual on a Friday night with boisterous college students ready to let off a little steam. As they walked to their table, it was fun to watch the other girls. Their eyes became huge as they looked at Justin with dreamy eyes that drank in his jaw dropping good looks. Then, they would see her watching them and hastily look away. Yep, they made one great looking couple and Caitlyn felt good knowing she was the one Justin wanted and had chosen to be with even though he could have chosen anyone.

Justin was silent and moody during dinner. The guys kept teasing him, saying if he didn't lighten up, someone else would need to take Caitlyn to the party in order to save her from the sheer boredom of being in his gloomy company. Justin glared at them and said through clenched teeth, "I don't think so."

Caitlyn put her hand on his arm and laughingly said, "He's just joking. Babe, are you okay?"

Justin looked at her and nodded his head, then leaned over. He placed his hand behind her head, brought her face toward him, and gave her a long, thorough kiss that left no doubt in anyone's mind as to his claim on her.

Her mind went blank from sheer pleasure. When he finally released her, she slowly sat back in her chair with a dazed look on her face. Trying to breathe and act normal, Caitlyn tried to pick up her fork but her hand was shaking so she leaned over to take a drink in order to recover her composure.

Justin's moodiness continued throughout the meal. He made it a point to keep touching her. He slid his fingers up and down her arm, rubbed her back and neck, played with her fingers, and lightly caressed her thigh.

Her breathing remained shallow and erratic as tingles overtook her senses. Her skin felt warm and sensitive everywhere as Justin continued to touch her. Thoughts drowned in a swirling sea of pleasurable sensation. Conversation became almost impossible and it took every ounce of effort to listen and respond to the lighthearted chatter of the rest of the group.

Justin didn't even pretend to be interested in the conversations going on around them; he kept his attention focused on Caitlyn. After paying the check and gathering their things, everyone headed out into the cold, frosty night air to make the trip to Steven's house. Justin had a room there because he had decided that one year in the dorms was enough for him. Denny had coughed up the money to pay his share of the rent for the entire year, which included utilities, so Justin just had to budget for his share of food and extras, like sharing the cost of this mid-finals party.

Caitlyn had only come over a couple of times, mostly on nights when there were only two roommates hanging around because Justin didn't want her hanging out when all five of the guys were home. He said they acted like a bunch of goons, trying to have her attention with lame jokes and wrestling and stuff, and he wanted her all to himself.

The house, large and spacious with sports posters pinned up haphazardly around the room and an old cover, probably from someone's bed, thrown over the couch. A keg sat in the center of the living room floor and a second one provided ready access in the kitchen. A ping-pong table had been set up next to the keg in the living room. Miss a volley, take a swig from the keg. Justin and Phillip started playing ping-pong and trash talked each other after every missed shot. Caitlyn steered clear of that game. She wasn't much of a drinker and hated the taste and smell of beer. She hoped there would be more to this party than drinking.

Everyone was loud and having fun and people came and went. It was good to see Justin finally loosening up and having a little fun. Caitlyn didn't understand why he had been so moody lately. He kept talking about how he hated the fact that she wouldn't be with him during the holidays and it wouldn't be Christmas without her. How was he going to bring in the New Year if she wasn't there for him to kiss? No matter what she said, he kept going on about how much he needed her, he needed to know she loved him and would be his forever.

Caitlyn headed toward the back room where Steven had a television set up with movies to watch. Some kids were watching a sci-fi so she grabbed a pillow, found a spot on the floor and became comfortable. The atmosphere in the room was nice and relaxed, just what she needed after all the intensity of dinner.

About halfway into the movie, Justin came in looking for her. His face was flushed and she could tell he had lost the ping-pong game. He looked irritated and wasted. He plopped down beside her, wrapped his arms around her and started nuzzling her neck. Instantly, the warm, delicious sensations from earlier came flooding back.

Whispering huskily, Justin asked her to come to his room. Feeling a little nervous, she whispered back, "I don't think that's a good idea. Let's stay and finish the movie, okay?"

Justin dropped his arms from her and got up off the floor. Looking down at her, he said, "Fine. If you don't trust me, stay here," and turned to leave. Everyone had stopped watching the movie and watched their emotional tug of war.

"Hey girl," said someone she didn't know, "Don't you be stupid and go off with him. You might get more than you want."

"Shut your face," snarled Justin and looked at her through squinted eyes. Caitlyn bit her lip and took a quick breath.

This is Justin, my Justin.

She placed her hand in his, nodded and allowed him to pull her up off the floor.

"Don't say I didn't tell you so," yelled the same person from inside the television room. "You'll be wishing you had listened when he's through with you."

She dropped her head and tried not to listen as Justin led her by the hand.

They went upstairs to his room and he closed the door behind them, leaned against it and stared intently at her.

"I'm sorry about that. I know you hate when people make scenes in public, but I just wanted some time alone with you. You'll be leaving soon and I can't stand the thought of being apart from you. I love you so much and I have to know you love me, too. Say you love me. I'm dying inside, please say you love me." Justin started walking slowly toward her. He held out his hand and waited for her response.

"I do love you." She placed her hand in Justin's hand.

"Say my name when you say it. Please," whispered Justin as he began drawing her toward him.

"Justin, I love you," she whispered.

He sighed with pleasure and folded her within his arms then slowly started rocking her from side to side.

She placed her arms around his waist and relaxed within his embrace.

He didn't hurt me or grab me. He just wants to hug me.

Justin's hands began to stroke slowly up and down her back. Soft, gentle kisses dotted the side of her neck and his breathing became faster and faster. He cupped her chin and turned her face up to receive his kiss. His lips were soft and gentle and as he deepened his kiss, Caitlyn couldn't tell where he ended and she began. She felt as if her legs wouldn't hold her up any longer.

Justin moaned deep in his throat as he felt her respond to him. He backed her up and began to lower her to the bed.

A warning bell went off in her head as she realized her compromising position.

No, not like this, at a stupid party while he's wasted and his friends are just on the other side of the door.

"Justin, let's talk, or watch television and cuddle. We need to slow down," whispered Caitlyn.

He threw a leg over her and pressed firmly against her side as he slid a leg between hers.

He captured her mouth again and began caressing her thighs. "Justin, please. We have to stop. I'm not ready to do this." He began sliding the edge of her dress higher.

"I love you so much. I just want you to know how much I love you before you leave. Maybe you'll stay with me instead of leaving. I can't stand being away from you. I want you to be mine forever. Please love me back. Am I enough for you? I just want to make you so happy that you'll want me the way I want you. I want you to stay with me. I need you."

"Justin, I do love you, but I don't want to do this, not here, not like this."

"You're going to leave me. I don't want you to leave."

She tried pushing him away but he rolled completely on top of her and continued kissing her. The kisses became harder.

No, I don't want to do this.

She broke free of Justin's kiss.

"Justin, stop it. You know I don't want to do this," whispered Caitlyn. He kissed her neck and rubbed against her body with increasing force.

"Yes you do. I can tell. You wouldn't kiss me back if you didn't want me, too. I told you, I love you. I'll love you forever. Now, you'll be mine and you'll never doubt how I feel about you."

"Justin, no. I don't want to..." Caitlyn sucked in a breath.

How did this happen? We were just supposed to kiss.

Her stomach and thighs quivered and ached. She couldn't get enough air into her strained throat and her arms felt heavy and laden. Her wrists ached with the pain of his grip as Justin continued to squeeze both of her wrists with his right hand. Tears slid down her cheeks and pooled in her ears as she tried to close her mind off to the reality of what was happening.

I don't want this invasion.

The lingering scent of beer on Justin's breath was nauseating and revolting and the air was tainted with the sour smell of his breathing. She tried to turn her head away but Justin forced her head back and continued kissing her. Her bottom lip burned as the skin split. She hated the sound of his breathing and the force of his body as he picked up speed. His obvious enjoyment was another blow to her shattered heart. Crying silently, she willed herself to lie completely still.

This stranger forcing his will on her wasn't the Justin she loved. She didn't know this man. She wanted him to stop and leave her alone. She closed her eyes tightly and tried to block everything out. She pictured a box, stepped inside and closed the lid. Safe, she was safe inside the box.

Nothing could hurt her inside the box. Justin couldn't hurt her inside her box.

Justin started planting soft kisses on Caitlyn's face as his breathing returned to normal. "I love you so much. It'll be better for you next time, I promise."

He continued to surge gently against her as he stroked her hair and body.

"Caitlyn, why aren't you saying anything? Tell me you love." He brought his face up to meet her eyes.

"Why are you crying? I tried not to hurt you. I told you I wouldn't hurt you again. I'm sorry if it hurt. I'll try harder next time, I promise."

His words broke through her brain fog.

"Get off," said Caitlyn through clenched teeth. "Get off me, right now. Get off, *get off*, **get off**!"

Pushing against Justin's chest, she was able to push him off. She straightened her clothing, stood up and turned to look at him. He quickly fixed his clothing, sat up, and reached out to catch her hand.

"Caitlyn, sit down. Tell me what's wrong. I just needed to show you how much I love you. I was hoping if you knew how much I love you that you'd stay with me instead of leaving. We can have our own holiday and winter break together, just you and me. What's wrong with that? You're my family, the only family I ever want."

She snatched her hand back out of his reach.

"I'll tell you what's wrong. You knew. You knew I didn't want to do this. Not here and not now in this way, but you made me. You took away my choice. I had the right to say when, where, and how, but you took that away. I don't want you to touch me *ever* again."

She backed her way to the door, keeping Justin in sight. When she turned the knob, she found the door locked.

This was his plan all along!

"Caitlyn, you liked my kisses. You touched me back. I tried to go slow and be gentle. I'm sorry if I hurt you. I said I would try harder next time and it'll get better for us, I know it will.

You can tell me what you like and I'll only do what you want next time. I just wanted to show you how much I love you..."

"Stop saying that! You just don't get it, do you? If you loved me you wouldn't have made me do something you knew I didn't want to do. You knew when you brought me here what was going to happen. That's why you locked the door!"

"No! You came with me of your own free will. I didn't pick you up and carry you here. You came because you wanted to. I didn't lock the door to keep you in, I locked the door to keep those goofs I live with, out! This is supposed to be the night when you finally see how much I want to be with you forever."

A shred of truth from Justin's words caused a stabbing pain in Caitlyn's heart. Doubt began to creep in.

Did I come in here knowing what was going to happen? Caitlyn realized she had to deal with her thoughts. She had to leave, now. She unlocked the door.

Justin jumped off the bed and tried to stop her from leaving. He tried to hug her but she twisted out of his arms and pushed him back, away from her. He stepped back but held out his hand to her, palm up. Reaching out, he attempted to stroke her check.

"Caitlyn, please, please don't go. You can sleep here and we can talk, just talk. I won't try anything, I promise. Please don't go, don't leave me. I need you so much and I'll go crazy if you leave now. Talk to me, please."

Caitlyn moved out of his reach but looked up into his eyes when she heard a break in his voice. They were filled with tears.

She stepped back and willed herself not to be moved by his eyes.

"I want you to hear me, Justin. Don't come around me anymore. Don't call me, don't text me, don't email me or try any other way to contact me. I-want-you-to-leave-me-alone."

Justin heard the determination in her voice.

"You don't love me, not like I love you. How come you can't love me the way I love you? You're all I ever want. I'll do whatever you want, please, just stay so we can talk about this."

At her continued silence, he dropped his hand and backed away from her while tears slowly slid down his face.

"You promised you wouldn't hurt me again..."

"I said it gets better..."

"Again, you just don't get it. You hurt my soul and you broke my heart. I will never trust you again."

* * *

Justin sat down on the bed and watched as Caitlyn turned and walked out. He curled up on the bed and buried his head under his pillow, then he dragged himself off the bed and asked Steven to take her back to campus. He stood in the hall and watched them leave, then turned, walked back to his room and climbed into bed and covered his head with the sheet.

* * *

Caitlyn had to look away from Justin. She couldn't deal with his feelings when she had her own pain to get through. She left his bedroom and made her way downstairs where she found one of Justin's roommates. She was about to ask him for a ride until she saw him stagger toward her.

Great, no purse, money, or ID.

Steven came up behind her and tapped her on the shoulder. "Hey Caitlyn. Justin said you might want a ride home and asked me to take you. Do you want to leave?" He noticed the tear streaks on Caitlyn's face.

"Are you okay? What's up? Did you and Justin split up? You can tell me. He's been a real piece of work lately, so touchy that none of us can stand him. I don't know what's up with him. Don't worry about it, though, you'll be able to make him come around. He's crazy about you and I know he'll do whatever you want."

Steven kept up a continual stream of chatter as they walked out to his car. He gave Caitlyn an inquisitive look at her continued silence. When he saw tears still streaming down her cheeks, he tried harder.

"Caitlyn, what's up, really? Are you okay? I mean, Justin didn't do anything stupid did he? The boy seems crazy about you, but, sometimes stupid happens. Was he stupid? Do you need to see a doctor or the police or anything?"

Caitlyn felt herself cringe at the questions and shook her head. "No. Please Steve, just take me home. Wait, have you been drinking?"

"No. I'm one of three designated drivers tonight. I don't want anyone leaving a party at my house and trying to drive, so we always have two or three people who agree not to drink."

Steven let Caitlyn keep her own company during the drive back to campus. He stopped in front of her dorm but stopped her from leaving the car.

"Caitlyn. I think I know what happened. If you want to talk or anything, I'll listen. If you want me to kick his butt, I'll do that, too. You just say the word and it's done."

She looked at him silently, her eyes, large and shiny with tears. Her voice was hoarse as she replied. "No. Don't kick his butt, but thanks for the offer. I really have to go now. Thanks for the ride."

"Seriously, if you want to talk about it, let me know. Are you sure you're okay? It's not cool that anything shady happened at my house. I can take care of it, but you have to let me know what really happened. My mind can come up with some real heavy images and this just ain't gonna sit well with me."

"Steven, I need you to let me deal with this my way. It's my problem and I can't... I just can't ... I ... I ... I have to go. Please." Head down, Caitlyn turned her shoulder away from him, fingers clenched together in her lap.

"Okay, for now. But if you change your mind about Justin gettin' a butt whooping', just say the word. And Caitlyn, take care of yourself."

Caitlyn nodded, bounded out of Steven's car and headed into her dorm.

Some kids were coming out the door just as Caitlyn arrived so she was able to get inside the building without anyone paying attention to her less than perfect make-up. No one noticed the tear stains on her cheeks or the haunted look in her eyes. She had placed her room key on a chain around her neck, under her dress and pulled it out to get in her room. Melinda had a movie on and glanced over as she came inside. She noted tear streaks but hunched her shoulders and looked away.

Caitlyn gathered some nightclothes and quietly walked into the bathroom. Turning on the water, she adjusted the temperature so that it was almost scalding. Her shaking hands made it difficult to strip off her clothing. The material felt cloying and dirty against her skin. As she started to step into the water, Melinda knocked on the door. "Caitlyn. Are you okay?"

Tears began to slip down her cheeks. "Yes. I just need to take a shower."

Melinda opened the door, came in and grabbed her arm before she stepped into the shower.

"If he attacked you, you shouldn't take a shower. You should call the police and go to a hospital. You need to press charges against that prick."

Horrified at the thought, Caitlyn shook her head. "No. I just want to take a shower and go to bed. What are you doing in here anyway? Don't look at me. Get out of here and leave me alone."

She crossed her arms and tried to hide as much of her body as possible, then pushed Melinda backwards and closed the door.

"Why are you going to let him get away with this?" Melinda's eyes were narrowed as she glared at the closed bathroom door.

"Ahh! Fine. Do whatever you want. See if I care." She smacked the door with her hand.

"Get away with what? I thought you didn't care. Isn't that what you told me? *Leave me alone.*" Caitlyn glared at the closed door and shook her head.

Why does Melinda have to act like she cares now? It's too late. What's done is done.

"Fine. Don't talk to me. What-ev-er." Caitlyn could hear Melinda slamming things around in the room. Then there was silence as Melinda slammed the outer door to the room.

Stepping into the shower, Caitlyn let the water run down her body while tears continued streaming out of her eyes, mingling with the hot water.

Betrayed, that's what you did. You betrayed my trust. You took a part of me that wasn't yours to take. You said you loved me. How could you take me when you knew I wasn't ready? Why would you do that if you love me? You don't love me. You're a liar. Your words are lies. Do I have to give myself away to prove I love you? I think I hate you. How come you didn't stop when I asked you to? What does that make me? How can I trust myself? My body will heal, but how do I heal my heart?

The questions kept running through her mind. Putting her hands over her ears, she tried to block out the sound of her own voice. She tried to concentrate on the pounding of the water against her scalp. Listening to the water was better than going inside her head. If she went inside, the questions were there, waiting to pounce and assail her all over again.

She grabbed the body wash and the loofa, poured a generous amount and began to scrub her body. The coarse texture felt soothing against her arms and shoulders. The hot water added an unexpected sting to the newly scrubbed skin and provided a distraction from her thoughts.

The stinging pain of each new area seemed to extend and blend with the area scrubbed before and kept the questions at bay. Inside the pain, there was no room for self-doubt. Inside the pain, she could not hear the questions that kept trying to shout inside her mind. Those questions fought to drown out the sound of the water so she kept scrubbing, trying to find new areas that weren't already blazing with a searing sting.

New pain, this time it wasn't soothing. This time, there was a concentrated burning that went deeper than the stings on the surface of her skin. Good. More pain made the questions harder to hear.

When she looked down at her thighs, Caitlyn noticed blood oozing out of long scratches that extended from her genital area down to her knees. She dropped the loofa, put her hands over her eyes and started sobbing. She dropped down to her knees and leaned her head against the shower wall.

Was this my fault? I didn't want this, I didn't, I didn't, I didn't! Oh Justin, why? How could you do this to us? I thought I loved you. You promised you wouldn't hurt me again and now you've stolen my freedom to choose you. You said you loved me. I thought you were the man of my dreams. Why couldn't you wait? I would have loved you forever. How can I love you now? How can I love me now?

She wrapped her arms around her legs and leaned her forehead against her knees. Just when she thought she didn't have any tears left she found herself crying again.

Caitlyn heard the bathroom door open and tried to muffle her sobs. "Caitlyn, come out of there. You've been in here for over an hour."

"Leave me alone." The words came out in a hoarse whisper. Her throat was raw from crying and her body felt weak and shaky. Her mind felt blissfully numb and her eyes were heavy and swollen. She laid on her side and closed her eyes while the shower continued to send a never-ending rain of hot, pelting water against her tortured, tender skin.

"Caitlyn, if you don't come out, then I'm coming in. Come on now. I've got your robe." Melinda opened the shower curtain and found Caitlyn curled up in a fetal position. Her eyes were closed and she was mostly non-responsive. Her skin had long scratches all over, as if she had tried to take off a layer of skin. After reaching over to turn off the water, Melinda crouched down in front of her.

"Caitlyn. Give me your hand. I need to get you out of here." Caitlyn heard a whisper from somewhere far away.

How funny. It sounds like Melinda. That can't be right because this voice sounded kind. Melinda is angry. She's angry, all the time, and usually at me. Where is my box? I need my box.

Caitlyn tried to open her eyes, but they were so heavy. Her brain kept trying to bring down a dark curtain to block out awareness.

She slowly became aware that the shower was no longer blanketing her with its warmth. Without the warmth of the hot shower, the heat in the room quickly gave way to a penetrating cold. Caitlyn shivered and moaned. She squeezed her eyes as a fresh stream of tears began to make their way down her cheeks. She couldn't deal with Melinda's anger, not now.

Melinda pulled her up by her arms and propped her back against the shower wall. She wrapped an arm around Caitlyn's torso, braced her feet and slowly hoisted her off the shower stall floor.

Caitlyn didn't notice when a second pair of arms joined Melinda. She kept hearing whispering. Who was talking and what were they saying? She couldn't concentrate. Her eyes felt heavier by the minute and her brain didn't form comprehensible thoughts. She closed her eyes and allowed herself to drift further into the blanket of fog that beckoned like a faithful friend waiting to hold her safe and protected within its thick embrace.

Melinda and Tanya managed to get her into bed and covered her up with a comforter.

They dimmed the lights, looked at Caitlyn sleeping and discussed whether they should call campus security. Melinda locked her fingers together to still their shaking.

"This is beyond me. Did you see her skin? I don't even know what to think. How can I talk to her? What do I even say?"

"Dude. Just watch her tonight. I don't think she's even gonna wake up. She looks pretty messed up. I don't think she should be alone. I'll bring some food over tomorrow so you don't have to leave to eat. Or, I can babysit her while you take a break. I don't know, maybe you're right about calling someone. This is awful." Tanya looked at Melinda, then back at Caitlyn and shrugged her shoulders.

Melinda shook her head. "No. She was really freaked out when I mentioned calling the police earlier and now I think she's even worse. I have a number to a crisis hotline. They should be able to help or at least, tell me what to do. Thanks for your help tonight. There was no way I was going to be able to get her out of that shower and into bed by myself."

"No sweat. I'll come by tomorrow morning. Let me know if you need anything before I get here, okay?"

"Yeah. Hey Tanya? Don't tell anybody, okay?" Melinda ran her hand through her hair, rubbed her eyes and the back of her neck.

"Like I would. You know me better than that. I'm not into that whole gossip thing. But, if one of us thinks she's going to do anything else to hurt herself, we sure better tell someone. I would feel awful if she died because we tried to keep this a secret instead of telling someone so that she can get help."

"I'll watch her. I promise I'll call the hotline if I think she isn't going to be okay. I won't wait." She looked at Caitlyn, motionless and oblivious to everything going on around her. She appeared to be sleeping, but Melinda couldn't be sure.

* * *

Irritating morning light invaded the healing cushion of brain fog. Swollen, heavy eyelids slowly parted. She put up her hand to block out the light and noticed Melinda sitting on her bed watching her. She looked down. In her bed, in pajamas. Her last recollection was being in the shower.

How did I get here?

It didn't matter. She turned over and faced away from Melinda without speaking. She closed her eyes and tried to find her way back to the fog where she could escape the questions and pain that waited to pounce.

* * *

There were whispers again and this time, the smell of toast and the warm scent of cinnamon and clove wafting through the air. The scent disturbed the fog she desperately wanted to remain within. Caitlyn put her pillow over head but that didn't do any good. The delicious smells caused her stomach to growl with hunger, reminding her that she was still in the land of the living.

Crap freakin' ola. Why does my body have to want food when I just want to sleep? Caitlyn flung the blankets back, sat up and glared at Melinda and Tanya in silence. *What are they doing and why are they looking at me?*

"Caitlyn. Tanya brought us some breakfast. How about it?" Melinda held her breath as she waited for a response.

Caitlyn looked down and slowly nodded her head as tears filled her eyes and began to slip down her cheeks again. She slid out of bed and made her way over to the small table. "Thank you, Tanya," whispered Caitlyn while offering a small smile. She took the toast and her tea and made her way back to bed. She flinched as the material from her pajamas got caught and pulled on the scratches on her thighs. She climbed carefully into bed and started eating. Once again, her body was betraying her. Her brain wanted protection by staying in the fog but her stomach wanted food. Last night, her brain said no. As the memories and heartbreak began intruding again, she found her appetite gone. She set the food down, slid further under the covers and pulled her pillow over her head again. She didn't cry loudly this time. Instead, she simply let the tears find their way into the sheet that covered her bed.

* * *

Caitlyn slowly became aware of someone rubbing her back and hair. Looking up, she met Melinda's dark eyes. Melinda didn't say anything, just continued to rub Caitlyn's hair. Caitlyn was glad to have the time and space to begin to heal without guilt, anger, or recriminations.

Tanya too, offered silent, steady support. Caitlyn found that Tanya or Melinda was always there as her constant companion. They were with her before, between, and after classes. She called her mom and told her she wouldn't be able to come home for Thanksgiving. Tanya and Melinda also stayed so she wouldn't be alone.

One question Tanya asked kept running through Caitlyn's head.

"What did you do that was so wrong? You kissed a boy you thought you were in love with, right? How was that wrong? He's the one who crossed the line. That wasn't your fault. A few kisses doesn't equal an invitation for him to take advantage of your feelings, let alone your body. Don't keep beating yourself up. You're human and it's okay to like a boy."

Caitlyn accepted Tanya's words and began to forgive herself. Melinda gave her a number to the crisis hotline, but Caitlyn couldn't bring herself to call it. Amazingly, Justin didn't try to contact her. He sent a few messages through his friends asking her to contact him and to forgive him, but he didn't show up in person. After a couple of weeks, Caitlyn worked up the nerve to see a counselor off campus. The first visit was free. No one gave her strange looks and she felt comfortable with the counselor. Weekly sessions became encounters she looked forward to for the remainder of the semester. Her counselor gave her the confidence to begin trusting her emotions again. She began to build confidence to face each new day, not with dread or fear, but with anticipation that her inner strength would see her through whatever the day would bring.

She kept one question locked inside.

Can I be strong enough if I see him again?

17

The sudden ring of the phone startled Caitlyn and Penny. Victor's voice brought them back to the reality of the night.

"Caitlyn. I'm sorry about the way I left. I need some time to think. I don't want to hurt you, but I don't know how to be with you without your past coming between us. I'll call you later in the week. Bye." Caitlyn heard the catch in Victor's voice and felt her heart break all over again.

"Penny. What am I going to do?"

Penny looked at her in silence. She and Caitlyn were friends, but that friendship succeeded because of their light, casual encounters. Penny said a silent prayer, reached out, drew Caitlyn close and gave her a hug.

"I'm so sorry about everything you've been through. I can't imagine what your pain must feel like." She felt tears build and let them slide unchecked.

"I can't stand this. Why can't I forget about what Justin did and be at ease with Victor? I keep thinking about Justin and I don't want to, I really don't. I used to be able to keep thoughts and feelings about him quiet in my brain. I would say the words the counselor told me to say and everything would be fine. Now, they don't work. I don't want to feel this pain anymore. I want peace." Caitlyn sighed. She felt physically weak from all the crying and emotional turmoil. She closed her eyes and tried to let her mind grow blank.

I can't think about this anymore. Peace, peace, peace.

"Caitlyn, is it okay if I pray for you?" Penny bit her lip as she waited for a reply.

"You pray?" asked Caitlyn, her voice rising in surprise. "Sure, I mean I guess so. Go ahead. I don't think it'll do any good though. If there is a God, I don't think He likes me. I don't like me sometimes, so how can I expect Him to like me? I'm confused though. You go dancing and you date different guys. I didn't think you were a bible-thumper."

Laughing, Penny asked, "What is a bible-thumper?"

"You know. A bible-toting prude. That's not you, though. How can you go to church and still go dancing?" Caitlyn seemed genuinely interested.

"I love to dance. The bible doesn't say I can't dance. When I go, I go with friends. I look nice and have fun. There is nothing wrong with that."

"If you prayed for me, what would you say?" whispered Caitlyn. Keeping her eyes closed, she waited for words that might give her some kind of hope or peace.

Taking a deep breath, Penny waited a moment. "God. Hear my prayer for my friend Caitlyn. You know her heart and you see her pain. Please bring peace to her mind and comfort her hurting heart. Amen."

Feeling her eyes begin to close, Caitlyn sighed. "That was nice."

Penny looked down at Caitlyn and realized she had fallen asleep. She propped a pillow under Caitlyn's head, eased off the couch and made her way over to phone. She called Jarrell and told him she needed to stay with Caitlyn. Eleven o'clock. Caitlyn's story had taken three hours. She thought about the Justin she had met and the Justin from Caitlyn's past. How could he be the same person? The Justin she met didn't seem capable of hurting anyone. Penny went into Caitlyn's room, grabbed a blanket from the closet and settled down on the bed. She set the alarm on her phone for 6 and tried to relax.

* * *

Caitlyn woke up to the smell of something sweet and coffee. She sat up, rubbed her face, then looked around and stretched her stiff body. Her limbs felt weighted down, her eyes felt swollen, and her mind felt blissfully numb. She walked into the kitchen and found Penny sitting at the table eating breakfast.

"Smells good. Did you make enough to share?" Penny smiled at Caitlyn's attempt at normalcy and replied, "You know it. Grab some."

Caitlyn plugged in her kettle and pulled out a bag of Earl Grey. Tea sure did sound good right now.

"Thanks for listening last night. Today's going to be rough. It's a good thing I restocked my make-up because I'm sure I look like a wreck." Caitlyn kept her eyes down as she spoke. She felt a little awkward. Would Penny start talking about God? Where was God when she had her heart broken? She didn't know how she felt about this whole God thing and she wondered why she hadn't known about Penny's faith before now.

Who is Penny? I thought I knew her, but maybe I don't know her any more than I knew Justin. Am I that bad at reading people? What does that say about me?

"Caitlyn! So, can I borrow some clothes or not?" Caitlyn looked up and focused on Penny.

"What? I'm sorry. I was off in my own world for a moment there. What were you saying?" Caitlyn offered a tentative smile in apology.

"I said that I won't have time to go home before going to work so I wanted to know if I could borrow some clothes for today. What about it?" Penny got up and started washing her dishes as she waited for Caitlyn to give an answer.

"Sure. I bet I have something that'll fit. Let's go and find you an outfit." After placing her own dishes in the sink, she and Penny started going through clothes, trying to find something that would fit Penny. After a little bit of searching they were able to find a suitable skirt and blouse that would work.

Penny showered while Caitlyn finished cleaning up in the kitchen. She thought about the events of the night while she washed up the few remaining dishes. Her reunion with Victor had started out so great. His kisses and embraces were everything she wanted. Then, those old feelings had to intrude.

Where do I go from here? Why can't I move forward? Will I ever be able to trust someone to love me without hurting me? One step at a time, one task at a time.

She forced her mind to close off and wiped away a tear. She took a deep breath and headed toward her bedroom, but paused when she heard Penny's whispered voice coming from inside the room. Caitlyn waited until Penny was finished, then rattled the doorknob and entered the room.

"All yours. Thanks for the loan of the clothes. I'm going to head out so I can get coffee at Cross Over before going in to work. Do you want anything?" Penny was whirling around the room gathering her belongings and talking a mile minute.

Caitlyn couldn't help laughing. This was the friend she was used to, this energetic non- stop talker who was upbeat and lively.

"No. I've had some tea and I'll have another mug on my way. That's enough caffeine to last for a while. I'll see you at work." She walked Penny to the door and gave her a tight, silent hug. Penny squeezed her back and headed out the door.

Caitlyn looked at the clock and hurried into the bathroom.

Great, less than an hour to throw myself together and get out the door. This is good. Being rushed leaves less time for thinking. I just need to breathe.

* * *

She arrived at the office and found most of the staff crowded around Janice's desk admiring her beautiful daughter. She walked over and smiled as she met Janice's eyes.

"Oh, I'm just here for a visit. My princess is due for a check-up so I thought I would stop in and play the proud momma role for a while before she gets grumpy from her examination.

"How are you, Caitlyn?" Janice waited for a reply while taking in the dark shadows under her eyes.

Caitlyn glanced into Janice's eyes and then down at the baby. She shrugged her shoulders and answered with a small smile.

"Things are good. I wish the weekend was a day or two longer, but who doesn't?"

This wasn't the time or place for a serious talk so Janice decided to let it go for now. She stood up and gathered the baby from the last pair of arms to hold her and prepared to continue on her way. Janice called farewell to Mr. Wingate on her way out the door and threw a promise over her shoulder about meeting a deadline.

Caitlyn headed over to her desk and passed Penny, who was on the phone setting up a time to meet someone. She picked up her own messages and found a message from her mom mixed in with her assignment.

"Caitlyn, please come over for dinner. I have a surprise for you. Love, Mom. P.S., come over by 5:30."

Smiling, she picked up the phone and called her mom to confirm that she would come over for dinner. As she continued going through her messages, she found one from Victor reminding her they were having dinner at his apartment with his friend Dawn. Caitlyn bit her lip and frowned as she tried to decide what to do.

She called Victor's office, then sighed with relief when his voice mail clicked on.

"Victor, my mom wants me to come over for dinner at her house at 5:30. I said yes before I saw your message. I didn't think you would want to see me right now. Can I have a rain check, please?" Caitlyn quickly hung up the phone before she changed her mind and begged him for a chance to come over. She took a quick breath and forced herself to concentrate on the tasks at hand.

* * *

Victor let the machine run as Caitlyn left her message canceling out on dinner. He sucked in his breath at the sound of her voice. He put his head in his hands and leaned forward until his head rested on his desk. After a few minutes, he took a deep breath, sat back and ran his hands through his hair. He pinched the bridge of his nose and took a deep breath to force back tears, then squinted his eyes and squared his jaw.

He called Dawn and let her know dinner for tonight was off, then smiled as Dawn relayed exciting news. She was going home on Tuesday because she and her husband had decided to start their family now.

"I still want to meet Caitlyn. I'm not flying out until 11:30 tomorrow night so you'd better find a way to get her over here for dinner."

Victor let Sheila know he was going to spend the day putting together the photos from the Buffalo Soldier shoot. He allowed his mind to drift during the solitude. As he sorted through the photos and lined up the photos with his notes and timelines, he found incorrect breaks in the timelines that showed the number of times he had stopped to think about Caitlyn.

Victor sighed and stood up to stretch then began to pace around his office. He found the stack of pictures he had taken of Caitlyn, sat down on his couch and flipped through each picture. The open expression in her eyes captivated his attention.

Here she was throwing food at him. Here, playing peek-a-boo with a pillow and here, she was laying on her back and smiling up into the lens of the camera directly over her face. In one picture, she held her stomach as she tried to control the snorts that had come out accidentally as she laughed. The images began to blur as tears began streaming down his cheeks.

Victor gently laid the pictures down with shaking hands and leaned his head back.

18

Caitlyn made her to-do list, gathered her things and headed to her mom's house. As she walked out to the parking lot, she glanced up and saw Victor by her car. He looked as tired and worn out as she did. She leaned her head against his chest and tried to contain her tears as Victor wrapped his arms around her, and kissed the top of her head.

"I got your message about going to your mom's house for dinner. I brought over a couple of the pictures I took of you. She might like them. I know I do. I like the pictures, but I love the girl in the pictures."

As he met Caitlyn's eyes, he smiled and leaned down for another quick kiss before she had time to respond. He pushed away from the car and released her as he handed her the envelope.

"So, have a good time and tomorrow, have dinner at my place. Don't stand me up, okay? By the way, tonight seems like the perfect time to tell your mom about me." Not giving Caitlyn time to respond, he took another kiss and walked away.

As she watched him, Caitlyn couldn't help smiling as she unlocked the door and sat down. He hadn't given her a chance to say yes or no to dinner and part of her felt relief. She wanted to go but she hadn't been sure to face him. Instead, he had come to her.

She smiled and wiped away tears, warm with the knowledge that he still enjoyed kissing her. That had to count for something. She took a moment to flip through the pictures and found herself in awe of his talent.

Is this how I really look? Is this what he sees when he looks at me?

What she saw was a young, beautiful girl whose eyes were full of life and confidence. Where was the scared girl she had inside, the one so fearful of really letting Victor in? That girl wasn't in any of the photographs.

I want to be this girl all the time.

Included was a photograph of Victor. He looked so handsome. He stood in front of a huge stack of boulders that marked the entrance into an area that had once served as a place of sanctuary for a group of children whose parents had died during a flashflood. He had been shooting petroglyphs in the area and found their shelter. The children ranged in age from thirteen to four. The pictures Victor captured highlighted the dangers of being unprepared for the devastation of flashfloods. Those pictures had gone a long way toward cementing his career. He had contacted the authorities who were able to connect the children with family members.

Caitlyn felt her mouth go dry as she continued to gaze at his picture. She looked into his eyes and nodded her head. Yes, tonight was the night.

As she pulled up in front of her mom's house, Caitlyn saw a rental car parked in the driveway.

That's strange. Mom didn't say anything about guests.

She gathered the pictures from Victor and made her way up the sidewalk to the door. As she got closer, she heard laughter going back and forth in lively conversation. Opening the door, she let herself in.

The smells coming from the kitchen were divine. Rosie had pulled out all the stops for dinner tonight. Caitlyn smelled homemade bread, freshly chopped vegetables for a salad and her favorite, vegetable lasagna. That meant there would be a sumptuous dessert following dinner.

I wonder what the occasion is?

Her mom heard her and came out of the kitchen to meet her.

"Caitlyn my love! I'm so glad you came and you're right on time. We have visitors. I was so surprised when I got the call but I just knew you would be excited to meet them. Come in honey, come in."

She wrapped her arm through Caitlyn's and pulled her into the large family room to meet the guests who had her so excited. Her mom announced her presence as if she were introducing royalty.

"This is my lovely daughter, Caitlyn. Caitlyn, this is Justin's mom, his step-dad and little brother. They are in town for a meeting about a project that Denny's company is bidding on and they wanted to come and meet you. They've heard so much about you from Justin that they thought this would be a great time to spend the evening with you."

Caitlyn felt rooted to the ground. Her mom kept going on and on about what a great opportunity this was for *'the families to get to know each other'*. Rosie acted as if this was a meeting between the families of a bride and groom.

Oh no! Is Justin here?

Caitlyn looked around wildly and searched for his face. All she saw were the faces of their families. She breathed a small sigh of relief and fought for control.

I can do this. I just have to get through dinner and then I can tell mom the truth. Of course, I may break her heart, but at least she'll know there's no chance Justin and I will be anything more than past history. I thought Penny said God loves me. If You love me, then why are Justin's parents sitting in my mom's house? What's the deal, God?

She sat down in a nearby chair, smiled politely and nodded her head. She looked at Robert. He was just as cute as she had pictured after listening to Justin, but he looked more like Denny and he didn't have Justin's gorgeous eyes. She was glad about that. She didn't want to spend the evening gazing into Justin's eyes even if they did belong to someone else.

Caitlyn glanced at Denny. He looked at her with a small smile that looked more like a sneer. Or was it a leer?

Is he leering at me with his wife sitting less than two feet away?

She felt creeped out and quickly looked away towards Justin's mom, Karen.

Even though her early years had been hard as a single mom, Karen was still incredibly beautiful. Caitlyn couldn't believe she was the same woman Justin said had left him alone so often to go out hunting for men. Drinking had been a large part of her life but her skin still looked supple and healthy. Her eyes were clear and open as she calmly met Caitlyn's gaze. She had a kind, comfortable smile. Caitlyn timidly smiled back even as she fought against the urge to like her.

Karen proved to be just as charismatic and charming as Justin. She entertained everyone with tales about cute little things Robert had done recently, all the girls he was charming in his classroom, and of course how great Denny was as his father. She seemed to blossom in the spotlight and made it clear she was saving the best stories for last, those about her beloved Justin. When she started talking about him, she made eye contact with Caitlyn and smiled broadly, relishing the idea of making her son sound wonderful for the girl he had spoken about so often.

Caitlyn sat there during Karen's tales, a smile plastered so tightly across her lips she felt like her face would break into tiny pieces if she tried to change her current facial expression. She felt glassy-eyed from keeping her eyes stretched wide open and her cheeks were burning from the effort to keep her smile in place.

How much more can I take?

Her mother and Darius were laughing and talking as if they had just been reacquainted long-lost friends. Every time she made the mistake of looking at Denny he would leer and wink at her. She finally turned her shoulder toward him by angling her chair toward Robert.

Dessert consisted of a luscious crème brulè with fresh whipped cream and ripe, red berries. Rosie had worked really hard to master the technique so the inside had a decadent creamy filling and the top had a solid crunchy shield that crackled with each scoop.

Karen dutifully raved about the wonderful dinner and fancy dessert and Rosie beamed with the plethora of compliments that flowed her way. Caitlyn forced down as much food as her churning stomach could hold and told her mom the food was wonderful. In order to find a way out of any further conversation, she started gathering dishes and offered to do the cleanup. "It's the least I can do since you made such a wonderful meal."

Karen offered to help her with the dishes and Caitlyn ground her teeth and swallowed a groan as her chance for a break flew out the window. When they started the dishes, Karen continued her stories about Justin.

"He used to talk about you all the time. My Justin is a man who loves deeply and he's very loyal. Once he commits, he commits for good and he seems to have his heart set on you Caitlyn. You seem like such a lovely girl. As a mother, I have to tell you I only want the best for my boys. I can't claim to have been the best mother in the world and Justin has had some rough times with Denny, but I did the best I could. My Justin, well, he's a good boy and I hope you love him as much as he loves you. You haven't said much tonight so I don't know how you feel."

After she dried the last dish, Karen turned and placed her hand on Caitlyn's arm. She placed a hand on Caitlyn's cheek and as their eyes met, she whispered, "Please don't break his heart." Wiping away the tears that trickled down Caitlyn's cheeks, she smiled gently and continued.

"If you don't love him, please, let him go gently, but quickly. You have to tell him or he'll keep trying to win your love." She gave Caitlyn's arm a quick squeeze, turned and quietly left room.

Caitlyn stayed in the kitchen, grateful that Karen had given her some time alone. She gathered her thoughts while Rosie and Darius said their good-byes to Justin's family. When she heard the door close, she walked into the family room and retrieved the pictures Victor had given her earlier. She sat down on a chair and waited for her mom and Darius to come back into the room.

"Caitlyn, you should have come to say good-bye. Justin's mother is such a lovely woman, every bit as charming as her handsome son. I can see where his gift of gab comes from. My oh my how that woman can talk. She sure does love those boys of hers. I could tell she liked you, too Caitlyn. I don't know about that Denny, though. He seems like he could be really difficult if it suits him." Rosie looked over at Caitlyn and waited for a response as she noted her continued silence. She patted the cushion beside her and motioned for Caitlyn to come over and join her.

Caitlyn went over to the couch, knelt on the floor in front of her and gathered Rosie's hands into hers. She took a deep breath and looked up into her mother's eyes.

"Mom, I need to talk to you, about me, about Justin, and about Victor. I'm sorry I haven't been honest with you before now. I was surprised Justin's family was *the surprise* you were talking about when you invited me over for dinner. Never in a million years would I have thought that his family would set foot in this house. I know you've been keeping in contact with him and I don't mind, really I don't, okay, actually I do mind. I hate the fact that you still talk to him. Justin and I will never ever, ever be together again. I need you to really hear me, mom.

Please don't think it's just a matter of time or Justin giving me the right present or saying the right thing. There is nothing he can say or do that will ever make me change my mind. He and I are through, forever."

"Caitlyn my love, tell me what happened? I just don't understand. You both seemed so happy the last summer you were together. Sometimes, to have a long and steady relationship, each person has to make adjustments to make things work. We find out the person we love does have feet of clay, but honey, if you can look past the flaws in the other person and look at the heart, the love will stay strong. You and Justin...."

Caitlyn squeezed her mom's hands and gave them a little shake as she interrupted her. "Mom, there is no me and Justin. There is me living my life and there is Justin, doing whatever it is he does now. Please, *please*, **please** hear me! We are not, nor will we ever again, be a couple. He broke my heart, mom. There's no going back for me, *ever.*"

"People hurt each other all the time when they're in love, honey. That's why we have to work at keeping our relationships alive every day. We can't take those we love for granted. If you just gave him another chance..."

This time, Darius interrupted her and gave Caitlyn a gentle smile of encouragement. "Rosie, love of my life, give Caitlyn a chance to finish what she's saying." He sat down across from Caitlyn in his favorite chair and gave a nod to indicate she should continue.

Caitlyn took a deep breath and stood up. She paced back and forth, deep in thought. "Justin was the first boy I was ever really serious about. He was handsome, witty, charming and he swept me off my feet. He paid attention to me and made me feel so special. I felt beautiful and pampered. He made me laugh and worked so hard to please me. It made me feel good that he cared enough about me to want to develop a relationship with you.

He wanted me to say I would marry him before coming home for Christmas my last year at NAU. He kept pushing me and pushing me to say I would be his wife. I couldn't do that, not right then. If he had his way, we would've been married over Christmas break.

I wanted to travel after graduating. I wanted to find my place in the world, you know? How could I agree to go straight from being a college student to being a wife and mother? He wanted babies right away, mom. I'm managing to take care of myself but there's no way I could take care of kids, not now and especially not then. I mean, can you even imagine me with a kid or two? That's just crazy, but that's what Justin wanted."

Caitlyn's pacing increased, her words pouring out. As she talked, her hands restlessly moved from being clasped behind her back to fists pounding her thighs. Head down, she didn't see the floor. All she saw was Justin pestering her to marry him. Justin, continually pestering and pestering her to have sex with him. Justin, always pushing and making sure anyone within viewing distance knew she belonged to him.

"Do you remember how depressed I was when I came home during my last Christmas break at NAU? I couldn't talk to you then, and part of the reason was because you kept asking me about Justin this and Justin that. I could tell how much you liked him. How could I tell you he had to stay part of my past? Could I break your heart? I never wanted to break your heart or make you sad. You're my mom. I want you to be proud of me."

Caitlyn looked at her mom and searched her eyes. Seeing tears streaming down Rosie's face, she walked over and knelt down beside her. She wiped away the tears and laid her head on her mom's lap. She sighed, closed her eyes and rested for a moment while soaking in some much needed comfort.

Rosie stroked her hair and tried to speak. She looked up at Darius and he squeezed her shoulder as he offered silent encouragement.

"Caitlyn honey, did Justin hurt you? I have to know. I love you so much and I only want the best for you. If he hurt you, I just don't know what I'll do. I thought he was a nice young man and he seemed so crazy about you, but don't you know I love you more than I could ever love him? You can tell me anything Caitlyn, anything. Please, tell me if he hurt you." Rosie held her breath and waited for an answer. She wanted to hear the truth, but she was also afraid of hearing her baby had been hurt.

"Yes. He did hurt me. He broke my heart and broke my trust. Justin still doesn't understand there isn't any going back. He came back here and acted like we could just pick up right where we left off. It's almost like he refuses to believe he did anything wrong, like we just had a fight and everything will turn out fine.

Then, I come for dinner and I see flowers from Justin, and now, his mom and step-dad are guests here for dinner? I couldn't believe it. You went to a lot of trouble to make such a nice dinner. You went all out to make the evening special for them and it makes me mad that Justin is behind it all. He's still trying to have all the control and make us all do what he wants. I need him out of my life, forever. I don't want to see him or think about him or hear about him."

She was amazed to find a sense of calm, peace, and strength flowing through her.

Speaking the words confirmed her determination to close the door on her past with Justin. She smiled as she realized she could breathe. The truth hadn't been as bad as she had feared. She sat back up and gathered her mom into her arms for a fierce squeeze.

Rosie pulled back and placed her hands on either side of Caitlyn's face. She looked deep into her eyes.

"Caitlyn, did he rape you? If he did, we can still call the police and have him arrested. I mean, he should not be allowed to get away with what he did."

"Mom. For a long, long time now I've fought against the pain he caused. I tried so hard to keep it hidden because I didn't want anyone to see inside of me. I was afraid people would judge me or blame me for what happened. So, instead of trusting you or anyone else for that matter, I kept it all bottled up inside. But do you know what I've learned? By keeping everything inside and not trusting anyone, I think I gave him power over me. Thoughts of him would pop up when I didn't want them to. Memories and the pain he caused had control over my heart and mind. I let him keep me from trusting anyone. I wouldn't even date because thoughts of Justin would have me questioning the motives of men who were probably very nice. He even got in the way of my feelings for Victor. It's like I couldn't control how I felt about myself, about other people, or relationships. But, I'm ready to move forward now and I won't let Justin or memories of him have any more control. I'm taking back my life."

"Honey, you are a strong, beautiful woman. I will always support you and stand behind you. I am so proud of you. Wait, who's Victor?"

"His name is Victor Knoble and he's a photographer. I went to interview him when Janice went into labor. We sort of hit it off and I've been seeing him ever since. I wanted to bring him over to meet you but I wasn't sure you would like him the same way you liked Justin. He's so great mom. I feel relaxed when I'm with him."

"Honey, you look happy and of course you should bring him over here. I would love to meet him. If you like him, I know I will, too." Rosie sat back as Caitlyn retrieved the pictures from the table beside the couch and showed the photos from Victor.

"Oh my, these pictures of you are so beautiful. Look at your smile. Even your eyes are smiling. Is this Victor? He's handsome and he has kind eyes." Rosie smiled at Caitlyn when she saw softness in her daughter's eyes as she gazed at the photo of Victor. Darius left the room, leaving mother and daughter huddled together.

* * *

Caitlyn headed home and enjoyed the peacefulness of the evening air. The sky was clear and it was easy to see the stars in the huge, black canvas of night. Caitlyn was surprised at the clarity of her senses. It was almost like blinders had been removed and she was finally seeing things clearly. She inhaled the fragrance of gardenia flowers that filled the lawns along her route home. There was no trembling in her stomach and for the first time in a long time, her nerves didn't feel frazzled.

19

Sleep came easily for the first time in a long time. Caitlyn slept deeply and woke up rested and at peace. She remembered that Victor wanted her to come over and have dinner. She was going to meet his beautiful friend. She looked forward to meeting her, but still felt a little silly at being jealous of her. Old insecurities had bubbled up and sent her off on a solitary trip that could have wreaked irreparable havoc between her and Victor.

Lucky for me he hung in there and cared enough to think we're worth the effort to make this work.

Caitlyn stopped at Cross Over for coffee and treats in order to surprise Penny at work. She couldn't wait to see the surprise on her face and felt good about this impromptu gesture. Treats may not seem like a big deal but since she usually didn't splurge, Penny would be surprised. She laughed as she thought about Penny.

She thinks I'm so predictable, ha.

"Caitlyn! You do love me! How did you know I needed coffee and breakfast?" Penny smiled, gave her a hug, dived into the bag and snagged a couple of pastries to devour.

Caitlyn laughingly answered, "You always need breakfast, my friend. Today, it's on me. Enjoy."

Walking over to her desk, Caitlyn started to sort through her messages and then checked her schedule for the day. The day promised to be long and tedious as she had two stories to start researching and submit for review plus numerous calls to make in order to verify information and facts she needed for her current assignment. When her phone rang, Caitlyn distractedly answered.

"This is Caitlyn." She cradled the handset in the crook of her neck and picked up a pencil to write down anything important.

"Caitlyn," came Victor's warm husky voice. She felt her breath catch in her throat and fumbled the phone, catching it before it hit the desk. She couldn't believe that just hearing his voice produced this tidal wave of sensation.

"Hi, Victor." She tried to control her breathing. Did her voice really sound as breathy as she feared?

Good gravy I hope not.

"I just wanted to call you early to make sure you're still coming over for dinner tonight. Say you're going to come." Victor tried to sound causal as he waited.

"Yes, I'm coming. Should I bring anything?" Her body came alive just thinking about him. She heard a sigh before he answered.

"Good. Can you come over right after work? Dawn has to be at the airport by 10:00 and I want us to be able to have plenty of time without rushing. You don't have to bring anything. I'll take care of everything."

He gave her directions and the code she needed to enter his gated community. Caitlyn hung up the phone, took a deep breath and fanned her hot face. She told herself to concentrate and get back to work but her mind kept drifting to images of Victor's mesmerizing face. Caitlyn realized she was doing it again and forcefully jerked her mind back to the task at hand.

"I will get this finished even if it kills me," she mumbled. She took a swig of her tea and buckled down.

After she took care of phone calls and set appointments, she went to see if Penny was free for lunch.

"Penny, how about some lunch? I'm starving." She crossed her arms and leaned against the half wall that bordered Penny's desk while she waited.

"Yeah. Lunch sounds really good. How about we go for Ethiopian food today? We haven't done that in long time." As usual, Penny was talking up a storm.

Caitlyn tried reading her but Penny kept averting her gaze. Penny moved papers around on her desk and as Caitlyn watched the movements, she noticed that while it appeared Penny might be searching for something, she was actually covering up messages.

Caitlyn gave an exaggerated yawn and plopped her purse down on Penny's desk, right on top of a pile of messages she hadn't been able to cover up yet.

"Penny. Do you want me to wait for you outside? I drove last time so it's your turn to drive today." She looked at her and tried to act casual as she waited for a response.

Penny sighed, stopped shuffling papers and looked at her, then gave a little smile and indicated Caitlyn should lead the way. Caitlyn reached down and scooped up her purse with both hands, and with it, the messages she had covered up before Penny could place papers on top of them. She smiled brightly, turned and led the way to the door. As she walked, she glanced back over her shoulder and saw Penny give one more glance at the papers on her desk before she turned to follow Caitlyn out the door.

Penny kept giving one or two word responses so Caitlyn gave up trying to make small talk. At the eatery, Caitlyn left Penny waiting for the table and went to the restroom. The messages she had scooped up were burning a hole in her hand and she couldn't wait any longer to find out what Penny was trying to hide.

She smoothed out the first one and saw a message from Tim, the manager she needed to meet for her current assignment. Pulling out the next message, Caitlyn froze as she read it.

"Penny, call me. Justin." The message had been taken at 8:10. She felt her heart begin to accelerate and her breathing became shallow. She pulled out the next note and saw that it was also from Justin. The time was 8:45. The third message, 9:45, again from Justin. Caitlyn wasn't sure what to think

What are you doing, Justin? Why can't you just go away? Caitlyn pounded the wall, then bit her knuckles to keep from screaming.

She splashed her face and neck with cool water and then headed out to meet with Penny. "Hey Caitlyn, I went ahead and ordered you hot tea. I can't decide what I want to eat today. I think we should share the vegetarian platter. I've always wanted to try it. What do you think?" Penny seemed more relaxed and Caitlyn decided right then to trust her friend. Still, it was going to be hard when she knew Penny harbored secrets, especially since the secret concerned Justin.

"I think I'll have a salad. I'm having dinner with Victor tonight so I don't want to have a big lunch and then a big dinner. He said I'll love his mom's stuffed shells recipe. I'm excited."

"We need to get together, you, me, our guys, and go dancing or something. I still can't believe you're dating Victor Knoble. That's just crazy."

"I know. I can't believe it myself. But he's so great. I want you to get to know him. I still have to take him over to meet my mom." They paused a moment as their meal was served. The smell of the ginger, cloves, and cardamom made Caitlyn's stomach gurgle. Penny peeled off a piece of injera, scooped some cabbage and carrots and took a bite before she continued.

"Is it serious enough for you to be taking him home to meet your mom? You sure you're not moving too fast?" Penny watched Caitlyn's face intently as she waited for her to respond.

"We're taking it one day at a time. Victor knows my mom was crazy about Justin and I think he wants her to get to know and like him as well. I think he also wants to make sure I'm serious about putting Justin in my past. If I have him meet my mom, I think that will convince him I'm sincere. That's my guess anyway."

Penny nodded her head and quietly started eating again.

Lunch continued to be relaxing and Caitlyn was glad their time together was filled with fun conversation and laughter. She knew she needed a distraction so she could put the messages back before Penny discovered they were gone.

The drive back was a lot more relaxed and Caitlyn enjoyed the banter during the drive.

When they arrived back at work Caitlyn settled down to finish her tasks. She peeked over at Penny periodically and waited for the chance to put the messages back.

After about an hour, she saw Penny go into the bathroom and took advantage of the opportunity. She looked at the pile of messages and the way Penny had organized them by date and time. Caitlyn tried to insert the messages into their correct spots before Penny returned. She managed to get the last one into the stack just as Penny turned the corner heading back to her desk. Caitlyn went to the lounge door, grabbed the handle and turned toward the hallway, as if returning from a break.

"Hey Penny. So, I thought about what you said, about getting together with the guys. We should plan dinner for later this week. What do you think?" She tried to sound casual and forced herself to lean against Penny's desk. She took deep breath and made herself meet Penny's eyes.

"I can't even think about food right now. I feel like a stuffed balloon from lunch. But that would be fun. You don't know Jarrell so we could all eat dinner and then go dancing. You can get to know him and I can talk to that hot man of yours. But you better watch out because I think I have been infatuated with him ever since I first saw his picture. Mmm, he is fine."

"Whoa Nellie, I've got dibs, remember? Okay. Dinner and dancing sounds great. Let's plan on Thursday or Friday. I'll have to find out if Victor can do it. You know, I don't even know if he likes to go dancing. Anyway, I've got to get back to work so we can talk about when and where later." She gave Penny a big smile and a pat on the arm, then breathed a sigh of relief and headed back to her desk.

Penny watched her leave and wondered again how she was going to get Justin to stop calling. She picked up his last message and started writing out possible responses.

20

Caitlyn followed the directions Victor had given her and found her way to his apartment without any trouble. His apartment was located on a hill and the location gave him a great view of the sprawling valley to the south.

Caitlyn found the guest parking spots, parked and started walking up the slope toward Victor's apartment. He was located at the top of the slope, on the second floor of the first building. The buildings on both sides of the street had small, curved flowerboxes attached to the balconies. The profusion of colors was a brilliant contrast against the ruddy color of the buildings. The wrought iron railings had sculpted designs that differed by building.

She rang the bell and waited. She had to work hard not to bite her lip. Victor answered the door, smiled, and grabbed Caitlyn's hand, pulling her quickly inside. Dawn waited by a doorway that led into the kitchen. Her beauty was breathtaking and Caitlyn suddenly felt all of her old insecurities begin to claw their way back to the surface of her consciousness.

"Dawn, I'd like you to meet Caitlyn. Caitlyn, this is Dawn." Victor stood by Caitlyn's side as Dawn silently gazed into Caitlyn's eyes. Suddenly, her whole face lit up as she smiled and reached out to take Caitlyn's hand. If it was possible, she became even more beautiful. It was easy to be drawn in to the warmth of her smile.

"Caitlyn. It's very nice to finally meet you. Victor has told me a little bit about you and I'm looking forward to getting to know you." She pulled Caitlyn's arm through hers and they walked over to the living room where they sat down on the sofa.

"Has Victor told you we are practically brother and sister? We used to play together all the time since we lived next door to each other. We also had some pretty good fights, as all brothers and sisters do. We used to drive our parents crazy because they felt like they had more than they bargained for with an extra kid around all the time. Now of course, I'm glad I can stay with him when I have to come here and work. I get tired of staying in hotels all the time. Now, enough about me. I'm dying to hear all about how you two met. You are simply beautiful. I can see why Victor loves photographing you. Your eyes are quite lovely."

Caitlyn looked over at Victor, sitting in a chair watching their interaction. He gave a little smile and said, "She's dying to hear your version. I told her you came to my office to interview me and we hit it off. She thinks I may be leaving out some details."

Caitlyn smiled, grateful he hadn't told Dawn about that stupid fantasy she had shared at the restaurant.

"Victor was so great. He was supposed to be interviewed by Janice, my mentor, but she went into labor. He could have refused the interview but he agreed to let me complete the job. I was really nervous but he helped me relax. He even helped me out of a sticky situation and stayed around to make sure I was okay. He's a really nice guy."

"A sticky situation, hmm. That sounds mysterious. Want to elaborate?" Dawn smiled and quirked her eyebrow as she gazed back and forth between Victor and Caitlyn.

"Dawn. Enough. You'll have time to continue the inquisition another day. Let's eat and relax before you have to jet off to the airport. That husband of yours will have my head on a platter if you miss your flight." Victor grabbed Caitlyn's hand and pulled her into the kitchen while Dawn followed.

Caitlyn leaned against a counter and Victor placed a hand on either side of her and rubbed his forehead against hers. He gave a small sigh, wrapped his arms around her, then placed a gentle kiss on the side of her neck.

"I sure am glad to see you. I love having you here." He rubbed his nose up and down the side of her neck, from ear to collarbone. His soft whisper tickled her skin and Caitlyn felt a shiver run along her spine as her stomach and body flushed with warmth.

"Victor, Victor, Victor. I thought you said you wanted to eat. I have a flight to catch, or did you forget about me already?" Dawn laughed, picked up a kitchen towel and pulled the garlic bread from the oven.

Victor smiled against Caitlyn's neck, sighed and released her. He looked into her eyes, winked and leaned forward to steal one last, quick kiss before pulling the stuffed shells out of the oven.

Caitlyn, as always, felt dazed from the rush of emotions that came with touches from him.

Dawn smiled and nodded as she saw the dreamy look on Caitlyn's face.

Dinner was a fun affair. Dawn talked about some of the good times she and Victor shared growing up. Caitlyn asked her what it was like to be a famous model. Dawn grew a little bit somber as she talked about the rumors that constantly surrounded her and how they caused a strain on her marriage.

"I'm lucky my husband knows how much I love him and that I'm committed to him and our marriage. If he had insecurities about us, the rumors would be daggers that killed us as a couple. It gets hard. You know, every time I stay with Victor, rumors fly that this is our little love nest. Can you believe that? He's my brother and this is a refuge, but instead of being able to relax, I have to hear sleazy rumors. Did Victor tell you I'm going to take a break from my career to start a family?" Dawn's eyes grew large and round and she sat straighter as she delivered this tidbit of news.

"No, he didn't. That's great, congratulations."

Caitlyn felt relaxed and found herself enjoying the conversation as Dawn went back to painting a picture of a young, mischievous Victor Knoble.

He managed to give it right back, telling Caitlyn how Dawn hated being the tallest girl in their classes, had braces, and wore huge glasses as a kid.

Caitlyn laughed as she pictured a tall, scrawny, gangling girl. She understood the insecurities Dawn felt as a young girl, unsure of herself, uncomfortable in her own body. Looking at her now, Caitlyn saw how those earlier experiences had given Dawn an empathetic and tender heart. As Dawn prepared to say her good-byes, Caitlyn was glad she had taken this opportunity to spend time with someone special to Victor.

Victor told Caitlyn he would be right back and gathered Dawn's bags and carried them down to the car that had arrived to take her to the airport. Dawn gave Caitlyn a big hug, then gathered her purse and a sweater to wear on the plane.

While Victor was gone, Caitlyn looked around the living room and saw several pictures of Victor with friends and family. She picked up one that had to be his parents. His mom was smiling, but there was no mistaking the tears on her cheeks.

"Parents. Sometimes they talk about how great things are going to be when they can have the house all to themselves again, but there's no way you can believe they really mean it when their sadness is plain to see."

Caitlyn jumped; she didn't hear him come up behind her. "Where were you going?"

"I was moving here. I was offered a position in D.C. which would have allowed me to go home for holidays, special occasions and long weekends. My mom wasn't happy when I chose to move across the country to Phoenix instead. This picture was taken the day I left and my mom couldn't stop crying. She said she was happy for me but I knew she felt sad about not being able to see me every couple of weeks. If she has her way, I'll end up moving close enough for her to be able to see me a lot more often."

"Where is home? Your parents look sweet and that's a nice view of your house."

"My parents live outside of Roanoke, Virginia in a boating community. I love going back, but that isn't my home anymore. I've been spoiled by the winter weather here in Phoenix and I can't see myself living anywhere on a permanent basis except here. I manage to go back every year and my parents fly out and stay with me once a year. I'll be going back out for a visit in July. Speaking of parents, how was dinner with your family?"

"Nice segue, my friend. How long did it take for you to think of a way to bring the conversation around to my dinner?" Caitlyn smiled as she teased Victor.

"Actually, I've been thinking about it all day. So spill. What happened?"

Caitlyn set down the picture of Victor's parents and walked over to his sofa. Sitting down, she stared at the carpet for a moment as she tried to calm the sudden increase of her heartbeat and accelerated breathing. She wiped her sweating palms on her slacks and took a deep breath. Then she gathered her hair and pulled it over her right shoulder where she started braiding and unbraiding it. She looked over at Victor as he sat down next to her, released her hair and clasped her fingers together between her knees.

"Dinner was interesting to say the least. I walked in and found Justin's mom, step-dad, and little brother there, all waiting to meet me and share dinner. I ..."

"Are you telling me that Justin was there, in your parent's house?" Victor interrupted.

"No, he wasn't there but he might as well have been. I had to listen to his mom go on and on about how great he is. His brother, Robert, is a cute little kid, but Denny, his step-dad, gave me the creeps. Just the way he looked at me made my skin crawl." Caitlyn's eyes squinted as she relived the discomfort of being with Justin's family.

"Did you know they were here in town?" Victor watched her closely.

"No. I don't think my mom would have been so excited about the dinner if she had been having regular conversations or visits with them. She used to talk to Justin all the time. I'm sure that if she had been talking to his mom she would have told me. I think they must have contacted her and she invited them over for dinner."

"How did the evening end?"

"Well. I told my mom that Justin will never again be a part of my life. I showed her the pictures you gave me and she really loved them. I also told her I've been seeing you. She wants to meet you."

Victor breathed a sigh and pulled her into his arms for a gentle hug. Pulling back, he placed his hands on either side of her face, looked into her eyes and then leaned in to place a gentle kiss on her lips. Feeling her lips match his caress, he stopped and gazed silently into her eyes, and slowly leaned forward to take another, longer, deeper kiss.

Caitlyn closed her eyes and gave herself over to the delicious feelings that flowed through her body with each second that passed.

Leaning back, Victor pulled Caitlyn onto his lap and tucked her head under his chin. He rubbed her back and leaned his head on the sofa and smiled.

"So, when do I get to meet your mom and Darius? I think it should be soon."

"Why are you in such a hurry to meet my mom?" She whispered as she rubbed her nose against his throat and placed gentle kisses along the base of his neck.

"I have to meet her before you change your mind. So, what do you say about this weekend? We could go over and have a barbecue or something."

"I'll talk to my mom and see if that's okay. I'll let you know. It's getting late and I should probably get going. Tomorrow is going to be a long day." Caitlyn slid off Victor's lap and walked toward the door.

Victor caught her hand. "Can't you stay a little longer? I'm really glad you told your mom about me, but we need to talk about Justin."

Caitlyn placed her hand on his chest and looked up into his eyes. "I know you have questions about him. Please give me a little more time. I have to work this out in my mind before I can share my thoughts and feelings with you. Trust me when I tell you that he will never be a part of my future. I'll call you tomorrow about this weekend and I'll try and be ready to share what I've worked out by then. Okay?"

Victor sighed, nodded and silently opened the door. He closed it behind him and took her hand in his as they began the walk down the slope to her car. The night sky was clear and Caitlyn was awestruck at the view of the beautiful city. The lights against the dark night sky lit up the city like a postcard.

As they walked, Caitlyn reminisced. "Walking up and down this hill kind of makes me think about San Francisco. I went there once with my sister, after she and her boyfriend broke up. She was determined to go and start her life over there, in a new city. Boy was that a work out. We walked everywhere and my legs hated me for a while. This isn't as bad as those hills, though. Do you like having to park down at the bottom?"

"It's not bad. I get a little bit sick of it around the beginning of September, but we're all a little bit ready for a break from the heat by then. Will you remember how to get in with the code the next time you come over?"

"Sure. I put it in my phone. Are we okay, I mean, for now?" Caitlyn waited with bated breath for his response.

Victor nodded and gave her a quick hug. "Sure we are. I'll wait for your call about this weekend." He opened her door, then moved away from the car so she could leave.

Looking at him, hands shoved down into his pants pockets, Caitlyn smiled, nodded, and pulled away from her parking spot.

* * *

Caitlyn fixed a cup of tea, pulled out her calendar and called her mom.

"Hi mom. How are you doing?" As Rosie started a monologue about her day, Caitlyn settled against the couch cushions and waited for an opportunity to jump into the conversation.

"So mom, can Victor and I come over for dinner on Saturday? He thought maybe we could do a bar-b-que. What do you think?"

"That sounds like a good idea. What should we have? Oh my. I think ..."

Caitlyn smiled and gave an occasional, "um hm," as Rosie held a conversation with herself about possible meal choices.

"Mom, just call me and tell me what to bring, okay? I need to get to bed so I'll talk to you tomorrow. I love you, goodnight." Caitlyn hung up the phone after Rosie said goodnight and climbed into bed. She thought about the events of the day as she drifted off to sleep.

What are you hiding, Penny? Why is Justin calling you so much? I think I hate him.

21

Jarrell was late. Pacing back and forth in front of her couch, Penny kept checking her watch and glanced out the window over and over as she waited for him to arrive. He had agreed to arrive before Justin showed up.

Penny heard a car door and glanced out the front window just in time to see Justin emerge from his car. She checked her watch again and gritted her teeth. Justin rang the doorbell and Penny sighed, then opened the door and invited him in.

"Hi Justin. Come on in and have a seat. I'm glad you could come." She cleared her throat and tried to lower her voice pitch back to normal. She forced herself to meet his eyes but found herself glancing away after a second.

"Thanks for inviting me over. I'm glad you're willing to help me talk to Caitlyn again. You're a good friend, to both of us. Is she here, yet?" Justin came in and seemed animated. He rubbed his hands together and then ran his fingers through his hair as he waited for her reply.

"Yeah, about that. See, the thing is, Caitlyn isn't here and she isn't coming later. I invited you here so you and I could talk. Caitlyn ..."

"Why do I need to talk to you? It's Caitlyn I want to speak with. Call her." Justin's eyes squinted and his cheeks flushed with color. He spit out the command through gritted teeth as he stared at Penny.

Justin's voice had become hard and unfriendly in less time than it took Penny to gather her thoughts. Penny backed away from him and positioned herself behind the sofa.

"How about something to drink. I have some raspberry iced tea. Have a seat and I'll get you a glass, okay?" Penny quickly walked into the kitchen before Justin could stop her and leaned against the wall. She pulled her phone out of her pocket and sent a quick text to Jarrell, letting him know Justin was here and asking him to hurry up. She placed the phone on vibrate, set it on the counter, grabbed a cup and poured some tea for Justin.

"Hey Justin, are you hungry? I'm starving. Give me a minute to throw together some nachos. They're really good with black beans, avocado, and sour cream..."

Penny jumped when she heard a thud against the wall to her left and turned to find that Justin had come into the kitchen behind her. The picture on that wall now slanted down on one side.

"I just want to talk to Caitlyn. I thought you said she would be here and that's the only reason I agreed to come over here instead of going to your job."

"Listen. We'll talk, I promise. Just let me get a snack because I'm no good when my stomach is sticking to my backbone. And, I did not say Caitlyn was going to be here, I said I wanted to talk to you *about* Caitlyn. There is a difference. Now, how about you put those black beans in the microwave for me. Put a microwave cover over them so they don't splatter all over the place. You're gonna love these nachos. They're so great after a long day of work that sometimes I make them as my dinner." Chattering non-stop, Penny breathed a sigh of relief as she watched Justin follow her directions with putting the beans in the microwave.

Penny heard the front door close and heard the heavy tread of Jarrell's footsteps. "Hey woman! Where are you?" Jarrell playfully yelled.

"We're in here, babe. Are you hungry? Nachos are on the menu." Penny grabbed a napkin and wiped sweat off her face and neck.

"Who's we?" Jarrell asked as he came into the kitchen.

"Oh, hey Justin. Good to see you again, man. How are you? Now I remember Penny said you were stopping by. Thanks for helping with those nachos." He gave Penny a quick kiss and a gentle squeeze as he took a moment to gaze into her eyes.

"I'm going to change so I can get comfortable before we get this grub on. You good in here?" He looked at both Penny and Justin.

"Yeah babe, we're almost done. No onions for you tonight, so don't even ask for them. Just letting you know beforehand." Penny laughed and swatted Jarrell on the butt as he walked away.

He left, muttering under his breath about bossy women. Jarrell had brought some clothes over and left them so it would look natural for him to be here when Justin came over.

Justin and Penny fixed themselves plates, and Penny fixed a plate for Jarrell. They took the food and drinks into the front room and made themselves comfortable. Jarrell came in, sat down next to Penny, and picked up his plate of food.

"So, how are things going with you, Justin? Penny tells me you're into construction. How long have you been in that field?" Dressed in a pair of jeans, a burgundy thermal top and socks, he looked comfortable, at ease, and handsome.

Justin bit a chip and took a moment to finish chewing before he answered. He wiped his mouth on a napkin and looked at Jarrell.

"Fine. Things are fine. I was hoping to be able to talk to Caitlyn, though. I came here to see her." He looked at Penny after he spoke.

"I was surprised to find out you and Caitlyn already knew each other. When Penny said she was going to introduce you to Caitlyn, I thought it was going to be a first meeting. How do you know her?" Jarrell watched Justin as he waited for his reply.

"We went to the same college. We even dated for a while, but then we separated and took different paths after college. She was the one that got away." As he spoke, he clenched and unclenched his fists.

Jarrell looked over at Penny and noticed she wasn't eating and had tears in her eyes. "So what happened? Back in college, I mean?" Jarrell continued to eat between questions.

"We were in two different places back then. I was ready to get married, have kids, the whole bit. Caitlyn said she just wanted to have some independence, find herself, that sort of thing. I rushed her too much and she walked away. I don't plan on making the same mistake twice."

"That sounds rough. You have a game plan?" Jarrell tried to sound casual and friendly.

"Well, for one thing, I'm going to let her know we can go as slow as she wants this time around. All I want is another chance. I just need the chance to talk to her. Penny, can you help me?" Justin looked at Penny.

Penny took a breath and placed her hand in Jarrell's.

"Justin. When I met you, I was excited about being able to introduce a good-looking man to my friend. Caitlyn didn't talk about the men she dated in college..."

"Caitlyn didn't date around in college. She dated me." Justin interrupted.

"Well, anyway, I had no idea you two knew each other. I mean, Phoenix is huge and people come here from all over the place. What are the odds that the one guy I want to introduce my friend to is a guy she's already dated? How crazy is that?"

"We're meant to be together. What are the odds that of all the people I meet after I finally decide to start dating again is a friend of the one woman I want to spend the rest of my life with? I'm telling you, this is my shot. Will you help me, Penny? My heart is in her hands but I need your help."

Penny felt her eyes fill with tears and struggled to push words past the knot in her throat. "I can't, I can't do this. Excuse me," Penny said as she stood up and walked quickly into the kitchen.

Jarrell followed her and gathered her into his arms as she cried and rubbed her back. "Babe, I know this is hard, but we have to go back out there and let him know that his dream of being with Caitlyn is a dream he has to let go of. I'm here and I'll help you get through this, okay?" He wiped the tears from Penny's cheeks and gave her another hug and soft kiss before taking her hand and leading her back out to the front room.

Justin looked up as they entered the room and watched as they settled themselves on the couch, then noticed that Jarrell continued to hold Penny's hand. He looked from Penny to Jarrell then Penny again, but she refused to look him in the eye.

"You're not going to help me talk to Caitlyn, are you?"

"Justin, Caitlyn is seeing someone. Since I've known her, she's never shown the slightest interest in anyone, but the man she's seeing now, well, you should see her eyes. She just lights up when she talks about him. I know she's serious about him. I'm sorry to be the one to have to tell you this, but you have to give up and move on. The faster you accept this, the better. You'll see. You'll be able to meet someone else and I know you'll be happy."

Penny's voice trailed off as she watched Justin shake his head.

"No. Caitlyn is the only woman for me." Justin's voice had grown deep and raspy and he kept clearing his throat.

"Justin, she asked me to make it clear to you that there was no future for the two of you. She said she doesn't want to see you ever again and she was terrified, truly terrified that I might have given you her address. You have to believe me when I tell you that now is the time to start thinking about a life without her."

Justin took a deep breath, stood up and ran his fingers through his hair. He gave Penny and Jarrell a silent nod and walked toward the door.

"Justin, wait a minute. I know you'll be okay. It'll take a little time, but you'll find the right girl. I know you will."

"I found the right girl. Now I just have to find a way to let her know she's the one."

"Justin. How are you going to convince her of anything when she doesn't want to see you? She was totally serious about that. I can't tell you where she lives and you won't be able to come and see her at work. You really have to walk away. I wouldn't tell you any of this if I thought there was a chance for you."

"It's okay, Penny. I have to do this on my own now. I have to go now." Justin left without looking back.

Penny looked at Jarrell with wide, disbelieving eyes.

"He didn't listen to anything I said. He still thinks he can have a future with Caitlyn. I feel so responsible. If I hadn't invited him to go out with us to meet my hot friend, he wouldn't know where she works, he wouldn't have found her again, and he wouldn't be thinking that his dreams can still come true. And, to listen to him, the only thing he did wrong was to push Caitlyn to marry him. He didn't own up to the fact that he violated her."

"Penny, you tried. That's all you can do. Let Caitlyn know that Justin refused to listen so she can be on the look out for him at work. As for what Justin did, in his mind he didn't violate Caitlyn. He probably thinks they just hooked up and it was no big deal. Guys like him want what they want. He's a smooth talking creep if I ever saw one."

"What do you think he meant when he said he has to do this on his own now? I can't even imagine what that means. Oh no. You don't think he'll do anything crazy do you? What have I done?" Wringing her hands, Penny sat down on the couch. So much for her plan of getting Justin to back off.

Jarrell sat down beside her and pulled her into his arms.

"Babe, it'll be okay. You have to let Caitlyn know so she can protect herself. Give her a call and tell her now so that she can start making some decisions."

"What if she hates me for this? I don't want to lose my friend." Penny seemed to be gazing off into space.

"I think it'll all work out. Caitlyn is strong. She fought her way back from that assault and landed on her feet. She didn't let his actions beat her. I think she's stronger than you think. She'll be able to handle this but you've got to tell her so she can be prepared."

Penny sighed and nodded her head. "You're right. I better give her a call. She was going to dinner with Victor but she may be home by now. I'm so glad you were here tonight. Thank you for all your support." Penny gave Jarrell a long tender kiss, leaned against his chest and rested her head on his shoulder. After finishing the nachos, she picked up the phone to call Caitlyn.

22

Thoughts of Penny, the messages from Justin and possible secrets mingled with dreams as Caitlyn drifted off to sleep after dinner with Victor and Dawn. The sudden trill of her cell phone startled her awake and drove away the vestiges of sleep.

"Caitlyn. Thank goodness you're home. I need to talk to you."

" Hey Penny, how are you? What's up?" She heard Penny catch her breath as if she had been crying.

"Are you hurt? What's going on?"

"Caitlyn, I talked to Justin tonight. I tried to tell him you were seeing someone else and he needs to move on and forget about having a future with you."

"What!" Caitlyn felt her whole body become tense with anxiety. The hand that gripped the phone began to shake.

"What did you tell him?" She could feel her body tremble and she had to swallow a burst of hot bile that filled her mouth.

"I told him you were seeing someone and he needed to leave you alone. I tried to make it clear to him there was no chance for him, but he didn't listen, Caitlyn. It's like he has this image in his brain of having the perfect family and you're part of that image. He kept saying you're the only girl for him. I'm so sorry. I don't know what else to do." She waited for a response but heard silence from the other end of the phone.

"Caitlyn? Caitlyn? Are you there? I'm so sorry." Penny's voice rose in pitch as she implored Caitlyn to respond.

Caitlyn remained frozen, an image of an angry, determined Justin in her mind.

Justin, fists clenched. Justin, nostrils flared, eyes squinted, and lips tightly pressed together.

"Did you tell him where I live? Please tell me you didn't tell him where I live."

"No Caitlyn. I would never tell him where you live. But honey, he does know where we work. I think he may show up there and try to talk to you. He said something about *having to do this on his own*. I don't really know what that means, but he thought he was going to be able to talk to you tonight at my house. He was angry and disappointed you weren't there. I don't know what he'll do, but he really wants to talk to you. He said he needs to show you his heart."

"He probably will come to the magazine. Can you do me a favor?"

"Sure. Anything. I feel so awful about all of this. I hope you can forgive me. I didn't know he was someone who had hurt you in the past. I'm so sorry."

"It's not your fault. Please don't be hurt, but I have to ask you not to come over here for a while. I don't trust Justin and I wouldn't put it past him to follow you so that he can find out where I live. Are you going to keep talking to him?"

"I'll try not to. He has been calling me at work, but I won't return any more of his calls. Do you think that'll help?"

"I don't know. I hope so. If you do talk to him, please don't tell him I'm seeing Victor. I don't know if he would go and talk to Victor or not but I don't want him to have any more information than he already has. I hate the fact that he knows where my mom's house is. Now I'll have to be careful about going over there. Why can't he just leave me alone?" Caitlyn threw a pillow off the bed onto the floor and leaned her head against the headboard.

"Honey, he thinks he's a man on a mission to regain his lost love," Penny whispered.

"I don't want anything to do with his idea of love. If that's love, then love stinks and he can keep it."

"Don't give up on love. It's glorious and liberating when it's true love."

"Well. I don't know anything about that kind of love, at least not yet. Justin's idea of love was control. I had to think, act, and move the way he wanted, when he wanted, and how he wanted. No thank you. Never again."

"Caitlyn, I hope your idea of love gets a makeover. Maybe Victor will be able to help redeem your belief in love." Penny gave a small chuckle and Caitlyn could almost see the wink that came with her statement.

"Maybe. We're not there yet so we'll see. Anyway, don't come over for a while, okay?"

"Sure thing. That's the least I can do since I helped to create this whole mess. You be safe, all right? Call me anytime and I'll be there for you. Goodnight. I'll see you tomorrow at work."

Caitlyn hung up the phone and decided to go and take a shower to wash off the sweat that had accumulated on her body during the call from Penny. Her nightclothes felt sticky and clammy as they clung to her frame. The warm, soothing water felt wonderful and Caitlyn felt a little more relaxed as she changed into new sleepwear. She didn't know what to think. She had no idea what Justin might do. He could show up anywhere, at any time and there was no telling what was going through his head.

How can he possibly think he has any chance with me?

Caitlyn picked up the phone and decided to let her mom know what was happening.

"Hi mom. How are you?"

"Caitlyn! It's so good to hear from you. We're doing good over here. How are you? What gives us the pleasure of hearing from you tonight?"

"Well, I wanted to let you know that Justin seems to be living here in Phoenix."

"What? How do you know? Has he bothered you? Are you okay?" Caitlyn heard the panic in her mom's voice.

"Mom, slow down. I'm okay. I actually saw him, not tonight, but I did see him a couple of weeks ago. I went out with Penny one night because she wanted me to join her on a double date. She had met Justin and invited him out to meet me. She didn't know that we already knew each other and she didn't know he was the only person walking on the planet that I didn't want to see again." The right side of Caitlyn's lips turned up in slight grimace and she shook her head.

"What happened when he saw you?"

"Well, he grabbed my wrists and tried to force me to talk to him. Victor was there and made him leave. He knows where I work now. He can't get in to see me, but he does know where the building is."

"Caitlyn, you'd better be careful. Do you want me to drive you and pick you up from work?"

Caitlyn laughed, thankful for this wonderful, never ending support her mom always offered.

"No, but thanks for the offer. I'll be okay and I'm going to be careful. But, the thing is, he told Penny he still thinks I'm the only one for him and he seems to think that if he can talk to me, I'll fall head over heels for him or something. I just don't get it, mom. I told him in college and again the at Palisades when I saw him that I never want to see him again. Why he thinks he still has a chance with me, I'll never know."

"Maybe you should have Penny tell him that if he doesn't leave you alone, you'll call the police." Caitlyn heard an angry tone in her mom's voice and she could picture her pursed lips.

"I'll see where this goes. Maybe he won't do anything and everything will be fine." Caitlyn sighed, rubbed her face and fluffed her hair with her fingertips.

"What about Victor? What have you told him?"

"He was there when I saw Justin."

"Yes, but does he know that Justin knows where you work and that Penny talked to him? Does he know that Justin still wants to be a part of your life?"

"I don't know if I want to say anything just yet. Hopefully, Victor won't find out because Justin will go away before there's anything to find out. There's no reason to tell him about something that might not even be a problem. That would be one more headache I don't need."

"Well. Just think about it, okay?"

"Sure thing, mom. I'll talk to you later. Goodnight."

Caitlyn finished getting ready for bed and hoped sleep would eventually come.

* * *

Sleep had been largely elusive and when she did finally drift off, her dreams were filled with Justin's face. She decided to give up a lost battle, got up and got ready. Going in early meant she could leave before six and that would be a good thing in case Justin decided to show up at the end of the day. Penny was already hard at work when she arrived.

"Hey Caitlyn. You're here early. You look tired. Did you get any sleep last night?

I know I'm tired. I tossed and turned all night long. I just can't believe Justin had the nerve to ignore everything I told him about you seeing someone. He's just like every other man who doesn't listen, you know what I mean? I swear ...." As usual, Penny rambled on and on without waiting for or expecting any kind of response.

Caitlyn sighed and started going over the submission she had been proofing yesterday. Penny came over when she didn't respond and started chattering again.

"Caitlyn! Are you listening to me? What are you going to do about that?"

She looked up with a confused look. "What am I going to do about what? I missed what you just said."

"I said that even though I didn't tell Justin, Victor's name, he's bound to find out since it's not like he won't see his face somewhere. What are you going to do about that?" Penny stood with her arms crossed and rocked back and forth on her heels.

"I didn't think about that. Hopefully he won't remember what Victor looks like."

"Well what does Victor think about all this?"

"I haven't told him. So far, there's nothing to tell. I don't want to make an issue out of something that may turn out to be nothing, you know?"

"Mmm, I know Jarrell would be totally ticked off if I kept something like this from him. He'd say I was keeping secrets and he'd make me miserable."

"Well, I'll talk to Victor about it if Justin proves to be a problem."

"Okay. I guess you know what you're doing, at least I hope you do. Sometimes it's better to take the bull by the horns and control the situation instead of letting the situation control you. Then, all you can do is react, you know what I'm saying?"

"Yeah, I've heard that before and I'll be ready." Caitlyn stretched and yawned, then gave Penny a slight smile as she went back to reading over the submission material.

Penny sighed and walked over to her desk and sat down, shaking her head.

Caitlyn was thankful Penny had finished her inquisition. She was too tired to deal with her nonstop chatter today. She headed to the break-room to prepare a cup of tea. She breathed in the calming fragrance of the Earl Grey and tried to will her stomach to cease its constant quiver. Walking back to her desk with her mug, Caitlyn felt a huge smile spreading over her face when she saw the beautiful flowers waiting for her. Victor must have placed his order for these beautiful flowers last night after she left. She reached for the card and expected to see his beautiful handwriting.

Beautiful flowers, for my one and only beautiful flower.
Justin

Caitlyn sat down in a stunned daze.

Of all the nerve of. Are you really so delusional that you believe I would forget about your betrayal just because of some beautiful flowers? Arrrgh!

Caitlyn ripped up the card, grabbed the vase and walked into Janice's office. "Good morning Janice. These were sent over for me but I would love for you to have them. Is it okay if I leave them on your table here by the door? I know you're only here for a couple of hours but feel free to take them home."

"Are you sure? Those are absolutely gorgeous. The man who sent them must think mighty highly of you."

"I'm sure. Enjoy them." Caitlyn set the flowers down and quickly left the office before Janice could shoot any questions her way.

Work crawled and concentrating proved to be difficult. Caitlyn called Victor after eating some lunch.

"Hi Victor. I talked to my mom last night about having dinner on Saturday. She's looking forward to meeting you. How does your schedule look?"

"You tell me what time and I'll be there. Better yet, what if we go together? I could come over to your place, we could hang out, and then head over to your mom's house. How does that sound?"

"You don't have any work you need to do?" Caitlyn smiled at the eagerness in Victor's voice.

"I do, but I can bring it with me and do it at your place. Or, you can come over to my place and I can still get my work done. Then we can think of some way to fill the rest of our time before heading over to your mom's house." Victor's voice had become soft and husky as he continued.

Smiling, she pictured herself wrapped in Victor's arms, whiling away the lazy hours.

"Caitlyn? What do you say? Should we spend the day together at your place or mine?"

"I can come over to your apartment after I run some errands. I think I'll make a dessert to have after dinner. By the way, do you even like dessert? I feel like there's still so much I don't know about you." She bit the right side of her bottom lip and frowned a little.

"Yes, I do like dessert. Fruit pies are my favorite. You name it and I'll eat it. As far as not knowing much about me, I have an idea about how we can fix that."

"How?"

"Well. We can start by spending hours and hours and hours together. Then, you can pick my brain for answers and I'll do some picking of my own."

She laughed at the sultry, comical voice Victor chose to use and agreed to go over to his apartment between 11:30 and 12:30. That would give them about four hours before they needed to head over to Rosie and Darius's house for dinner.

* * *

Caitlyn managed to get all of her articles ready for submission by the end of the afternoon and had a conference call with Janice to discuss upcoming assignments. As she prepared to go home, she walked slowly out of the building, scanning the parking lot and sidewalks before heading to her car. She half expected to see Justin skulking around. She breathed a sigh of relief when he was nowhere to be seen.

She scrambled into her car and locked the door before relaxing and laughed at how silly she must have looked as she walked quickly, swiveling her head from side to side with every step. Still, she was very glad she hadn't seen any sign of him.

Maybe I don't need to worry after all. I can deal with flowers and if that is going to be his tactic, then Janice and every other woman in the office will benefit from having beautiful flowers on their desks.

* * *

After fixing a light dinner, Caitlyn settled down on the couch with a glass of sweet red wine, ready to unwind and relax after a long day that had stretched out because of a restless night. Her concentration was interrupted by the sound of the doorbell.

Frowning, she got up and headed over to the door.

23

Caitlyn peered through the peephole and a smile of joy brake out on her face and she felt her heart leap in excitement as she saw Victor on the other side of the door.

"I'm glad you came over. Come on in. What made you decide to drop by?"

"I didn't feel like eating alone in my apartment. Have you had dinner yet?"

"Yeah, I just finished but I have some stir-fry left that you can have, if you want."

"Sure, that would be great. Thanks. I wasn't sure if you'd be home or not but I decided to take a chance. I was thinking about dinner on Saturday and thought it might be fun to bring my camera. Do you think your mom would like some new pictures? I could take some that are posed and some candid shots. What do you think?"

"That would be great but you don't have to. I don't want you to feel like you have to work for your supper or anything, you know? You're supposed to be a guest."

Caitlyn warmed up the stir-fry and put some on a plate. They walked into the front room and sat down on the couch as Victor kicked off his shoes and made himself comfortable while he ate.

"I think it would be fun. If your family is like mine, I bet it's been awhile since you all had any family portraits taken. I can take some nice ones. Besides, I have to make sure I get on your mom's good side."

"No worries about that. She's looking forward to meeting you and if I know her, which I do, she's going to love your smile. Once you flash that, she'll be putty in your hands, my friend."

"What makes you think that's all I have to do?" Victor smiled as he waited for her answer.

"Well, I can't think straight when you smile at me, so..." Caitlyn smiled but averted her gaze.

"All I have do is smile, huh?" Victor put his plate down and moved closer to Caitlyn on the couch. Catching her chin in his hand, he leaned forward.

"How do you feel when I do this?" Softly kissing her, Victor pulled back slightly before kissing her again, this time brushing his lips back and forth.

Caitlyn opened her eyes and found Victor staring at her face.

She couldn't look away. Victor had a pleased expression that he didn't even try to hide.

"I love the way you look right now. Soft, relaxed, and open." He slipped one hand behind her neck and let his other hand glide beneath her knees. Victor slid Caitlyn down to a side position on the couch. Lying beside her, he wrapped his arms around her, slid one leg between hers and continued the soft, gentle touches that increased the tingle in Caitlyn's lips and made her feel as if every inch of her skin was alive and on fire.

Victor sighed against Caitlyn's neck and pulled back so he could look at her face. She met his gaze head on and he felt his heartbeat kick into overdrive. Caitlyn's eyes did not show any fear or confusion. He gave another quick kiss, but didn't linger against her lips.

"I have a job I have to wrap up. I'll be down in the Bisbee, Tombstone, Ft. Huachuca area until Friday. I should be back sometime Friday night so I won't be able to see you again until Saturday. Are we still on for hanging out at my place around 11:30?"

"Yep. I'm going to make a couple of desserts and you get to help." Caitlyn stretched her arms over her head and settled herself closer to Victor.

"As long as I get to be with you, it's all good. By the way, I don't have a problem with you having things you need at my apartment. If you have things there, then we wouldn't need to worry about cutting our time together short because you don't have something."

"I appreciate your thoughtfulness. If I need to leave something there, it's nice to know you don't mind. What are you going to be doing in Bisbee?"

Leave things? It's still early days. Hmm.

Victor smothered a smile and started telling her about his current job. "Maybe you can come with me next time. I should have good reception so call me anytime. Well, I'd better get going while I still can. I'm going to miss you." Victor leaned over and captured Caitlyn's lips again, then heaved himself up off the couch.

"I'll miss you, too. I love going to Bisbee. I haven't been there since I was a kid. We only went a couple of times but I remember there was this little shop that sold all kinds of honey, flavored in different ways. We would buy jars and jars of it and these big bags of pretzels. Then, we'd eat the pretzels by dipping them into the honey. My parents let us pick a flavor and it was fun to try different ones. I haven't thought about that in years. Those were good times."

"Do you want to come with me?" Victor paused from putting on his shoes and looked at Caitlyn.

"Sounds like fun, but I can't take time off at the spur of the moment and you'll be working. I was gone for a week, remember?"

"How could I forget? You drove me crazy worrying about you. Promise me you won't do that again. If you're ever worried or have questions about how I feel about you, just ask me. If we're going to move forward, we have to be honest and open with each other and you're going to have to trust that I'll never force you to do anything you don't want to do."

"I promise. I do trust you. It's me I don't trust, but I'm trying. Can we change the subject? I'd rather talk about Saturday. If I know my family, people may be coming in and out. If you're going to take pictures, you'll be busy trying to keep up with everyone."

"Not a problem. It'll help me get to know everyone. Now, give me one more kiss and I'll be off. I have a lot to do before I leave in the morning." He gathered Caitlyn close and gave her a quick kiss and a squeeze before heading out the door.

* * *

Caitlyn cleaned up his plate and prepared for bed, feeling good about how relaxed she felt in Victor's arms. He hadn't made her feel awkward about her previous reaction and that made it easier for her to relax in his arms tonight. She was surprised at feeling a little out of sorts at the thought that she wouldn't see him for three days. It felt so right to have him in her apartment.

She began to drift off to sleep thinking about his arms, then got back up and called him.

"Hi Victor. I just wanted to let you know that it's going to be a little weird not seeing you for three days. I hope you have a good trip, though. Bye."

Victor got out of the shower and noticed that he had a message. He smiled when he heard the message.

24

Caitlyn stopped by Cross Over's before heading into work. Tea and a fresh fruit tart sounded really good today. Feeling really good, Caitlyn decided to treat Penny even though it was her turn to do the treating.

As she entered the building, she walked with a light, carefree gait. There, waiting on her desk, were more flowers.

"Ooo. Those are beautiful. If you don't want them, I'm sure I can make room in my office for another vase," joked Janice as she walked by.

Lips pressed together, Caitlyn picked up the card, prepared to hand over the flowers.

Again Justin? You need to give it a break because this is getting really old. I don't want to play this game anymore.

Caitlyn, I'll see you Saturday. Victor

Smiling, Caitlyn leaned over and breathed in the heady fragrance of the beautiful flowers. No way was she going to give these flowers away, they were all hers. She headed over to Penny's desk with the morning treats, still smiling over the flowers from Victor.

"Caitlyn! Did I ever tell you I love you?" said Penny as she dove with excitement into the bag of pastries.

"You're the best friend a hungry girl can have. I have a really hectic day and I know that those two cups of coffee are going to be long gone before lunch. Call me later, okay!" Caitlyn laughed as Penny flew out the door in a whirlwind of movement.

She walked back over to her desk and got started on the day's work. She didn't see much of Penny for the rest of the week. The days began to blur into one another, filled with the routine and mundane tasks of taking care of local stories. She had brief conversations with Victor and her evenings were quiet. She was glad when Friday finally came. She felt excited about being able to see Victor. It was going to be great having him finally meet her mom.

As she headed to the store after work, Caitlyn decided to stop near work for the pie ingredients. She browsed through the produce, took her time smelling the fruit and checking to see if it was ripe. While she stood in line to pay, she chuckled and shook her head over the exaggerated headlines of some of the magazines that were strategically placed near the checkout registers.

As she turned to leave, she froze. There, standing in front her, between her and the door, was Justin. Her stomach immediately began to tighten and Caitlyn felt her fingers begin to shake. Luckily her items were in a paper bag with handles because her arms felt weak.

"Hi Caitlyn. It's good to see you," said Justin quietly.

Caitlyn hated that he looked so calm.

Why do I have to feel this nervous while he looks like he just stepped out of a magazine? It's not fair!

Caitlyn looked past Justin without speaking and tried to step around him. "Caitlyn, I was wondering if I could talk to you? They have a coffee bar here and I would love to buy you a cup." Justin continued to maintain a soft, slow tone.

"Move."

"Caitlyn, please. It's just a cup of coffee. I promise, if you talk to me this one time, I won't bother you again. If you tell me to stay away, I will. Please."

Caitlyn closed her eyes and sighed. "I'll give you five minutes, that's it.

And you don't touch me. Deal?"

"Whatever you want. Let's go and find a table. Can I carry your bag?"

"No, I can carry my own bag." She hated the sudden cheeriness in his voice.

Justin walked with Caitlyn over to a table in the coffee bar and they sat down across from each other. He gazed at Caitlyn while he tried to collect his thoughts.

"Your five minutes started the moment I agreed to listen to you," said Caitlyn as she deliberately looked at her watch to note the time.

"Can I get you some coffee?" asked Justin quietly.

"No. You have four minutes left." She was unable to still the flutters in her stomach that seemed to be multiplying by the second.

How come he doesn't look scary? He should look scary.

"Caitlyn, do you remember the first time you ever talked to me?" Justin clasped his hands together on the table and waited for Caitlyn to respond.

A picture flashed in her mind. She had been clearing tables and he was sitting at one of the tables, watching her. When she got ready to pass his table, he reached out and handed her a flower.

Caitlyn tilted her chin up and looked Justin in the eye.

"No. I don't remember. What I do remember is that you took away a choice I had every right to make, that's what I remember." Caitlyn kept her arms folded across her chest and continued to sit up straight in the chair.

Justin continued without acknowledging Caitlyn's response. "You were bussing tables and I could tell that you were really tired. Your hair was pulled back into a ponytail and it was obvious you had pulled it back in a hurry because you missed a few strands. I offered you a flower and you were so surprised. I loved the expression on your face. I tucked your hair behind your ear and asked you out. You said, yes and every-thing felt right in the universe."

"You have two minutes left." Caitlyn fought hard against the tears she felt pricking her eyes. She didn't want to feel sorrow at the loss of that early, young, and carefree love.

"I never wanted to hurt you, ever. I know I could have been a better man, but I didn't know how. I listened to other guys and did what they did and really, they didn't know any better, either. I know it's not an excuse, but all I ever wanted to do was to show how much you meant to me. I would have done anything if it meant showing you how much I loved you."

Fearing that she wouldn't be able to maintain her composure any longer, Caitlyn stood up and picked up her bag, preparing to leave.

"Caitlyn, wait, please. You told me once that you didn't believe people were all good or all bad. If you truly believe that, then why can't you have the same belief about me? How come I can't be given the benefit of doubt?" Justin's voice had become a little more urgent.

"Do you believe people deserve a second chance or not? All I'm ask-ing is that you give me a chance to show you I'm not the same, pushy guy you knew in the past. I won't ask for much, just a cup of coffee, please."

As she looked into Justin's pleading eyes, Caitlyn didn't see the monster from her memories. She only saw the pleading eyes of the boy who had first charmed her with a flower.

"I want you to leave me alone. I don't want flowers, I don't want to see you and I don't want to have a cup of coffee with you. I want you to go away." Caitlyn gripped the handles of her bag and turned to leave.

Justin stood up and caught her arm. "I will leave you alone if you just hear me out. One conversation, that's all I ask. All I ever wanted was you, by my side, forever. Please."

Caitlyn pulled her arm loose and looked at Justin. His eyes looked calm and sincere.

"Fine, one conversation. After that, you leave me and my family alone, deal?"

Justin smiled and nodded his head. "Deal. When and where? You say the word and I'll be there."

Caitlyn hesitated, then answered. "Sunday afternoon at the Japanese Garden. 2:00."

"Done. You won't regret this Caitlyn, I promise. I know you'll understand everything after we talk." Justin leaned over as if to give her a kiss on the cheek.

Caitlyn jerked back and held her bag against her chest. Squinting her eyes, nose and lips turned up in a grimace, she spoke sharply in response to his actions.

"I told you not to touch me. You don't have that right, not anymore. You want to talk to me, you play by my rules this time or you can get lost now for all I care."

Justin's eyes grew large as he listened to her. When she finished speaking, he nodded and stepped back.

"I'm sorry, okay? I promise to try it your way, no touching. Thank you, Caitlyn. I'll see you Sunday." His voice had lost its cheeriness. As he turned and walked away, his head was down and his shoulders appeared slumped.

Caitlyn placed her hands on the table and eased herself down on the chair. Her hands and legs felt shaky and she felt numb. *"What have I done?"*

25

The vibration from Caitlyn's phone startled her. Victor's eyes stared at her as the addictive strains of Miles Davis broke her train of thought. Caitlyn picked up her phone, then set it back down and allowed the call to go to voicemail.

I can't talk to you right now, Victor. I need time to think.

"Excuse me, Miss. Are you okay?"

Caitlyn looked up and met the eyes of a woman wearing a uniform with a name tag: Shanae.

"Yes, yes. I'm okay. Thank you." Caitlyn averted her eyes and pulled her keys out of her purse.

"I don't mean to pry or anything, but can I talk to you for a minute?"

"Yeah, sure. Have a seat." Caitlyn waved her hand toward the chair across from her and Shanae sat down.

"It isn't any of my business, but I heard you tell that man not to touch you." Caitlyn looked at Shanae, then averted her eyes.

"Yes. He used to be my boyfriend but those days are long gone. I can't seem to get it through his thick skull that he needs to leave me alone. It'll be fine though."

"I know it's hard for you to look at me, people always pretend they don't see me or look everywhere except my face. But I didn't always look like this. My husband drank a lot, and that beer did something to his brain because he would get angry after drinking and when he got angry, I ended up with a busted lip, a black eye, and once, he even knocked out a couple of teeth. Of course, he always said sorry the next day but that sorry didn't keep his fists from my face or body the next time."

"I'm sorry about your suffering. Why did you stay with him?" Caitlyn forced herself to look Shanae in the eye after glancing quickly at the deep jagged scar that ran down the right side of her face, from her temple to her bottom lip.

"We had two kids. I didn't know how I was going to take care of them by myself and besides, who else would want me? Paul always said he loved me and he was the best I was ever going to get. I believed I couldn't do any better and he looked so sad whenever he said sorry. How could I leave a heartbroken man?" Tears slid from her eyes.

Caitlyn reached for a tissue and handed it to Shanae. "Why did you want to tell me your story?"

"My dad used to knock my mom around when I was growing up. I used to say I was going to find someone who treated me better. I begged her to leave my dad, but she never did, not even after he started hitting me and my sister. Paul hit me while we dated and my mom told me to do better than she did. I thought I was so smart back then." Shanae's voice drifted into silence as she shook her head, her gaze unfocused.

"Paul was popular, handsome, and had a good job. I ended up pregnant but I thought I was one lucky girl to end up with him even if he did get mad and hit me once in a while. After I married Paul, my mom told me I had made my bed and I needed to sleep in it. I ended up in the hospital more than once after he beat me. The last time was after he came home and decided I had ruined his life. He ended up cutting my face so bad I had to have surgery. My mom took care of the kids while I was in the hospital but she wasn't happy about keeping them. When I was getting ready to leave the hospital, I called my mom to come and get me. She said I needed to call my husband and think about keeping my family together." As she spoke, Shanae clasped and unclasped her fingers, tore off and rolled torn pieces of a napkin and made circles on the table top with the pad of her index finger. She took a deep breath, then continued her story.

"I told my mom I couldn't go back home because Paul might kill me next time. If I died, who would take care of the kids? Then my mom said I should have thought about that before I went ahead and got pregnant." Shanae looked down at the table in silence.

Her shoulders were slumped and she crossed her arms and cried.

Caitlyn waited, tears streaming down her own face. She reached across the table and rubbed Shanae's forearm.

"I'm sorry, I don't mean to take all your time, but I have two daughters. I try to talk to them about relationships but kids don't listen to their parents and my oldest daughter blames me for us not being with their dad and changing their lives. I don't want them to make the same mistake I made, but I don't know how to make them understand that they don't need to hurry and settle for the first guy who comes along. Maybe if they hear someone else's story, they will understand what I've been saying. You're someone's daughter as well and if I can save you some pain by hearing my story, then I've done good. I won't be quiet anymore."

"Can I ask you another question?"

"Sure, go ahead." Shanae looked at Caitlyn without trying to minimize the appearance of her scar, more evident since her tears washed away the make-up she had used.

"What happened to Paul? Do you or your children have any more contact with him?"

"Remember how my mom wouldn't come get me? Well, Paul didn't show up either. He was at home getting drunk and feeling sorry for himself. One of the nurses who took care of me asked me if I was ready to go back home. I told her I never wanted to go back. She asked me where I wanted to go and I said Phoenix. Two hours later, she handed me three bus tickets and some cash. She said my future was now in my hands. I called a cab, picked up my kids, went to the bus station, and never looked back. Paul found me and tried to squirm his way in to my new life, but I got a restraining order. He left and went back to Louisiana. He calls and threatens me every month when he sees the receipts for child support."

"Are you ever afraid he'll come back, maybe hurt you or the kids? I'm sorry. You don't have to answer that if you don't want to."

"It's okay. I do worry about that. I know I'll never feel safe again, no matter what I do or where I go. I always look over my shoulder and I hate shadows because I always see him lurking in the dark. He's the burden I will always carry and I would give anything to feel safe again."

"I want to feel safe, too. All I have to do is think about him and I feel my wrists hurting. I don't know how to get past everything."

"You never will. The only thing you can do now is keep yourself safe and don't make the same mistake by thinking everything is suddenly different because he said sorry. A snake is still a snake."

"Thank you for sharing your story with me. I think it took a lot of courage for you to talk about what you've been through. I have a lot to think about. Would it be okay if I come back and talk to you again?"

"Sure you can, anytime. Be safe."

Caitlyn gathered her bags and walked out to her car, scanning the parking lot until she was in the car with the door locked.

26

Deep in thought, Caitlyn distractedly finished her errands, her agreement to meet with Justin and the conversation with Shanae weighing on her mind. Two blocks from her apartment, she turned her car around and headed back to Dante's.

Strumming her fingers on the steering wheel, Caitlyn leaned her head back on the headrest and closed her eyes. She sighed, took a cleansing breath and pulled the keys from the ignition and started walking toward the building. She placed her hand on her trembling stomach and tried to ignore the shakiness in her legs.

"I can do this, I can do this, I can do this." Caitlyn mumbled all the way to the offices, where a scant few staff members continued to work.

"Excuse me Mr. Wingate, can I have a moment of your time?" Caitlyn stood just inside the doorway of the office and clasped her hands together and tightened the muscles in her thighs.

"Is it necessary?" Jack responded without looking up from the paper he was reading.

"I really need to speak to you about a story that can only be written by me." Jack looked at Caitlyn but didn't say anything.

"This story needs to written..."

"Ms. Matthews, there is a protocol in place for the submission of story ideas. That protocol does not include interns coming to my office and pitching ideas without first going through the assigned mentors."

"I understand the process, Mr. Wingate. The thing is, this story..."

"Need I explain the protocol again? I suggest you approach your mentor with your story idea..."

"No sir. I'm going to write this story tonight and if you aren't interested in having the first shot at publication, then you should know that I will find a way to make it known by any means necessary."

"Are you giving me an ultimatum?" Jack laid the paper down and stood up as he continued to stare at Caitlyn.

"No sir. It's just that my story is the same story as so many other women and I can't keep silent any longer. Shanae is great and doesn't deserve to feel horrible but he cut her face and she knew it was hard for me to look at her and her life will never be the same and she's still having to deal with him. I wasn't hurt like that but now he's back, just when I thought everything was finally going right and I put him in my past and then I find his parents sitting in my mother's house and I feel like I'm going to explode and ..."

Caitlyn jumped when she felt a hand on her shoulder and looked up to find that Jack Wingate had crossed the room and now stood beside her. He held out a tissue to her, guided her over to a chair and shut the door to his office. He sat in one of the chairs facing his desk, next to Caitlyn.

"Tell me your story."

* * *

Exhausted, Caitlyn leaned her head back on the headrest and closed her eyes, the conversation with Mr. Wingate running through her mind. A knock on her window made her jerk upright.

She opened her eyes to find Victor standing next to her door. She climbed out of the car and stood next to him.

"Hi. I left you a couple of messages. Are you okay?" Victor frowned as he noted the smeared mascara beneath Caitlyn's eyes.

"Yeah, I'm okay. It's been a long day and I have a story to write that I need to finish tonight. I was going to call you, but I had a meeting with Mr. Wingate about the story and it took a long time to work out some of the details. Are you still game to meet my mom tomorrow? And how did you know to come here?"

"You bet, about meeting your mom and you're a writer. I took a chance when I didn't hear from you. I figured the odds were in my favor that you would be here, and, I was right. Are we still going to make something to take over?" Victor reached out and tucked several errant hairs behind Caitlyn's ear.

"Your eyes are a bit red and you look tired. Are you okay?"

"Yes. It's been a rough day and the story I'm working on got to me. I should be able to head over around 10:00. Does that work for you?"

"I'll take what I can get. Call me when you're on your way. Good luck with the story." Victor leaned over and gave Caitlyn a gentle kiss before turning and heading over to his car.

Back in her apartment, Caitlyn kicked off her shoes, set her purchases down, wolfed down some leftover vegetable fried rice sat down and began to type.

27

Bleary-eyed, Caitlyn squinted at the alarm and groaned as she peeled off a sheet of paper plastered to her face.

"So not ready to face the day." Caitlyn yawned, stretched and straightened up in the chair, rubbing the small of her back. She flexed her fingers and shook out her aching limbs, grimacing as pinpricks began to tingle up and down her arms.

She gathered the supplies needed for her dessert, threw herself together and headed over to Victor's apartment. The bags felt heavy as she trudged up the hill to his building. Victor answered the door before the ring of the doorbell faded away.

"Hi Caitlyn. Come on in." Victor held out his hand and took her bags, then backed up and made room for Caitlyn.

"Good-morning. Thanks for taking those bags. They feel like they weigh a ton today. Maybe it's because I'm exhausted. I was so tired after I finished my story that I fell asleep at my desk." Her voice trailed off as she noticed Victor's tense expression and lack of response. She watched as he placed each item from her bags on the kitchen counter with studied care, his back facing her.

"You're quiet, is everything okay? I mean, are your mom and dad alright?"

"They're fine, thanks for asking." Victor placed his hands on the counter and leaned on his arms, head down for a moment before turning to face her.

"I received an interesting call from my publicist, Tom. He proposed an opportunity for a huge story, captured in words and pictures, and at any other time, I would jump at this chance, but now, I don't know what to think." Victor stood, arms crossed, watching Caitlyn.

"You don't seem happy with this chance. Why not?" Caitlyn tilted her head to the side as she waited for his reply.

"The problem I have with this is you're central to the outcome. You're the reason for this turn of events and without your involvement, there isn't an opportunity."

"Me? What are you talking about?"

"Your boss, Jack, told Tom about the story you're working on. You know, the story where you spill your guts to the world even though you couldn't tell me anything." Victor's voice broke as he strode past her into the living room where he sat down on the couch and buried his face in his hands.

Caitlyn stood in the kitchen, mouth agape. She sucked in a breath, lifted her chin, then followed Victor and sat down beside him.

"His name is Justin and I met and dated him in college. I still can't believe how stupid I was to believe his lies." Caitlyn gave a little laugh and shook her head, then continued.

"Penny didn't know him and I never told her about my jerk of a boyfriend. My roommate used to tell me I was an idiot and deserved every bruise because I kept taking him back after he acted sad and said sorry with a puppy dog face. I guess I did deserve it back then, but I walked away. Now he shows up and thinks he can waltz back into my life as if nothing ever happened and now, because of him I've hurt you. I think I hate him."

"Why tell your story now? What's changed?"

Caitlyn's brow puckered as she stared at Victor, then shook her head.

"You happened, and I guess, I happened. I ended up talking to Justin yesterday when I shopped for the dessert ingredients. He was in the store and asked me to have a cup of coffee with him so he could plead his case." Victor started to interrupt but Caitlyn held up her hand.

"Please let me finish. After I listened to him, a woman who works at the coffee shop came up to me and told me her story. She's a woman who managed to escape with her life and kids, but at great cost. I realized that part of her story is part of my story and I know that my story is part of someone else's story. We're all connected. Shanae's story helped me see that I do have the strength to live and love on my terms. I hope my story helps someone else discover a hidden reserve to make tough choices."

"So what's next? Do you think that telling your story will make Justin leave you alone?"

"Hopefully. I did agree to meet with him tomorrow afternoon and I plan to tell him about this story."

"I don't like the idea of you going anywhere near him. Why do you have to meet with him in person?"

"It's important to me to work through my fears. I have to do this. I have to face my demons and tell him to stay away from me once and for all."

"You don't know what finding out about this story will do or how he'll react. He could become violent, then what?"

"I've got it under control."

"Let me go with you. I can give you privacy but be close enough to help if he decides to put his hands on you."

Caitlyn reached out and laid her hand against Victor's cheek.

"I love the fact that you want to protect me, but you can't save me. No matter how all of this turns out, I have to save myself."

Victor pulled Caitlyn close and touched his forehead to hers, his hand behind her head. He closed his eyes and sighed.

"Promise me you'll be careful."

"I promise."

Victor kissed her and held her in silence.

"Okay, we better get to making that dessert or your mother may not feed me." Victor hauled Caitlyn up off the couch and held her hand as they made their way into the kitchen.

* * *

As Victor and Caitlyn got of the car in front her mom's house, her sister's boyfriend looked away and her sister hurried out of the house with a couple of plates of food, said a hurried, "Hi, good to see you. Sorry I can't stay," climbed into her boyfriend's car and off they went.

"That was my sister. You'll probably never meet her because we only see her once in a while. Come on. Let's get this party started."

They saw her nephew Larry first, sitting on the couch engrossed in his phone. "Hey Larry. How are you doing?"

"Good." He didn't look from his phone.

Caitlyn smiled and led Victor past the living room out to the backyard.

"Caitlyn. Come on over, honey." Rosie wiped her hands on a dishtowel and held her hand out to shake hands with Victor. "You must be Victor. It's wonderful to meet you." She held onto his hand for a moment as she gazed into his eyes. She smiled and nodded her head as she released his hand and turned to give Caitlyn a hug and a kiss.

The next door neighbors came over with their kids and everyone began eating and talking while the kids ran around and played in the pool.

Victor sat down next to Darius and Caitlyn watched as they laughed and talked. Penny arrived with Jarrell and her younger sister, Mandy who went to the same school as Larry. They formed a two person team against the younger kids in a game of water volleyball.

Victor brought out his camera and everyone loved having their picture snapped. He offered to take family photographs and all the families cleaned up for a family photo by the famous Victor Knoble.

* * *

Back at her apartment, Victor played with Caitlyn's fingers as they lounged on the couch.

"I had a great time. Your family is awesome. Did your mom like me?"

Caitlyn smiled and shook her head. "You know she likes you. She thinks you're nice and you did good by taking pictures of everyone and talking. Did anyone ask anything too personal?"

"Nothing I couldn't handle. Speaking of handling things, are you sure I can't come with you when you meet with Justin?"

"I'm sure. This is my problem and I'm going to deal with it."

Victor sighed. "I guess that's it then. Call me as soon as you're away from him and back in your car, okay?"

"Yep, can do."

They watched a little television before Victor stood up and stretched.

"I have to get going. It seems that I need to clear up my calendar for the next four weeks or so for a new job that suddenly popped up."

"You're going to be taking photos of this whole project? Will you be traveling with me?"

"Yes. I'll be in the background capturing the stories through pictures while you do the interviews. Is it going to be strange for you to have me around while you work?"

"I don't know. I've never done anything like this before and I've never shared an assignment with a photographer before. I don't know what to expect as far as a professional interaction goes."

"I've worked with a lot of writers. When we're working, I'll be all about the job. I'll be tough if that's what needs to happen in order for this to be great. It won't be personal."

Caitlyn laughed. "Oh great. Are you telling me you're a prima donna on the job?"

"Not even. But, I won't be holding your hand and telling you something is great when it isn't, either. You should be able to handle it."

Caitlyn nodded her head and smiled. "That should be fine. I'm glad we'll be sharing this assignment. I felt bad when Shanae said she knew it was hard for me to look at her. I wish I could find a way to show her that she is still beautiful."

"She's had a hard time of it. Now, give me a kiss. I've got tons of work to get prepped." Caitlyn walked Victor to the door and gave him one last hug, then prepared for bed, Shanae's scar and Justin's face replaying in her mind.

* * *

Caitlyn hugged her purse against her stomach after getting out and locking her car. She looked around the parking lot as she made her way to the Japanese Friendship Garden.

Justin stood up as she approached, a broad smile on his face and held out a hand. Caitlyn stopped beyond his reach and shook her head.

"No. You don't touch me, ever. I agreed to meet with you, but that doesn't mean I will ever forget how we got to this point. Now, speak your piece."

"Let's sit down, okay? I bought some pastries and tea. I remember how much you love tea." Justin stepped back and pointed to a bench nearby where Caitlyn saw a box and two cups in a brown carry tray.

"Look Justin. Cut the crap. This is not you and me having a nice time and getting to know each again. You need to know that I've written my story and it's going to be published. I told everything and it's going to be part of a series about other women who've been hurt because of lies by someone they trusted."

"What the hell are you talking about? I never forced you. You're going to tell lies about me?" Justin's voice grew louder and he reached out to grab Caitlyn.

She jumped back out of arms reach and he clutched air. "They aren't lies. I told you to stop."

"I loved you. *I loved you!* You little ..." Justin closed the distance between them and grabbed Caitlyn's arm before she had a chance to snatch it away. She jerked back and slapped Justin as hard as she could. He let go of her arm and rubbed the side of his face.

"I told you not to touch me and I meant it! You will never touch me again! I thought you should hear about the story from me before seeing it in print but I don't need to hear anything else from you. Stay away from me, my family, my job, and my friends."

Justin clenched and unclenched his fingers as he stared at Caitlyn, his chest heaving with the force of his breathing.

"I'll sue. I'll sue you and that rag you work for. Your name won't be worth a pot to piss in after I get through with you," Justin snarled.

"So much for loving me. You only loved me when you controlled me. I don't expect to see you again."

Caitlyn walked away from Justin by backing up and keeping him in sight until she reached the corner of the sidewalk at the edge of the garden. As she turned the corner to the parking lot she saw Justin kick the box of pastries off the bench.

28

Caitlyn and Shanae stood in front of the room behind an old desk in the elementary school classroom. Every seat was filled and people lined the walls waiting for the meeting to begin. Caitlyn clasped her hands together, took a deep breath and stepped in front of the teacher's desk. Vivian, the group facilitator joined her and held up her hand for silence.

"Good evening. Our meeting today is going to be a little different. We have some guests who will be joining us and they've asked for a chance to speak first. Some of you agreed to speak to Ms. Matthews and share your journey with her. She and the other guests are here to see if anyone else is willing to share their story. We are taking this moment first to see if there are any objections to their presence. Please raise your hand if you protest."

Several hands lifted in opposition to the intrusion of outsiders. A murmur grew as people spoke to one another and Caitlyn leaned over and asked Vivian if she could speak. Vivian raised her hand again to gain everyone's attention.

"Ms. Matthews has asked to address the group. Let's give her our encouragement as we hear her out." The room filled with the snap, snap, snap of fingers and Vivian smiled and nodded her head at Caitlyn.

"Good evening. Thank you for allowing us to come and be a part of your meeting. You might be wondering why we've come and what this is all about. Please indulge me as I share my story." Caitlyn rubbed her palms down the sides of her hips, took a deep breath, and began to share the story of her journey.

* * *

Caitlyn wiped away the tears tricking down her cheeks with the tissues that appeared in her hands and looked into the eyes staring back at her. Some tear filled, some squinted and filled with intensity. Snap ... snap ... snap. The sound of snapping grew and Shanae linked arms with Caitlyn and gave her arm a squeeze.

"You did it. The snaps mean they accept you. Some of them will talk to you now."

Caitlyn touched her head to the side of Shanae's and smiled.

"Thank you for bringing me to your support group. I know the decision to let me into this part of your life took a lot of trust and thought."

"You've been open and honest with me. I trust you to do right by these gals."

Vivian signaled for silence. "Due to the earlier objections, Ms. Matthews and her group won't be sitting in on our meeting. Those who are willing to share their story with her will be able to do so next door."

Caitlyn and Shanae went to the next door classroom and waited. Victor came in and set up his equipment in a corner of the room.

Each person that came in gave consent for their story to be recorded and possibly printed. They met Victor and some agreed to be photographed. The interviews and photographs continued across six states, with meetings in schools, churches, gyms, and homes. Caitlyn sent in stories on a weekly basis to Jack while Victor worked on the complimentary photographs.

* * *

October 1st. Caitlyn smiled at Victor as he stood by the door leading into the foyer of the tall building.

"Are you ready to see the end result of all the meetings, interviews, and sleepless nights? Everyone is inside, ready to kick off Domestic Violence Awareness month." Victor stood by Caitlyn's side, just in front of the door.

"I'm ready, nervous, but ready. Have you been inside yet?"

"Yes. The place is packed, and Brandi, this year's spokeswoman is waiting. Jack and Tom are both here, as well as Vivian, Shanae, and a lot of the women we've worked with over the last couple of months. Let's get this show on the road." Victor smiled and inclined his head toward the door.

Caitlyn took a deep breath, squared her shoulders, nodded, stepped inside, and gasped.

The edges of the room were lit with soft purple lighting and trails of light marked paths on the floor that led to tall, vertical rectangular prisms that were lit from within.

Two of the four sides contained the photographs of a woman or girl that had been interviewed. One photograph was without make-up, one was a candid shot or a photo of her choosing. Some of the women requested a photograph with make-up, while others were photographed with their children, or other support. One side of the prism contained the story of the woman's journey. The last side offered words of encouragement, hope, or advice.

Tables with smaller prisms were placed intermittently through-out the room, against walls and at the intersections of connecting paths. Several of these prisms contained pictures and stories supplied by family members of women and girls killed by husbands, ex-husbands, boyfriends and partners. Many people were moved to tears after gazing at the beautiful faces of the children and families left behind.

As she walked through the room, Caitlyn thought about the women and their stories. She felt awe at the bravery and strength it took to take back their lives and piece together a future despite the heartache of shattered dreams. At the far side of the room, on either side of a set of microphones stood the prisms that contained her story and Shanae's story. Caitlyn looked at her pictures, then turned to look at Victor. One of the pictures showed Caitlyn crying and hugging a young woman. The other picture showed Caitlyn sitting down, asleep, against the side of a building, head back, and eyes closed with a sandwich uneaten in her hand. A third photo showed her smiling, looking into the lens of the camera.

"When did you take these? I didn't know you were there when I spoke with Nikki and I don't remember you taking my photo specifically."

"That's what makes me good at what I do. I see the real you." Victor took Caitlyn's hand and drew her to him, gave her a quick kiss and continued.

"This project has been eye opening for me. I've learned so much and I know it's important for these stories to be shared if there's any chance to make a difference in the life of even one person." Victor shoved his hands in his pockets and looked silently at the picture of a smiling Caitlyn.

Shanae came over and touched Caitlyn on the arm.

"Caitlyn, Victor. I'm sorry to interrupt, but I have to tell you how much I love my pictures. I don't look like a monster. Even with my scar showing, I can look at the pictures without cringing inside and the one with my children is a priceless gift. Thank you." She leaned over and gave Victor a quick hug, then hugged Caitlyn before walking over to join her daughters in front of one of the small tables.

Caitlyn watched as Shanae draped an arm over one daughter's shoulder and around the waist of her younger daughter as they gazed at the story on the table.

* * *

Brandi, the wife of a major league baseball player and victim of domestic violence, began to speak. Half an hour later, several women took the microphone and shared their stories. Tears flowed, hugs were shared and women linked arms, each one stronger for surviving, owning and sharing their journey.

* * *

Three months later, Caitlyn was still on cloud nine following the success of the series launch. Women continued to share their journey's at high schools, colleges, churches, and in support groups.

Caitlyn kept in touch with many of the women and wrote follow-up articles about the changes they made in their lives.

"Hi Shanae, it's Caitlyn. I'm calling to say hi. How are you?"

"I'm doing great. It's funny that you called. I met with a counselor at the community college and I've signed up to take some placement tests. My daughters have been encouraging me to go back to school. Can you imagine that? Me, a student again."

"I think that is wonderful. I'm so happy to hear that you've made this decision. I have no doubt you'll do great. Please keep in touch and let me know if I can help." Caitlyn smiled as she listened to Shanae speak about her nervousness of being a returning student and excitement of a brighter future.

As Caitlyn thought about some of the life-changing effects of the launch, a smile broke out on her face. She rubbed the back of her neck and looked at the pile of messages she needed to return, then glanced at the picture of Victor sitting on her desk. She looked at the calendar and smiled, then picked up the phone, dialed, and left a message.

* * *

"Hi Victor. I have a ton of messages that I need to answer, but I can't concentrate.

I keep thinking about our trip. I went shopping for a cute little something today during lunch. Pick me up by six. Don't be late."
Click.

She chuckled as she hung up the phone, leaned back in her chair, and stretched, then picked out the next message to return.